Millie Criswell

Asking for Trouble

HQN™

ISBN 0-373-77053-7

ASKING FOR TROUBLE

To Karen Solem

Thank you for your kindness, generosity of spirit, support and most of all, your brilliance!

CHAPTER ONE

IVY SWINDEL WAS ADDICTED to porn.

While most seventy-eight-year-old ladies were crocheting afghans or sipping tea from china cups, Beth Randall's great-aunt was viewing Internet pornography. The fact that the spinster's father had been a Methodist minister and the old lady still referred to sex as "matters of the flesh," made her behavior seem outlandish, if not downright abnormal.

But then, no one ever accused Ivy or her younger sister, Iris, of being normal. And at any rate, Beth considered normal to be highly overrated.

"I found the most interesting Web site this morning," the older woman stated at breakfast, blue eyes sparkling, and grinning like a naughty schoolgirl. "It's called 'Balls of Steel.' Isn't that colorful?"

Since Beth assumed the Web site had nothing to do with bowling or baseball, or any other kind of vertically played sport, she smiled tightly. Her focus shifted to her great-aunt Iris. She felt somewhat relieved that the woman's only addiction seemed to be Earl Grey tea, though she did harbor a worrisome fascination with witchcraft, which had the gossip-mongers in town working overtime. But even that didn't seem nearly as disturbing as the one Ivy had for naked men.

Her great-aunt had never admitted the reason she was so fascinated with male genitalia, but Beth suspected it had something to do with her desire to re-capture her youth. The old woman had been the wild child of the Swindel family, and the bane of her father's existence. She had never lacked for male companionship, or so she claimed. Ivy had admitted in a roundabout way that she'd sown her share of wild oats—a shocking concept in her day and age, when women were expected to be circumspect and ladylike—but had never found a man she deemed worthy enough to marry.

Apparently, Ivy was still looking.

Since that fateful day last year when Beth had given Ivy her old computer and she'd discovered the Inter-net, Ivy had become fascinated, then obsessed, and finally incorrigible, not to mention unrepentant, about visiting pornographic Web sites. And no matter how many times Beth had teased, cajoled and begged her not to, Ivy hadn't listened. Fortunately, she seemed in-terested only in naked men, nothing more sordid.

One had to be grateful for small favors, if one had an elderly aunt into porn.

Beth placed a plate of hot scones, fresh from the inn's kitchen, on the small round mahogany table in her aunts' suite of rooms on the fourth floor. Sipping the hot tea, she felt lucky to have these wonderful ladies in her life.

The Two Sisters Ordinary, named in honor of her aunts, had been the Swindel sisters' former home. Iris and Ivy had encouraged Beth to turn the historic Victorian into an inn so that others might enjoy it. She, in turn, had given them a life estate.

As was her usual custom, Beth proceeded to fill her aunts in on the day's upcoming events. "We have a new couple checking in today. The Rogers are from Columbus, Ohio. He's a dentist. They're coming to celebrate their twenty-fifth wedding anniversary."

"How wonderful! Will they be staying long?" Aunt Iris asked with no small amount of enthusiasm. Her aunt was an intriguing mixture of Mary Poppins and the Wicked Witch of the West and was quite possibly the most upbeat person Beth had ever met, though she was a stickler for the proprieties. Good manners were expected, as was circumspect behavior, which usually created problems where Ivy was concerned.

Ivy Swindel didn't know the meaning of the word *circumspect*.

"Just two days, possibly three," she replied, hoping for three because she needed the extra money.

"Is the man well endowed?" Ivy wanted to know, leaning forward to stare intently at Beth, who bit her lower lip to keep from laughing. "All the young men on the Web sites I visit seem to be. I do hope so. Maybe we can get those Chippendale dancers to come stay at the inn. Wouldn't that be lovely? I've been saving my dollar bills, just in case."

Iris gasped. "Sister, shame on you! What kind of talk is that, and in front of your niece? Children have very impressionable minds. I've told you that numerous times."

At thirty-four, Beth didn't think her mind was all that impressionable—warped, maybe; confused, at times; filled with self-doubt, always—she had her ex-husband to thank for that.

Greg Randall's constant criticism and verbal abuse had taken its toll. *"You're so stupid, Beth! Why the hell did I ever marry you? If I want your opinion, I'll ask for it."*

"I haven't met Mr. and Mrs. Rogers yet," Beth explained. And she certainly had no idea about any of her male guests' physical attributes, nor did she want to know. "This is their first visit to the inn." And would probably be their last, if Ivy started staring at the poor guy's...*um*...equipment, and she wasn't referring to dental drills. It was hard to believe that this male-nudity-addicted spinster was the same sweet old lady who used to read bedtime stories to her.

"I'm also expecting a young honeymoon couple to arrive at the end of the week," she announced. "Joan and Charles Murray are from Virginia. They sounded very nice on the phone."

"Oh good, that's sure to liven things up around here. Put them in the room with the big brass headboard, so we can—"

"Ivy Swindel!" Iris shook her head in warning. "Merciful heavens! That will be quite enough. What would Papa think to hear you say such things? I'm sure he's rolling over in his grave at this very moment."

Looking hopeful, her older sister grinned. "Do you think so?"

Sniffing the air several times at the acrid odor filling the air, Beth scrunched her nose in distaste. "What's that awful smell?" The lemon sachet, which usually permeated the large suite of rooms, had been replaced by something that smelled suspiciously like marijuana. Not that she'd ever smoked the potent weed, but her ex-husband had indulged, from time to time.

"Incense, dear. I'm trying out a new incantation and thought it would help set the mood."

"Iris is trying to raise the dead." Ivy grinned, which increased the multitude of wrinkles on a face that looked like a well-traveled road map. "I told her to start with Phinneas Pickens. That old coot could use some resuscitation. Why, I ran into him at the bank the other day and he pretended he didn't remember that I'd taught him eighth-grade English. Can you imagine? The man must be senile."

Iris was trying to raise the dead? Why on earth would she want to do that?

Beth decided she might have to reconsider which aunt was the nuttier of the two.

"Maybe Mr. Pickens is growing a bit forgetful," she offered, glancing at the ormolu clock on the mantel and knowing what she'd suggested was very unlikely. The man had a mind like a steel trap. "At any rate, he'll be here soon to inspect the inn for the loan I've applied for."

And she had no doubt he'd remember every debt she owed. Beth wasn't sure what she would do if she didn't get the additional funds or how long she could keep operating the inn. Business had been slow these past six months. And though she had bookings for the upcoming Thanksgiving and Christmas holidays, she wasn't sure the revenue would be enough to sustain her through winter, when tourism slowed down in the rural Pennsylvania township.

Mediocrity received its share of snow, but it wasn't reliable enough to base an entire industry on; and so the skiers and snowboarders went farther north, leaving only the die-hard antique lovers and Civil War buffs to spend tourist dollars in the quaint community.

"I wish we were able to help out more financially, Beth dear," Iris said, biting her scone daintily, and then wiping crumbs from her lips with an embroidered napkin. "We never meant for this house to become a burden when we gave it to you. Did we, sister?" Ivy shook her head.

"Don't be silly. I love this house. But it takes time to grow a business. There were repairs and alterations that needed to be done before we could open as an inn. This relic is a century old, after all."

Iris still didn't look convinced and Beth patted her hand reassuringly. "You'll never know how grateful I am that you and Aunt Ivy chose to share your home with me. I don't know what I would have done if you hadn't made the offer. You've always been there for me." Their generous gift had been a godsend to Beth, whose life had fallen apart after finding out that her husband of three years had been having an affair with one of his coworkers.

Greg was the athletic director for Mediocrity High School and head coach of the Miners football team. Penelope Miller, his paramour, was a physical-education teacher who coached girl's basketball and soccer.

Beth supposed their pairing had been inevitable. She'd never shared her husband's enthusiasm for sports, while her husband's lover fit his fantasy image of a female jock to a tee: big boobs, long legs and no brains, or at least none Beth could discern.

What seemed disastrous at the time had actually

turned out to be the best thing that could have happened to her. Greg's nasty moods and the venom that spewed forth from his mouth were now Penelope's problem to deal with. They deserved each other, as far as Beth was concerned.

Unwilling to turn tail and run after her husband's affair had become public knowledge, Beth had focused all of her energies on opening the inn, which had given her a chance to regain her self-worth and sanity, and a reason to get her life back in order, which hadn't been easy on many levels. But she was determined to succeed.

"This house was just too much for a couple of old ladies to manage," Ivy admitted. "And you love this Victorian as much as we do, so it seemed only fitting that you should have it. We wanted the house to remain in the family, and you're the only family we have left, aside from your mother, who is quite content with her life in California."

Thank God for that! Beth loved her mother, but she didn't like her very much and had no intention of living any closer to the woman than three thousand miles.

Margaret Shaw had a nasty disposition and made everyone around her miserable. Beth had thirty-four years of good reasons to dread her visits, which fortunately were few and far between. They argued over the most trivial things whenever they were together. Margaret took great delight in telling Beth in excruciating detail every little thing that was wrong with her. And she had a very long list!

"This house was the best part of my childhood and holds so many wonderful memories."

"You mean like the time you tried to help Elmer Forrest paint the front porch and ended up dumping a whole gallon of paint on his boots?" Ivy laughed and Beth smiled.

"Mr. Forrest wouldn't talk to me for months after that."

"Elmer felt badly about his behavior after we explained about your parents' divorce."

Thinking back to the heartache her parents' divorce had caused, Beth sighed. She'd often wondered if she'd been the cause of their breakup, but her aunts had assured her that Margaret and Melvin Shaw's failed marriage had been due to her father's wandering eye. She hadn't fully understood what that meant until the day her mother had explained in graphic, horrifying detail just what her father had done, shattering her childish illusions about a man she had worshipped and adored.

"My dear, are you all right?" Iris asked, her brow creased with worry. "You look positively glum."

Forcing a smile, Beth nodded, picking up the thread of their conversation. "Once I get the loan I'll be able to finish the landscaping and pay off the bulk of the debt I've accumulated trying to bring the inn up to code, which is why I intend to bribe Mr. Pickens with a jar of your damson plum jam. Mrs. Pickens is wild about it."

Ivy pursed her lips. "*Humph!* If you ask me, Finnola Pickens thinks too highly of herself. She was a very poor student—didn't know a verb from a preposition, as I recall."

Neither did Beth, but she wasn't about to admit that to the former schoolteachers. English, and grammar in particular, had never been her forte, though she adored reading, especially romantic novels. At least relationships in romance novels always worked out; they were required to have happy endings.

Too bad real life wasn't like that.

"We don't think you should show Mr. Pickens the cellar, dear. It's so cold and musty down there. We think it would be best if you just ignored it completely. Don't we, Ivy?" Iris appeared uneasy as she glanced at her sister, twisting her napkin into a tight knot.

"It's so damp down there," Ivy agreed. "And you know how much you dislike it."

Dislike wasn't quite the word Beth would have used. *Hated. Despised. Abhorred.* Those words fit so much better. "True. But I'm desperate. Don't worry. I'm taking Buster with me for moral support."

Aunt Ivy tsked, and then shook her head. "But you're terrified of the cellar, and that dog is useless as a watchdog. Why, he practically licks Mr. Jessup to death every time he brings the mail."

Buster was no Lassie, that was certain, but the black Labrador was the only good thing she'd gotten out of her divorce settlement with Greg, and Beth loved him. He'd given her unconditional love, something she'd never received from her ex—or any other man, for that matter.

"Don't worry. We'll be just fine. I'll be back up later this afternoon to let you know how my meeting with Mr. Pickens went. Until then, try to stay out of trouble."

The two old ladies glanced at each other before breaking into a fit of giggles.

HER RIGHT HAND TREMBLING over the rusty handles of the root cellar's wide double doors, Beth felt her heartbeat crashing against the walls of her chest like a wild hummingbird and nausea rise in her stomach. Fearing eruption was imminent, she breathed deeply several times to calm herself.

No way did she subscribe to that whole "when the going gets tough" scenario. She'd never gotten over her fear of the dark, dank, spooky place. Not after accidentally being locked in the cellar at the age of six by her aunts' cleaning lady.

But dammit! Mr. Pickens would be arriving at any moment to make his inspection and she needed that jam!

Beth might be chicken, but she wasn't stupid.

At Buster's morose whine, she inhaled deeply, and then swallowed with some difficulty. "We're going, we're going. Just be patient." But she couldn't get her feet uprooted. Her legs were shaking so badly the soles of her tennis shoes had attached themselves to the lawn like Mrs. Abernathy's ugly pink flamingos next door.

"I can do this!" A familiar feeling of panic started setting in. "Just pull the doors open," she told herself. "You haven't got all day."

Buster barked, apparently agreeing with her.

"Oh, shut up! Who asked you?"

Clasping sweaty fingers around the handles, she pulled up, holding her breath and praying the ghost of alleged murder victim Lyle McMurtry wasn't waiting on the other side to grab her. Feeling something furry on the back of her leg, she screamed, but then realizing it was only the dog, she frowned at the grinning animal.

"Stop that or you'll make me pee my pants!"

As she threw open the doors, Buster rushed in ahead of her, and Beth pointed the flashlight down the stairwell of the cellar, which smelled like hundred-year-old onions, despite the fact that none had been kept there for years.

Wrinkling her nose in disgust, she took her first faltering step. "I can do this! I can do this!" *Think of that woman from* Tomb Raider, *who ventured into scary places and kicked everyone's butt.* The wooden step creaked, and she halted in midstep, her heart pounding loudly in her ears. She was tempted to flee—so much for *Tomb Raider*—but knew she couldn't. Her aunts were counting on her to get that loan.

Where would Ivy and Iris live if she lost their house? Where would *she?*

Directing the narrow beam of light into the darkened room, she scanned the area, hoping she wouldn't discover a nest of spiders, or worse, rats hovering on the hand-hewn beams overhead. If there was one thing she hated worse than spiders, it was rats—big black ugly rats with skinny pink tails and gnawing sharp teeth.

Suddenly something scurried across her foot and she jumped back, nearly losing her balance. The flashlight flew out of her hand and dropped to the earthen floor with a thud. "Oh hell!" In its beam she saw the small, hideous face of a rodent, its whiskers twitching and tiny feet pawing at the metal stick. "Shoo!" She clapped her hands loudly to scare it off, hoping upon hope that it was the only one she would find.

The hell with Lara Croft; Beth was no Indiana Jones!

The inn's cellar had a rather nefarious reputation. It was rumored that a man named Lyle McMurtry had been murdered in it over fifty years ago. To make matters worse, the alleged victim had once been engaged to Beth's great-aunt Iris, which made the eccentric old woman and her sister suspect to the residents of Mediocrity. Everyone in town knew that Iris and Ivy were inseparable; where one went, the other followed.

Did that include murdering former fiancés?

A chill went through Beth, but she shook off the ridiculous notion that her aunts might be murderers and that McMurtry's ghost might be lurking about. Picking up the flashlight, she continued her surveillance.

Row upon row of her aunts' preserves, pickles and canned goods lined the rickety old shelves that were nailed to the walls of the room. A vintage 1950s rusted lawn mower and other assorted gardening utensils hugged one corner, and crates and boxes of every size and shape imaginable were stacked six feet high, making Beth aware of the fire hazard they presented.

The ancient dwelling, though up to fire code, would go up like a tinderbox if those cartons ignited. She made a mental note to discard them as soon as she could make the arrangements.

Grabbing a jar of damson plum jam off the shelf, she dusted it on the leg of her jeans, calling out to the dog, but he refused to come. "Buster, Buster, where are you?" She didn't intend to spend one more minute than necessary in the bowels of the Ordinary. "Let's go, boy. I've got a treat for you." But still the dog refused to heed the command.

Cursing softly beneath her breath, Beth moved cautiously toward the other end of the cellar, directing the shaft of light to reveal an old wooden worktable. There, resting on top was a small metal camp shovel. She searched her memory, finally remembering where she had seen the tool before. It had been the day her aunts had been arrested for shoplifting from Herb Meyer's Hardware Store.

On a whim Aunt Ivy had secreted the shovel beneath her coat to see if she could get away with stealing it. She hadn't. And it had taken all of Beth's persuasive powers and a promise to buy all of her gardening implements from Meyer's Hardware, even though they were twice as expensive as Builder's World, before the man agreed to drop the charges.

Guiding the beam of light to her right, she discovered Buster frantically clawing the earthen floor. "Stop that, you naughty dog!" Concerned the inquisitive pooch might accidentally expose and damage some old water pipes—a repair she could hardly afford—she moved closer to investigate.

"What're you doing, Buster? I told you we have to leave. Now!" Flashing the light on the dog's find, she gasped when she saw what looked to be a large, dirt-encrusted bone and stared in openmouthed hor-

ror as Buster's digging produced more skeletal re-
mains. She inched closer, unable to take her eyes off
the ghastly discovery.

*"We don't think you should show Mr. Pickens the
cellar, dear. It's so cold and musty down there. We think
it would be best if you just ignored it completely."*

Her aunts' emphatic insistence that Beth avoid
the cellar came flooding back and she started to get
a really bad feeling in the pit of her stomach. It might
have been the four scones slathered with strawberry
jam that she'd eaten that morning, but she didn't
think so. She clasped her churning stomach, feeling
as if she was going to throw up or faint—she couldn't
decide which—and inhaled deeply.

*Why had her aunts advised her to avoid the
cellar?*

It was pitch-black. The flashlight, waving up and
down because her hand shook so badly, didn't shed
much light or meaning as to what exactly she was
looking at. Or maybe it was the fact that she didn't
want to believe what she was looking at. She grasped
it tightly with both hands to steady it, and herself.

*What were those bones doing in her cellar? And
who had put them there?*

Her aunts were the only ones who ever ventured
into the bowels of the Two Sisters Ordinary on a
regular basis. They were fond of canning applesauce,

putting up jams and jellies, and they stored the canned goods in the cellar, where the temperature was cooler.

"Iris is trying to raise the dead."

"Lyle McMurtry." Beth whispered the name, then shook her head. The possibility was just too ridiculous to consider.

Or was it?

CHAPTER TWO

BETH CONTINUED to gape at the bones, and what she was thinking was…well, unthinkable.

Iris and Ivy had been acting stranger than usual of late, if that was possible. The old ladies had a reputation for eccentric behavior, and for being a bit off their rockers. She couldn't deny that they were both somewhat addled.

Shivers of foreboding tripped down her spine as she tried to decide what to do about the bones. After a few moments, Beth came to a decision: They had to be reburied. If anyone else found them, it would reflect very badly on her aunts.

But what if they're guilty?

What if Iris had done away with Lyle McMurtry and then had enlisted the aid of her sister to bury the poor guy in the cellar, as everyone suspected? As hideous as that thought was, it had to be considered.

If she reburied the bones, she'd be an accessory after the fact. Hiding evidence was a crime, not to mention immoral. But what other choice did she have? The old ladies were already suspects. Sheriff Murdock had made no secret that he thought they were responsible for McMurtry's disappearance. And she was responsible for them. They'd always been there for her; she couldn't abandon them now.

Picking up the camp shovel, she set to her task, vowing to get to the bottom of the mystery, and knowing that until she did, the bones would have to remain hidden. It might not be the wisest decision, but it was the best one she could come up with at the moment.

Beth knew she should go to the sheriff and report her find. But how could she? The whole scenario sounded crazy. And a reinvestigation into a fifty-year-old matter could jeopardize the lives of her aunts. Innocent people were convicted every day of crimes they didn't commit.

As nutty as the old women were, she loved them dearly and had to protect them, which is why she couldn't go to Iris and Ivy with her suspicions. It would hurt them tremendously.

But what if they're guilty?

She couldn't think about that now.

The officer from the bank was due to arrive at any moment. Once Mr. Pickens completed his inspection of the inn she would sit down and think long and hard about what she was going to do. But she wouldn't mention them to anyone. If Mr. Pickens found out about the bones, she could kiss her loan goodbye.

The wind whipped a spindly pine branch against the narrow dirt-covered window and Beth nearly jumped out of her skin. But no wonder she was nervous. She had a pile of buried bones in her cellar and a couple of loony aunts who were looking pretty guilty of a fifty-year-old crime.

Feeling chilled to the bone—poor choice of words—Beth proceeded with her task. A few moments later, a glimmer beneath the worktable caught her attention. Dropping the shovel, she moved toward it, kicking the dirt with the toe of her shoe until the object was revealed.

The gold locket was tarnished and appeared very old. She picked it up and, using her thumbnail as a wedge, attempted to pry it open. The lid finally popped to disclose two small black-and-white photographs. One was unmistakably her aunt Iris, looking young, radiant and happier than she'd ever seen her. The other was of a handsome, smiling man Beth assumed was Lyle McMurtry.

She stared at the locket in disbelief, shaking her head at the full import of what she'd just discovered—another piece of incriminating evidence.

Was this proof positive that her aunts were somehow involved? The locket was obviously her aunt

Iris's, and now here it was at the scene of the crime, if a crime had actually been committed.

Not only was she hideously lacking Lara Croft's chutzpah, she apparently had little of Nancy Drew's flair for mystery, either.

Dropping the piece of antique jewelry into the front pocket of her jeans, she got down on her hands and knees and began clawing the earth in the same fashion the dog had minutes before. She was filled with apprehension and dread, worrying and wondering what other items she would find that might shed light on what had occurred in this basement so long ago.

At first, her search came up empty and she breathed a sigh of relief. But then, just as she was about to give up, she spotted something white. Yanking hard to free it, she discovered a piece of old linenlike material. There appeared to be splotches of dark brown covering it. *Blood?* She swallowed hard. *Paint?* She prayed fervently, unwilling to take the chance it wasn't connected.

Beth gathered up the remaining pieces of material, which looked to be part of a man's shirt, and placed them in the ground with the bones. She had just dropped the last shovel of dirt onto the makeshift grave when the doorbell chimed.

If she didn't get this mess sorted out quickly, Mr. Pickens could become the next victim. After all, Aunt Ivy *had* seemed rather irritated with him.

Okay, so maybe I'm overreacting.

Surely there had to be a simple explanation for everything that had happened. She was too young to be an accessory to murder. And with her coloring, she would look awful wearing one of those hideous orange prison jumpsuits.

"I DON'T SEE WHY I had to leave school before Thanksgiving break. It's only a week away, and Missy Stuart's invited me to her slumber party. Now I'll miss out. And everyone's going to be there."

Out of the corner of his eye, Brad Donovan studied the sullen face of his twelve-going-on-thirty-year-old daughter while still managing to keep his eyes fixed on the traffic ahead. Congestion on Interstate 95 was always a nightmare at this time of morning.

He'd wanted to leave late last night, but had been faced with one medical emergency after another. First, Bobby Bartley had fractured his clavicle playing baseball, then he'd had to perform an emergency tracheotomy on a fifteen-month-old infant, who'd swallowed a piece of Lego toy that had lodged in his windpipe. So now he was doomed to sit in traffic and listen to Stacy whine for the next several hours.

"I've already explained, Stace, about Grandpa's disappearance. It's not like him not to call or let us know where he is."

"He sent you a postcard."

The postcard from the Two Sisters Ordinary was the only clue he had to his father's last known whereabouts. When he didn't receive a call back from the innkeeper after leaving several messages, he'd decided to drive to Mediocrity and see for himself if the inn's proprietor could shed light on his father's disappearance.

It wasn't like his dad to cut off all contact with his family. Robert Donovan was organized, punctual and thoughtful. The old man had lived with him and Stacy since Brad's mom passed away eight years ago. And though he seemed to have adjusted to life as a widower, to giving up his independence somewhat, Brad sensed that all was not well. His father had been morose lately. Brad had done his best to compensate, to offer companionship and support, but it hadn't been enough.

Six weeks ago, his dad had packed up his ancient Chevy Impala and announced quite unexpectedly that he intended to visit the Pennsylvania countryside, along with a few Civil War battlefields. Brad had offered to go with him, to make a family vacation out of the trip, but his father had been adamant in his refusal—almost rude, come to think of it. It was obvious the old man wanted to be alone. But why?

"Gramps probably just found some other stupid battlefield to see," Stacy pointed out, before opening her purse and taking out a tube of bright red lipstick. She applied it meticulously, blotting the excess, while viewing herself in the vanity mirror, her head tilting from side to side.

Stacy was growing up too fast. Since her mother's death four years ago to ovarian cancer, the young girl had turned from a downy chick into a fledgling swan, and Brad was often at a loss trying to figure out how to handle the difficulties of puberty and adolescence. The first bra and menstrual period had been traumatic enough, but now it was makeup, loud music and boys. Eight years of medical school and a pediatric residency hadn't prepared him for being the father of a pre-teen girl.

He and Stacy hadn't been communicating very well lately, and he wasn't quite sure how to remedy that. If he objected to the clothing she wore or the TV programs she watched, she called him old-fashioned. If he suggested that she spend more time on her homework, Stacy accused him of being overly critical—"in her face," as she put it.

It was extremely frustrating for a man who had chosen as his vocation the care and nurturing of children not to be able to figure out what was ailing his own daughter.

"Do you think I'm pretty, Dad?"

The question came out of nowhere, as they often did, and Brad downshifted the BMW into third gear before answering, ignoring the honking horn of the minivan behind him. "You're beautiful, Stace, just like your mom. I've told you that many times."

"Then how come Billy Carson said I was flat-chested and needed breast implants and that my front teeth were spaced too far apart?"

Billy Carson of the spiked green hair had little room to talk, but that had never stopped the loud-mouthed delinquent from giving his opinion. He was one of Brad's patients, but that didn't mean he had to like the kid, especially now that he knew he'd been staring at his daughter's chest. Little pervert!

"I doubt very much if Billy even knows what breast implants are. And you're not flat-chested, just slower to develop than some girls your age." He could tell she wasn't happy or convinced by his explanation, so he added, "In case you haven't noticed, all the top fashion models are pretty sparse on top. It's the look these days."

"Yeah, it may be the look, but boys still like girls with big boobs."

So did men, but Brad wasn't about to point that out to his impressionable young daughter. "I think you're going to like the inn where we'll be staying. It looks very quaint from the postcard."

Wrinkling her nose in disgust, she replied, "It's probably going to smell old and musty, like Grandma Ruth's house used to."

"Grandma was a bit old-fashioned, I guess. But there's always something to be learned from an older person."

"Then how come you're always telling Gramps how to do stuff? Maybe his way would be better than yours."

Before Brad could muster a suitable response about his responsibilities as head of the household, his need to have order and complete control, Stacy had put on her headphones, popped a wad of gum into her mouth and tuned him out, which was probably just as well.

It would be difficult to explain his need for normalcy and sameness since his wife's death. He really didn't understand it himself. He just knew that he needed his routine, his life, to remain uncluttered and uncomplicated.

Carol's death had turned his world upside down. He'd never realized, until she was gone, the depth of despair he was capable of, the gut-wrenching emotion, the emptiness inside him. For months after her death, his life had been chaos and confusion. Now that things were almost back to normal he wanted it to stay that way.

And driving to Pennsylvania in search of his errant father was not what he considered normal, or the way he wanted to spend his free time. And neither was dealing with rude country-inn owners who didn't return phone calls.

"I'LL BE IN TOUCH about the loan, Beth. And please thank your aunts for the jam. Mrs. Pickens will be delighted."

After the banker disappeared down the front steps, Beth slammed the door shut and leaned heavily against it, breathing a deep sigh of relief that the inspection was finally over.

Mr. Pickens's visit had gone on a lot longer than she'd anticipated. The man had been disgustingly thorough. He'd stuck his head in every oven, freezer and refrigerator, flushed toilets, turned faucets on and off, and she fully expected him to don a pair of white gloves to see if she had dusted the furniture that morning.

She hadn't.

But the worst had come when he'd ventured into the cellar, poking around at every little thing. She'd held her breath, waiting in fear that he would discover the bones and shirt, but fortunately the banker had found nothing amiss.

The grandfather clock in the foyer gonged four, and Beth knew her aunts would be expecting her to join them shortly for their daily ritual of afternoon tea, and to give them a full accounting of her meeting with the banker.

She had just turned toward the stairs when a knock sounded at the door. Thinking Mr. Pickens had forgotten something, Beth rushed to answer it.

Opening the door, she stared at the dark-haired man standing on her porch. He was tall and looked to be in his mid-to-late thirties, judging by the crow's feet appearing at the corner of his eyes. The stranger smiled, and she caught a glimpse of perfect white teeth. The man's parents had obviously spent a fortune on orthodontics when he was a kid. The money had been well spent. He was very good-looking, but then, he probably knew that. Most handsome men did.

"Mrs. Randall?"

"It's *Ms*. Randall. Can I help you?" she asked, and it was then she noticed the young girl standing next to him. The dislike in her pretty blue eyes gave Beth pause. Most people waited until *after* they'd spoken to her before deciding they disliked her.

"I hope so. I'm Bradley Donovan."

She held out her hand. "Welcome to the Two Sisters, Mr. Donovan." When he clasped her hand, she looked up to find that hundred-watt, hundred-thousand-dollar smile shining down on her and felt its warmth.

"Actually, it's *Dr*. Donovan. I've left several messages on your answering machine regarding my father, Robert Donovan. He was a guest here some weeks back and now he's missing."

Beth's heart began to pound. She remembered Robert Donovan. He'd played cards with her aunts on several occasions. She swallowed. Two gentlemen who'd been in contact with her aunts were now missing? She didn't like the odds.

"When I didn't get a response I decided to come in person to see if you could shed any light as to my father's whereabouts. My daughter and I are very worried about him."

Preoccupied with Mr. Pickens's visit, Beth hadn't had time to return his calls. "I'm afraid I can't be of much help, Dr. Donovan. I remember your father, but I have no idea where he's gone."

"I'm not worried about Gramps," Stacy Donovan blurted. "Just you are, Dad. I figure Gramps has gone off to visit some stupid battlefield. You worry too much. Chill, okay?"

"I'm sure you're right," Beth said, holding out her hand to the girl who responded by smacking her gum loudly, a sound only slightly less irritating than fingernails raking a blackboard. "I'm Beth. And you are?"

The girl hesitated a moment. "Stacy Donovan. My dad made me come here. I didn't want to. This place smells really old, like dead people live here or something."

The kid had a good nose; she'd give her that.

"Apologize to Ms. Randall at once, Stacy."

"That's okay. It's not—"

"Sorry." The young girl's apology lacked conviction.

"Come in," Beth said, remembering her manners and leading them into the front parlor. It was a cozy room, decorated in rose-and-green-floral chintz; the walls were painted a warm buttery yellow, with pretty lace curtains hanging at the double-hung windows.

"Actually, Stacy, this house is really old, over a century old, as a matter of fact. And the smell you're referring to is probably the incense my aunt is burning upstairs. I'll speak to her about it. I'm not crazy about the smell, either."

Her gaze lifted to the girl's father, and Beth had the strangest sense of coming home as she stared into Bradley Donovan's warm, comforting eyes. She shook her head to dispel the notion. "I'm very sorry about not returning your phone calls, Dr. Donovan. I'm not usually so inconsiderate, but I had several pressing business matters to attend to and forgot to check my answering machine." *Not to mention, there's a pile of buried bones in my basement, which may or may not belong to Lyle McMurtry. And for all I know, your father might be down there, too.*

Seating himself on the colorful sofa, Bradley Donovan yanked his daughter down beside him. "My father left our home in Charlottesville about six weeks ago. I know he stopped here because I received this postcard." He removed the card from his pocket, handing it to her; she recognized it at once.

"We give these postcards to the guests. They're in

all the rooms. But I can't recall anything unusual about your father's departure. Perhaps my aunts know something. They may have spent some time with him. I really can't be sure. I was just on my way upstairs to visit them when you arrived. I'd be happy to ask."

Momentarily appeased, he nodded, and then went on to talk about the attractiveness of the inn, the traffic he'd encountered on the interstate, and the weather. Though she did her best to listen intently, nodding at the appropriate times, she found herself oddly mesmerized by the color of his blue eyes. Beth had met many men since her divorce and had never given a hoot about the color of their eyes, or any other part of their anatomy, for that matter. Her relationships hadn't lasted long enough to find out if size really mattered.

Unfortunately, Stacy Donovan's eyes were shooting daggers at her. If looks could kill, Beth would have been buried in the cellar, right next to whoever was down there.

"The woman thinks you're hot, Dad. Let's get outta here."

Brad flashed his daughter an annoyed look. "That's enough, Stacy! What's gotten into you today?"

"I do not!" Beth shook her head in denial, her cheeks flaming bright red. "That never entered my mind." Nor would it. Fool me once was her motto.

The doctor looked amused by her discomfort, and

his dimpled grin made her eyes widen. "I'm sure it didn't, Ms. Randall."

Assuming a businesslike posture, she folded her hands primly in her lap. "Will you need to book a room, Dr. Donovan? I have several vacancies at the moment and can accommodate you."

He nodded. "I'm not sure how long we'll be here. I need to make inquiries about my father, talk to the local authorities, that sort of thing."

The authorities! Beth swallowed her fear and forced a smile. "I can put you and your daughter in a lovely twin-bedded room on the second floor. It has a view of the pond."

"That'll be just fine. And call me Brad."

"Hope our room's not next to yours!" Stacy told Beth, her pert nose wrinkling in disgust. "I don't want you bothering my dad. He doesn't like women."

Beth's right eyebrow arched, her attention shooting to the doctor, whose face was turning all sorts of interesting colors. "Oh? Well, I—"

"Stacy doesn't know what she's talking about." His daughter opened her mouth to say something else, but he cut her off. "Go out to the car and get your bag. Now!"

The girl heaved a dramatic sigh and sulked off. Beth wasn't sorry to see her go. She didn't have a great deal of patience when it came to children, especially mouthy, gum-smacking teenagers.

Unlike most women, Beth had no desire to have children. Her childhood had been so unhappy, her marriage such a disaster that she didn't feel qualified to dispense motherly advice. She enjoyed being an independent businesswoman with no husband to dictate and no children to tie her down.

"Don't pay any attention to Stacy, Ms. Randall. My wife died four years ago, and she hasn't adjusted very well. My daughter sees every woman I meet as a threat."

Beth smiled in understanding. "No problem—and it's Beth. I was twelve once, much to everyone's horror." And she'd grown up without a father since the age of ten, so she understood the girl's need to keep her dad close.

Their eyes locked and held for a brief moment, making Beth's heartbeat quicken, then the front door opened and Brad's daughter returned, breaking the spell, which relieved her to no end. She was already up to her armpits in complications; she didn't need another one, especially a handsome doctor with a missing father!

As she ushered Brad and his daughter up the stairs to their room, Beth wondered what she was going to tell the man about his father's disappearance. Obviously, her suspicions about the bones in her basement would not—could not—be a topic of discussion, not if she wanted to keep her aunts safe.

She felt the weight of the locket burning into her flesh, a painful reminder of gruesome possibilities.

Despite her best efforts not to, Beth found Bradley Donovan quite likable. He seemed kind and caring, and she couldn't help but notice how muscular his body was, how blue his eyes were. Of course, Greg was handsome, too, and he'd turned out to be the world's biggest rat bastard.

"Handsome is as handsome does," her aunts were fond of saying, and she wasn't about to forget that lesson.

Besides, she needed a man in her life right now like she needed another dead body in her cellar.

CHAPTER THREE

"OH, THERE YOU ARE, Beth dear. Ivy and I were wondering what was keeping you so long. The tea is getting cold."

Just the good doctor and his nasty daughter, she was tempted to say, trying hard to remember that she'd once been a pubescent child with a big mouth. Though she was positive she hadn't been as rude as Stacy Donovan, who had seen fit to flip her off when her father's back was turned. The young girl had passed annoying and was heading straight for unlikable. And though she knew there were reasons for her behavior, Beth had a difficult time accepting them.

"Sorry I'm late. Some unexpected guests just arrived—a Dr. Donovan and his daughter. I've been getting them settled in their room."

"I saw them out the window when they drove up," Ivy stated, perching primly on the edge of the red velvet settee and crossing her ankles, looking like everyone's idea of the perfect granny and making it hard to believe that the old lady had a salacious side.

"The man is quite handsome. You'd be wise to take notice, Beth. It's been a while since you've indulged, if you get my meaning, and he looks to be very well—"

"Aunt Ivy!" She held up her hand to cut off whatever suggestive comments her aunt was about to make. Beth had enough problems at the moment; she didn't need a matchmaking old lady meddling in her affairs.

"I'm not interested in Dr. Donovan, or any man, for that matter. I've told you both countless times that I'm content as I am. Besides, Brad Donovan's daughter hates me, so there's not really much point in pursuing any fantasies about him, if one were into fantasies, which I'm not." She lived vicariously through the heroines in romance books and movies. It would have to be enough.

Ivy smiled smugly, not believing a word of her niece's protestation.

Pouring tea out of a pink-flowered china teapot into three matching cups, Iris glanced up, eyes widening in surprise. "But why does the girl dislike you, dear? She doesn't even know you."

With a lift of her shoulders, she tried to explain. "Stacy lost her mother a few years ago. Apparently, she feels threatened by other women, sees them as competition for her dad's affections, which is totally ridiculous where I'm concerned, because I have no designs on the man."

"*Tsk-tsk.* That poor child." Ivy took the cup of Earl Grey her sister handed her. "She's undoubtedly lonely. I'll make it a point to befriend her. Maybe Stacy likes computers. I'll be sure to ask her the first chance I get. We can go online and—"

"But no pornography! You must promise, Aunt Ivy," Beth said firmly. "Most—" *normal* teetered on the tip of her tongue "—people don't think as liberally as you do about these kinds of things."

"Of course not!" Her aunt looked insulted that Beth would even suggest such a thing. "Though I don't know what all the fuss is about. There are statues of naked men in museums. Why, there's even one in the center of the town common. Nudity is a very healthy thing. If I were a bit younger and less wrinkled, I'd be tempted to join one of those nudist colonies. I think it would be a very exhilarating experience. I might just do it one of these days anyway."

The image of a shar-pei came to mind, but Beth blinked it away.

Iris's mouth fell open, and then recovering, she said, "That statue you speak of, sister, is a copy of the *David* by Michelangelo. It's a famous work of art."

"I'll say it is. That David was no slouch. Makes me want to travel to Italy to check out those Italian men."

"Do either of you know anything about Robert

Donovan's whereabouts? Where he might have gone after leaving here?" Beth interrupted, though she doubted the new topic would be any safer. "I was hoping he might have told you something during your visits."

The two women's faces reddened simultaneously and their eyes widened before exchanging what Beth construed to be guilty looks, even as they shook their heads in denial. "Why, no, dear." Iris smoothed the skirt of her print dress with quick, nervous movements. "We didn't associate with Mr. Donovan all that much. Did we, sister?"

Ivy shook her head. "No. Not at all."

"But I thought you played bridge with him a few times. I distinctly remember you telling me that." Her suspicions continued to grow. The old women were hiding something.

Dead bodies, perhaps?

Bonnie and Clyde. Iris and Ivy. It didn't have the same cachet to it. But still…

"Dr. Donovan is here to search for his father. He's very worried about him, says it's not like him to go off without leaving word."

Ivy scoffed. "Oh, I'm sure he'll be just fine. After all, Robert—" Her cheeks filled with color at the slip. "I mean, Mr. Donovan is a grown man who undoubtedly knows his own mind. Young people should give older folks more credit for being capable.

Why, you'd be surprised what we can do when we put our minds to it."

Thinking back to the shovel, bones and locket, Beth had no doubt about that.

"Are you sure you've told me everything? It's very important that you confes…confide in me, if you know anything."

"Of course, dear," Iris answered in wide-eyed innocence, quickly changing the subject. "Now, why don't you tell us about your meeting with Mr. Pickens? I'm just dying of curiosity, and so is Ivy."

Heaving a sigh, Beth knew she'd get no more information out of the two old ladies today. They could be as stubborn as lint on black socks when they put their minds to it. Though she went on to reveal the details of her meeting with the banker, Beth couldn't shake the feeling that Iris and Ivy knew more than they were saying, which didn't bode well for her peace of mind, not when there were bones buried in her basement.

"I HATE LYING TO Beth, Iris." Ivy wrung her hands nervously and paced across the colorful Aubusson carpet her ancestor Isaac Swindel had brought over from England when he'd made the trip to the colonies with William Penn. "She's going to be madder than a flea-infested dog when she finds out what we've done."

Uneasy at her sister's prediction, for she knew it was true, Iris said, "Now, sister, you know it can't be helped. We don't want to involve Beth and get her into trouble. It's best to keep our own counsel, as we've already discussed. Besides, keeping information from someone to protect them isn't really lying—it's being responsible."

Blue eyes filled with uncertainty, Ivy pinched the bridge of her nose, trying to ease the pain centered there, and nearly dislodged her wire-rimmed glasses. "I'm going to take some Excedrin and rest a bit before dinner. I feel a headache coming on."

"All right, dear. I'm going to try that incantation one more time. I must be doing something wrong. It's just not working like it should."

"Maybe you should add some Viagra to your potion. It supposedly raises quite a few...*er*... things."

"Ivy Swindel! You are shameful."

The old woman smiled. "Yes, I know. But at my age I have every right to be. Life should be fun when you're as old as I am. In fact, I'm thinking about forming a chapter of that Red Hat Society here in Mediocrity. It's for women over fifty. They wear red hats, purple dresses and have oodles of fun. I may even let you join...or not," she tossed out before disappearing.

Iris shook her head and had just opened up *The Wicca's Guide to Potent Brews* when she felt someone's eyes upon her. She and Ivy rarely closed the door to their suite of rooms; they were the only inhabitants on the fourth floor, so it seemed unnecessary.

Her niece had insisted that they were too trusting of strangers and that someday one of the guests would walk off with their antiques and cherished possessions. But so far that hadn't come to pass, and Iris was doubtful it would.

Beth tended to be distrustful of people because of her unhappy childhood and the way her former husband had treated her. Not that Iris could blame the poor child. Greg Randall had proved to be a womanizing scoundrel. Still, it was Iris's belief that one had to have faith in the good of mankind.

Glancing over her left shoulder toward the open door, she found a young blond girl framed in the doorway and knew immediately that she was Bradley Donovan's daughter. "Hello?" She smiled in greeting. "Are you lost?"

The child, who was attired in jeans and a bright pink sweatshirt adorned with red hearts, shook her head. "Nope. I just wanted to see what was up here. I'm staying at the inn with my dad."

Apparently the sign stating Private Residence hadn't deterred the inquisitive child. "Come in. You must be Stacy Donovan. My niece, Beth, has told me a bit about you."

Nodding, the child stepped forward somewhat

tentatively and looked about at the heavy upholstered furnishings, red velvet drapes and ecru lace curtains hanging at the windows, then pulled a face. "This is really old stuff. Reminds me of my Grandma Donovan's house. At least you don't have those plastic things covering your lamp shades."

Shutting the book, Iris seated herself on the wing chair fronting the fireplace and motioned for the girl to sit down. "I don't get many visitors your age, and I always enjoy talking to young people." She missed her days of teaching school for that reason.

"No wonder no one visits," Stacy said, sniffing the air like a bloodhound. "It stinks in here. What's that smell? It's, like, totally gross."

Taken aback by the girl's bluntness, a soft blush touched the older woman's cheeks. "I've been burning incense."

Clearly impressed, the girl's eyes widened. "Cool. Do you smoke pot?"

Iris clutched her chest, looking horrified. "Heavens, no! Do you?"

"*Nah*. My dad would kill me. Besides, marijuana can be addictive and lead to other drugs. My dad's a doctor, so I know a lot about stuff like that. So how come you're burning incense?"

"I'm trying out a new incantation."

Stacy glanced at the book on the table. "Are you a witch or something?"

Iris smiled. "There're some around here who would say so."

"Cool."

"Would you like a cookie? I have some Fig Newtons left."

"Gross. I hate those." Then noting Iris's disappointed look, Stacy remembered her manners, adding, "No thanks, I mean."

"Tell me a little bit about yourself and your grandmother, Stacy. Do you visit her often?" Iris had always wanted children and grandchildren. But that had not been possible, not after… She pushed the painful thought away.

Plopping down on the lumpy chair, Stacy pulled a used wad of gum out of her pocket and unwrapped it, then stuck it in her mouth. "My grandma died when I was young, my mom, too. I just have Dad and Gramps now, only Gramps is gone. Missing, my dad says. He's real worried about him."

Pop! Smack! Pop!

The older woman held her tongue at the annoying sounds the child was making and replied, "Yes, my niece informed me of that, as well. I'm sorry to hear about your mother, dear. It's never easy when someone we love dies and leaves us." Iris glanced toward the window, lost in thought for a moment, and then looked back to find the young girl's eyes filled with tears.

"Mom had cancer. My dad took her death really hard. I used to hear him crying at night. It was kinda weird to know that he cried, too. I thought I was the only one."

Iris's heart went out to the poor child. It was clear Stacy was still grieving, and she knew what that was like. "I lost someone I loved, too. It was a long time ago, but his memory still lingers in my heart." As did the pain of his duplicity.

"Your husband?"

The older woman shook her head. "Lyle and I were never married, though we'd hoped to be one day. It…it just didn't work out that way. Sometimes God has a different plan for us, and there's nothing we can do but accept what He hands us." And try to go on. But that's never easy. Especially not when your life is destroyed by one single, impulsive act.

"Yeah, that's what my dad told me. Was your boyfriend cute? Most of the good-looking guys at my school won't give me the time of day. I think it's because I'm flat-chested."

Leaning forward, Iris swallowed her smile and patted Stacy's knee. "You have plenty of time for that sort of thing, my dear. You should enjoy your youth. You only get one go-around. I used to tell my niece that very thing when she would get impatient about growing up. But as you can see, Beth's turned into a fine woman."

The young girl looked as if she wanted to dispute that opinion. "I guess."

"And to answer your question, Lyle was very handsome—the handsomest man in Mediocrity." She smiled softly at the memory of dark hair and eyes as blue as her own. "Would you like to see his picture?"

"Sure."

Reaching into the drawer of the leather-inlaid mahogany drum table situated next to her chair, she pulled out a silver-framed photograph, handing it to her. "This was taken over fifty years ago, right before we were to be married."

The young girl studied the smiling man in the black-and-white photograph. He looked as if he hadn't a care in the world. "He's pretty good-looking, but not as handsome as my dad. All the women think he's hot, including your niece. But Dad's not thinking about getting married again. He still loves my mom." She said it with conviction, as if uttering those words would make it so.

Taking the photo from the girl's hands, tears blurred her vision as Iris gazed upon the man she loved and had thought to share her life with. But Lyle was gone, as were her girlish dreams of happily-ever-after. Gone, but not forgotten. Never forgotten. "He was a good man, in so many ways. We shared some wonderful times together."

Unable to disguise the emotion she felt, Iris could see she was making the girl uncomfortable and smiled apologetically. "I'm sorry. I tend to reminisce, to think about the past and what could have been, and it saddens me. It's part of growing old, I guess."

"Don't be sad." Stacy reached out, taking the old woman's veined, liver-spotted hands in her own small soft ones; her unexpected kindness touched Iris. "At least you still have his memory. My dad says whenever I'm sad about my mom I should think about all the good times we shared, the places we visited, the books she read and the songs she sang. They'll always be with me, if I keep her memory alive. And I intend to."

"Your dad sounds like a very wise man. I'm looking forward to meeting him."

"He's okay, for a dad, I guess." She rose to her feet. "I'd better get going. Dad'll be mad if he wakes up from his nap and finds me gone. He worries about me."

Iris nodded in understanding. "Come back and visit again, Stacy dear. I'd like to introduce you to my sister. I know Ivy would love to meet you."

"Is she a witch, too?"

"Heavens no!" Iris shook her head and smiled. "Ivy has *other* interests." Which would no doubt get her sister into trouble one day.

After promising she would visit again soon, the

girl departed. Iris clutched Lyle's photograph to her chest and heaved a deep sigh of yearning. It was hard growing old alone. But then, except for Ivy, she'd been alone most of her life. There'd been no man after Lyle McMurtry. In her heart and soul, they would always be one. Nothing—not time, distance or death—could dissolve a love such as theirs.

If only Lyle had been wise enough to see that. Things could have been so very different.

LORI COOPER WAS THE new head chef at the Two Sisters Ordinary and Beth felt extremely fortunate to have her working at the inn. The woman had shown up on her doorstep one day last September, asking if the inn needed a cook. It had been quite a fortuitous moment, for she'd been about to place an ad for a chef in the *Philadelphia Inquirer*.

The capable, creative chef had worked in some of Philadelphia's finest restaurants, cooking alongside some very accomplished chefs after completing her training at the Culinary Institute of America in upstate New York. Though she hadn't provided references Lori appeared to be honest, and her skill in the kitchen certainly backed up her claims, so Beth had no reason to doubt her.

Still, there was an air of mystery about Lori. The petite, dark-haired woman seemed unhappy, and she wondered if her heart held heavy secrets. Beth had caught her looking nervously over her shoulder a few times, as if expecting someone to pop out of nowhere and steal her away. Beth knew chefs tended to be high-strung, but Lori seemed more so than usual.

The grand opening of the inn's restaurant was scheduled for Thanksgiving Day, and Beth and her chef were working hard to get the kinks out of the menu and to finish the hiring and training of the kitchen and wait staff.

The two women were seated at the butcher-block table in the kitchen, evaluating the dishes Lori had prepared for this evening's meal, which the inn's guests had seemed to enjoy. They had filled out evaluation cards and rated the meal very highly. Brad Donovan had written *Excellent* across the bottom of his card, which pleased Beth greatly.

"The duck was a big hit. I think everyone liked the bing cherry sauce you served with it. And the rice pilaf was delicious, not to mention the pecan tarts. I'm going to get fat having you around."

Her chef smiled. "Then we should definitely keep duck on the winter menu, along with rack of lamb and scallops of veal. If I can find a good supplier for Dover sole, I'd like to include that, as well."

Making a few notes on the legal pad in front of her, Beth paused and looked up. "Are you going to be able to get the truffles for the stuffing?"

Taking a sip of the Diet Coke that was never far

from her reach, Lori replied, "Yes, but they're going to be expensive. I guess I could leave them out and substitute something else, if you'd rather not spend the additional money."

"Go ahead and order them. I want the grand opening to knock everyone's socks off. We already have quite a few reservations from Mediocrity's finest. Mayor Lindsay is going to be here," she explained, "and so is Hilda Croft, from the historical society, so we're sure to have a good turnout. Good word of mouth will help business during the off season when there are fewer tourists around."

The stuffing recipe was one of Lori's favorites, though she couldn't take credit for it. That honor belonged to world-renowned chef Bill Thackery, her former colleague. Though Bill might be absent, the one thing that wasn't was his prized recipe collection, which she had lifted prior to leaving Philadelphia, along with his favorite set of Henckels knives.

No doubt he was more upset about losing his knives and recipes than losing her.

Leaving Bill hadn't been an easy decision. He'd been her mentor, teaching her the finer points of culinary artistry, and she admired him greatly. But Lori felt she needed to get out from under his thumb, to establish herself as a chef in her own right, not just one of Bill's protégés. Though she counted him as a friend, she just couldn't work with him any longer.

He'd grown demanding and unreasonable, wanting everything to be done his way and stifling her creativity until she wanted to scream.

They bickered constantly about the correct way to do just about everything, like what ingredients to use in chili, the proper temperature for roasting duck, how much yeast was required when baking bread. You name it, they argued over it. In fact, they had argued bitterly the night before her departure over a duck pâté that Lori had created. Bill had pronounced it "bland." She'd stolen his knives and recipes for revenge.

The competition to outdo each other had finally gotten to Lori, who had decided one morning that she'd had enough, that it was time to make a break and get her own career off the ground. The Two Sisters Ordinary would give her that chance.

Lori hoped Bill didn't hate her too much. She still felt guilty about leaving him the way she did, with no note or explanation. But she figured he owed her for years of hard work and loyalty. The recipes and knives were a fair punishment for his obnoxious behavior and nasty disposition. She just prayed he wouldn't be able to track her down, because Bill Thackery *did not* like to be crossed.

"Is everything all right? You look upset. I meant what I said about the truffles. Just go ahead and—"

The dark-haired woman shook her head, smiling apologetically as she grabbed the edge of the table and pushed to her feet. "It's not the truffles, Beth. I'm just tired. If you don't need me for anything else, I'm going to my room and relax for a while."

"Of course. If you like, I can fix breakfast in the morning, so you can sleep later." Beth wasn't a fabulous cook like Lori, but she was proficient enough to slap bacon and eggs together.

"That's not necessary. I'll be fine by morning. But thanks for the offer."

Concern creasing her forehead, Beth watched her chef disappear and wondered, not for the first time, what was bothering the young woman. She didn't have time to ponder the possibilities, because the door from the dining area to the kitchen swung open and Brad Donovan entered.

He'd changed since she'd seen him at dinner and was now wearing jeans and a blue polo shirt. The jeans had been ironed, as evidenced by the perfect crease dissecting the pant legs.

Good grief! What kind of a man ironed jeans?

A man who was a perfectionist and wanted everything just so—a man used to genteel living, gracious surroundings and having a perfect wife—a man who was reserved, anal and her total opposite.

Still, the dimples in his cheeks when he smiled were awfully cute, and he had a way of looking directly into her soul—as if he knew exactly what she was thinking—that made her totally uneasy.

"Hope you don't mind, but I'm taking you at your word and making myself at home. Stacy wants a glass of milk, so I told her I'd bring one up to her when I retired, if that's okay with you."

"Of course. I'll get it for you." She made to rise, but Brad placed his hand on her shoulder and pushed her back down gently. His touch made her jump. "Please don't!" She shrugged it off.

"I'm sorry. I didn't mean—"

"Forget it, okay?" Beth had overreacted, but she didn't like to be touched in a proprietary way, not after Greg.

"I'd like to join you for a few minutes, maybe beg a cup of coffee, if I'm not disturbing you. Adult conversation's been at a premium at our house lately."

With an understanding smile, she pointed at the coffeepot. "Help yourself."

"Thanks." Fetching two mugs, he filled them with freshly brewed coffee and carried everything to the table, sitting down beside his hostess.

"You're not disturbing me," she said. "I'm just going over some menus."

"Your chef's terrific. I loved the duck. Very moist. And the skin was crisp, just the way I like it."

"Thank you. My hope is to have one of the finest

restaurants in the area. And with a chef as excellent as Lori I think I'm on my way."

"Without a doubt. So why did you decide to become an innkeeper? It seems an odd profession for someone so young. I always think of innkeepers as old married couples who crochet doilies, chop firewood and wear red-and-black-checked shirts."

Laughing, she sipped her coffee and started to relax. Brad Donovan was very easy to talk to and seemed genuinely interested in what she had to say. "I'm not as young as you think," she said, explaining about her aunts' decision to give their house to her, and hers to turn it into an inn.

"When I divorced my husband I was at loose ends. The inn gave me something to focus on. And I love everything involved in the operation of it. It's quite a challenge, but also very satisfying knowing that my guests enjoy what I do for them."

"I guess having people around all the time keeps you from getting lonely. That was the hardest thing for me after my wife died. I never realized how lonely being all alone could be." He stared thoughtfully into his coffee.

"How did she die?"

He looked up, his eyes filled with sadness. "Ovarian cancer. By the time Carol was diagnosed, it was too late. The cancer was too far gone."

"I'm so sorry. That must have been very difficult for you, especially with a young daughter to care for."

"It hasn't been easy. But Stacy keeps me focused on what's important. And I try not to dwell in the past."

It was clear he was still in love with his dead wife, and that said volumes about the kind of relationship they'd had. Beth had been deprived of that deep connection, that death-till-you-part kind of love in her own marriage and envied those who had it. Though not enough to ever look for it again.

"I don't get lonely very often," Beth said. Though sometimes at night when she lay in her cold bed, she yearned for a warm body to snuggle with. Buster came close to fitting the bill, but it wasn't quite the same. "I have my aunts, the guests, people around me all the time and, of course, my dog, so I'm rarely ever alone. There are times when that can be frustrating, like when I'm all set to watch a movie and I get interrupted."

"I can't remember the last film I watched. It's not as much fun now that Carol's gone. And Stacy's taste is so different than mine. I like the old black-and-white films, but she won't watch a movie if it's not in color."

"I guess kids Stacy's age like movies where everything gets blown up. My best friend, Ellen, is the same way. She's a huge Bruce Willis fan and doesn't understand the simplicity and humor in a classic film like *The Philadelphia Story,* which she thinks is boring. I love the classic films, too. I'm very addicted to my video and DVD collection."

While Beth went on to discuss a Humphrey Bogart/ Lauren Bacall movie she'd watched recently, Brad listened intently, surprised by the primal reaction he was having to her infectious smile, the sound of her voice and the sparkle in her big green eyes as she extolled the virtues of Bogart's abilities as an actor.

Beth Randall was a very attractive woman. He'd thought her cute at first glance, but he could see now that she was so much more. Brad hadn't felt such an overt response to a woman since he'd met Carol at med school, and he was stunned by it.

Of course, Beth and Carol were nothing alike. Carol had been a cool blonde, with pretty cornflower-blue eyes and a conservative air about her—the typical Southern belle. Beth, on the other hand, had massive amounts of coppery hair that tempted a man to run his hands through it. She was relaxed, casual....

"Is something the matter, Dr. Donovan? You keep staring at me as if I've grown another nose." She reached up to touch hers, hoping it wasn't dripping.

"No. In fact, your nose is very cute."

She turned fifteen shades of red, feeling the heat of embarrassment all the way down to her toes, which she was curling and uncurling under the table. "Thank you."

"I was wondering if you'd mind answering some questions about my father's stay here."

The question took Beth off guard and her stomach knotted. She tried to remain poised and nonchalant, schooling her features to reflect that. "I'm afraid I don't have much to add right now, Dr. Donovan."

"It's Brad, remember?"

"I haven't had a chance to speak to my aunts," she lied. "But I will. And soon."

"Do you think they know something? It seems whenever I bring up my father's disappearance you get nervous." He stared intently at her, wondering if she knew more than she was saying and hoping she didn't.

"Nervous?" Beth laughed one of those Katharine Hepburn *ha, ha, ha* laughs. Only hers didn't come off nearly as innocent or flippant. "Don't be ridiculous. I'm just tired. I've had a long day. So if you'll excuse me."

Before he could utter another word she bolted from the kitchen with lightning speed, not remembering about the milk for Stacy until she'd reached the haven of her room. But she had no intention of going back down.

There was no way she was going to face him again. Not until she knew who was buried in her basement.

CHAPTER FOUR

AUBREY FONTAINE PRIDED himself on having an uncluttered mind and a reasonably fit body, though his penchant for sweets, especially Krispy Kreme doughnuts, rendered him somewhat overweight. Still, for someone nearing fifty he wasn't in bad shape.

A man used to giving orders and having them obeyed, he wasn't accustomed to performing mundane chores, doing his own laundry, cooking meals or cleaning his apartment. He had a staff to do that. So, as he stared at the stacks of cardboard boxes, piles of old newspapers and magazines, and an assortment of what he considered first-rate junk that he'd found lying about his deceased mother's spare bedroom, Aubrey was not pleased about completing the menial tasks before him.

Isabel Fontaine had died from colon cancer five days before—a blessing, since the old soul had suffered cruelly toward the end. And though he'd done what he could to ease his mother's pain—excellent doctors, full-time duty nurses and a private room at the hospital—in the end it had all been for naught. Money couldn't save his mother. Only God could do that, and He had chosen not to.

Brushing impatient fingers through his thin graying hair, Aubrey heaved a sigh. He didn't have time to deal with this right now. He was a busy man, had a corporation to run and important financial deals in the works. He made money from investing, not from performing the duties of a garbageman. But he'd promised his mother on her deathbed that he would go through her private papers and attend to dispersing what little money she'd saved to her cousins, and that's what he intended to do.

Isabel had been a good mother, if a somewhat distant one, and Aubrey would honor her memory and do what he had promised. A man was only as good as his word. His many business dealings had taught him that. One didn't get to be a successful CEO of a company without having some integrity. Of course, he never allowed that integrity to interfere with making money. An honest man could still be successful; he just had to be smarter than the competition, and he had to be willing to look opportunity in the face and jump on it.

Aubrey never allowed *anything* to interfere with making money.

Removing his suit jacket and tie, he set them on a nearby chair, rolled up the sleeves of his custommade shirt and began wading through the mess, tossing old magazines and newspapers into the trash receptacle, and then removing his parents' old clothes that he'd found hanging in the closet. Chester Fontaine had died of a heart attack when Aubrey was twenty, and he gathered his father's suits, shirts and ties and added them to the pile he would donate to the Good Will, or one of the veterans groups.

Aubrey had never served in the military—a bad back had designated him 4F—but he always tried to do what he could for those less fortunate than himself. Besides, he needed all the write-offs he could get. Damn bastards at the IRS always had their hands in his pockets.

His cell phone rang. His assistant was on the other end, and she sounded frantic. Though extremely competent, Myra Lewis leaned toward hysteria, which he found annoying and very nonproductive. "Tell that asshole Connors there'll be no deal unless he meets our terms," he told the high-strung woman. "For chrissake, Myra, I'm not running a charitable organization! He either takes what I've offered for the property or the deal is off. Do you understand?" She stuttered that she did, and he clicked off, shaking his head in disgust.

He couldn't get through an hour without that

cursed cell phone ringing. For all its convenience, the damned invention definitely had its drawbacks. In the old days, a man could escape from the office and steal a few hours of peace and quiet, now he just carried it with him. Call forwarding, e-mail, photographs... There was no end to what those blasted phones could do.

Turning his attention toward the window and the small maple desk sitting beneath it, Aubrey heaved a sigh, dreading what came next. He switched on the metal lamp, sat down and began sorting through the clutter.

In the center drawer he found his mother's bankbook resting on top of her insurance policy. He was stunned to discover that she had nearly eight thousand dollars in savings, most of which he had provided over the years, to supplement the pittance his father had left.

"Well, well, Mama, you are full of surprises," he muttered, knowing how happy her vulture cousins would be when they discovered how thrifty Isabel had been. As primary beneficiary of her insurance policy, Aubrey stood to inherit a tiny bit more—ten thousand dollars, which would just about cover the cost of her funeral and burial.

Tossing the policy aside, he pulled out a brown leather portfolio buried at the bottom of the drawer and opened it to discover several yellowed newspaper clippings from *The Mediocrity Messenger*. He'd never been to Mediocrity, but knew it was a small rural town about a three-hour drive from where he presently resided, in a suburb outside of Philadelphia.

Aubrey didn't do rural. He was a city boy, through and through. The smell of cow shit gave him hives.

The first clipping was about a historic house that was owned by a family named Swindel. Searching his memory, he tried to remember if his mother had ever mentioned the name and was fairly positive she hadn't.

He prided himself on remembering names and minute details. It was essential in his business. The little things, the seemingly unimportant things that could make or break a deal, were what counted. And he didn't lose many deals.

The owner of the house appeared to be a member of the clergy. The paper referred to him as the Reverend Swindel of St. Mark's Methodist Church. Aubrey didn't believe in organized religion or luck. Smart people made their own luck. And as far as religion was concerned, he didn't need some pious man of God pointing out his sins. He knew full well what they were; he just opted not to atone for them.

Setting that clipping aside, Aubrey picked up the next, torn from the society pages, and read:

"The Reverend and Mrs. Josiah Swindel are pleased to announce the engagement of their daughter Iris to Lyle McMurtry, son of David and Louise McMurtry, of the town. A spring wedding is planned."

It was dated May 1952.

"I know you had a reason for saving all this junk, Mama, but I have no idea why." He was about to replace the clippings when he noticed the corner of an official-looking document peeking out from some old letters she had saved.

Curious, Aubrey scanned it to discover it was a birth certificate. He spotted his name at the top of the document, which was odd because his birth certificate presently resided in a safe-deposit box at Merchants Bank. The certificate read Aubrey *Swindel*, not Fontaine.

More than a little confused, his eyes widened as he read the names typed beneath his: **Mother's name: Iris Swindel. Father's name: Lyle McMurtry**.

Swindel. As the meaning became clear, his face turned an ugly shade of purple.

"Sonofabitch!" He'd been deceived. His whole life had been nothing but one goddamn lie after another.

"Jesus H. Christ, Mama! You really put one over on me, didn't you, you sly old bitch?" He continued staring at the document in disbelief. "How could you have deceived me like this, made me feel like such a goddamn fool? Are you having a good laugh over this? Are you, Mama?"

Aubrey hated surprises and he'd just been handed a whopper. No wonder the old woman had insisted he look through her papers. She wanted him to find this, wanted him to know that he'd been adopted and who his real parents were.

"But why didn't you just come out and tell me? Why did you hide the truth all these years?"

Because he'd been born a bastard, that's why. But then, there were those who'd been calling him that for years.

Crumpling the paper, he tossed it against the wall, and then kicked the garbage can so hard it upended, the contents spilling everywhere. He shouted every vile epithet he could think of at his parents, or the people he'd thought were his parents. He wasn't sure of anything anymore.

When his temper cooled, curiosity began to get the better of him. Why had Iris Swindel and Lyle McMurtry given him away? Why hadn't they wanted him enough to keep him? Was he so unlovable, so hideous a human that even his own mother hadn't wanted him?

He needed answers to his questions, and the only way to get them was to go to Mediocrity and see if his birth parents were still alive. If so, they had some explaining to do.

HARD WORK AND KEEPING BUSY had always helped Beth clear her mind. Her aunts were fond of saying that idle hands were the Devil's playground. To keep her mind off the problem in her basement, she'd decided that picking pumpkins and gourds from her garden would serve her quite nicely.

Beth was tired this morning; she hadn't slept very well the previous night. Thoughts about dead men buried in her basement and dreams of Dr. Bradley Donovan finding out about them had crept into her subconscious. Counting sheep hadn't helped and neither had studying the numerous holes in the ecru lace canopy over her bed.

When she had finally drifted off, Beth encountered bright blue eyes, dimpled cheeks, muscular arms and strong hands capable of healing. And she spent a great deal of time wondering what it would be like to be held in those arms, to feel Brad's hands healing her aching body and ailing heart.

To dispel those provocative but totally unwelcome thoughts she had tried thinking about Greg, the disastrous marriage they'd had, his infidelity, and all the misery that being involved with a man had caused her. But she knew deep down that Brad Donovan was nothing like the duplicitous, uncaring and judgmental Greg Randall. That would be like comparing a Boy Scout to Hannibal Lecter.

Greg had chewed up her heart and spit it out when

it was no longer palatable, and he hadn't even bothered to wash it down with a nice glass of Chianti. Based on what Brad had said about his marriage to Carol, she didn't think he was capable of such cruelty. Of course, he was still a man and that said a lot about why she needed to keep her distance. Not to mention that his father might still be an unwilling guest in her establishment!

The ground was cold where she knelt in the dirt, pulling weeds from between rows of vegetables and gathering up the items she needed for her autumn display. She looked up at the clear blue sky, the sun's warmth feeling glorious on her face.

"It's a pretty day, isn't it, Buster boy?" she said to the dog lying next to her, who thumped his tail in agreement. Placing several small pumpkins in the wicker basket, she cocked her head when she heard someone approach. The animal rose to his haunches and then wagged his tail as the visitor drew near.

Shielding her eyes, Beth glanced up to find Stacy Donovan standing over her. Though she smiled in greeting, she was not in the mood to spar with the ill-tempered young girl this morning.

"What're you doing?" the girl demanded, bending down to pat the dog, who responded by licking her hand furiously, making Stacy giggle. It was the first time Beth had seen her smile, and it transformed her pretty face.

"I'm gathering pumpkins and gourds, which I'm going to use to decorate the front porch." Beth always festooned the house for the various seasons and holidays, autumn being one of her favorite displays. She used corn husks, scarecrows and pumpkins to adorn the porch and handrails. Admittedly, she was a bit behind schedule this year.

Stacy made a face. "That's stupid. Why would you want to do that?"

"So the inn will look pretty. Would you like to help?" The offer was pure reflex, not an actual desire to have the kid around. When Stacy shook her head, Beth almost breathed a sigh of relief.

"I'm bored, but not that bored! Besides, my dad's paying good money to stay here. Why should I do your work for free? I'm a guest."

"You said you were bored, so I thought you might like something to do, that's all. You're certainly not obligated to help. Don't you like decorating for the holidays? It's one of my favorite things to do."

A haunted look in her eyes, the girl shrugged. "I used to before my mom died. Dad doesn't bother with it now. We didn't even put up outdoor lights last Christmas. And he bought a fake tree. We never had a fake one when Mom was alive. She hated them."

"I see."

"No, you don't! You don't know what it's like to lose a mom, so don't say you do."

Rising to her feet, Beth dusted off her jeans and tried hard to keep her temper in check. The child was like a wounded animal, striking out at everything she came in contact with, and she had to keep reminding herself of that.

"You're right. My mom's still alive and living in San Francisco, but my dad left when I was ten, so I think I know a little something about losing a loved one."

The child's expression softened momentarily. "Did he die?"

She shook her head. "My parents got divorced. But my dad may as well have died because I haven't seen him in many years." Her mother had chased the man away with vile invectives and threats of public humiliation. And even if her father had deserved Margaret Shaw's wrath, Beth still blamed the woman for forcing him out of her life.

But she blamed her father even more for never contacting her or making the effort to see her. She considered his behavior cowardly and unjustified. Beth had often wondered if her father had remarried and started a new family, if he had other children to bestow his love and affection on. The notion had bothered her a lot at first, but now she'd grown indifferent, though there were times, if she allowed herself to think about it, it still hurt.

She had given her heart to two men, and they had

both crushed it before abandoning her. She didn't intend to make that same mistake again.

Stacy scoffed. "That's not the same. My mom's never coming back. You've got a shot at seeing your dad again."

Beth thought that highly unlikely but chose not to argue the point. "You miss your mom a lot, don't you? Your dad said—"

Blue eyes flashing angrily, Stacy balled her hands into fists. "You stay away from my dad! He's not going to marry anyone, so don't get any ideas. A lot of women have tried to get him, but he loves my mom and no one else."

"I can assure you, Stacy," she began, taking a deep, calming breath, "I have no desire to marry your dad, or anyone else, for that matter. I was married. I'm divorced now. It was a painful experience and not one I wish to repeat."

"I can see why your husband left. You're not very pretty, or smart."

As if slapped, Beth rocked back on her heels, not knowing how to respond. She'd been plagued with self-doubt for years, and the mean-spirited comment hit a little too close to home. "Has anyone ever told you that you're not very nice?"

Looking somewhat stunned, the child stood there, her face expressionless, except for the red blush staining her cheeks, making Beth wonder if she was sorry for what she'd said. "Don't tell my dad what I said, okay? He'll be mad, and I'll get grounded."

"I'll think about it. But only if you promise to think before you speak from now on. Words can be as painful as bullets. I'm sure you know that." Junior high and high school had a way of humbling even the most brazen, outspoken child. There was always someone bigger, meaner and mouthier to bring you down to size. Stacy was going to find that out the hard way, if she hadn't already.

Running the toe of her white leather Nike back and forth in the dirt, Stacy finally nodded, agreeing in a small voice, "All right."

"Speaking of your dad, does he know where you are?"

"I told him I was going for a walk. Besides, he's busy right now and doesn't want me around."

"I doubt that. What's he doing?"

"He's sitting on the front porch talking to your aunts. He thinks they might know something about Gramps's disappearance."

A panicked feeling swamped Beth, and she swallowed. "Really?" The last thing she needed was for Brad Donovan to interrogate her aunts. There was no telling what the old ladies would say, or if they would incriminate themselves about what was down in the cellar.

Why did Bradley Donovan have to come into her life right now? It was very inconvenient, and not just because of the probing questions he asked about his father's whereabouts. Brad was making her feel things she had no desire to feel. Sexual attraction, physical awareness, giddiness and stupidity were feelings she couldn't allow herself to experience right now. Would never allow herself, she amended. She had too much at stake.

"I'd better go check on my guests. And I do need to get that porch decorated."

"Can Buster come with me on my walk? I won't go far."

Buster, who was wagging his tail and running circles around Stacy, seemed overjoyed with the idea; though Beth knew he wasn't likely to hang with the child long. When it came to adventure the dog had a mind of his own.

"All right. Just make sure he doesn't go into the pond. Buster loves the water, but it's too cold this time of year, and he might get sick."

As soon as both girl and dog took off across the field, Beth grabbed her basket and made a beeline for the front porch, praying Iris and Ivy were behaving themselves.

What were the chances?

She broke into a run.

"WOULD YOU CARE for more apple cider, Dr. Donovan?" Iris asked. "Our niece makes the best hot cider in the world. She uses real cinnamon sticks, not the powdered stuff."

Brad smiled at the two women, who were seated in the white porch rockers on either side of him, looking as if they'd just stepped out of a flower garden. Iris's dress was adorned with pink cabbage roses, while Ivy sported blue forget-me-nots. Their snow-white hair reminded him of tufts of soft cotton. They were sweet, if not a bit odd.

"No, thanks. It was good, but I think I've had my fill. Umm, I was wondering if you ladies would mind answering a few questions about my father. I'm really quite concerned about him. He's been missing for several weeks and it's not like him not to contact me." Brad had called his service for messages and checked his voice mail at home, but there had been no word from his father.

Exchanging a weighted look with her sister, Iris took a moment to consider, before asking, "What kind of questions, Dr. Donovan? As I told my niece, we didn't know your father well. He wasn't here that long, if memory serves."

"Sister has the worst memory," Ivy explained with an embarrassed smile, making Brad wonder if he was ever going to get any information out of the two old ladies. He'd been sitting on the porch with them

for twenty-five minutes. They had discussed everything under the sun except his father's whereabouts.
He couldn't help thinking they knew more than they
were saying. And that went for their niece, too. Every
question he asked had been dodged, dismissed or just
plain ignored.

The old ladies weren't very good liars, and neither
was Beth. Everything she thought was reflected on
her pretty face. He was certain, especially after her
abrupt departure last evening, that she was covering
up something, for someone.

"How did my father seem when you spoke to him?
Was he upset, angry, confused? It would help if I
knew his state of mind." He prayed his dad hadn't
been despondent. That was the one thing he worried
about.

Before leaving for his trip, Robert Donovan had
been depressed. And though Brad had suggested that
he seek professional help, perhaps get a prescription
for antidepressants, his father had flatly refused,
claiming there was nothing wrong with him that
fresh air and a change of scenery couldn't cure.

"I found Robert to be terribly unhappy," Ivy confessed, confirming Brad's worst fear. "After talking to
the poor dear, Iris and I were determined to help him
solve his problems in the kindest way we knew how."

"Ivy!" Shaking her head, Iris shot her sister a
warning look, then pasted on a smile when Brad

glanced over at her with a questioning, almost frightened look.

"I'm afraid Ivy is prone to exaggeration, Dr. Donovan. You must excuse her."

"What do you mean, the kindest way?" he asked. "You'd better explain what you mean," he said, staring at them intently and watching as the two sisters squirmed restlessly in their seats. It didn't look good. The more the old ladies talked, the more off-kilter they seemed, which was a nice way of saying they were a few slices short of a loaf of nut bread.

"My niece has conversations with herself. Did you know that, Dr. Donovan?" Iris asked, handing him a plate of scones. "Care for another?" She smiled sweetly.

"No, thanks. Now, about my father—"

"We're worried Beth will never find another husband," Ivy added. "She's always reading those romantic novels and watching old movies. She simply adores Cary Grant and Katharine Hepburn. She lives in a fantasy world, if you ask me." She tutted. "Not good. Not good, at all."

Distracted by the woman's comments, Brad took a moment to digest the information. "Really? I wouldn't have guessed that about her. I mean, I knew Beth liked old films, but she seems very well grounded. I've never heard her talk to herself. Does she do that often?"

"Oh, yes," Iris offered, "all the time. And sometimes she answers herself."

Brad's eyes widened. Did insanity run—*gallop?*—in the family?

"My niece suffered an unhappy marriage. I think she's looking for a knight in shining armor to whisk her away." Ivy placed two scones on her napkin before continuing. "Most young women these days aren't prepared for the harsh realties of life."

"Now, Ivy, I think you're being unfair," her sister said. "Beth does a wonderful job of running this inn."

"Yes, and it's a safe place to hide, isn't it? I don't think it's quite natural for a woman Beth's age to be holed up with a couple of old ladies, morning, noon and night. She should be out enjoying herself. I just pray that being married to that awful Greg Randall hasn't turned her against men and into a...well, you know."

Brad's mouth fell open. Beth might be a great many things, but a lesbian? He doubted that very much. In fact, the idea seemed quite preposterous.

"Ivy Swindel! What a ghastly thing to say."

The old woman shrugged. "I call them like I see them." When Brad turned to wave goodbye to the Rogers, who were off on a sight-seeing trip, she smiled and winked at her sister.

Checking her wristwatch, Iris frowned. "I wonder what's been keeping Beth? She told me she wouldn't be out in the garden long."

"Shall I go and look for her?" Brad suddenly felt the need to escape. He had just asked the question when the object of their discussion came bounding out of the house, slamming the front door behind her and carrying a wicker basket filled with pumpkins and gourds. Beth's cheeks were rosy and her hair something of a disaster, but her smile was as radiant as ever.

"Good morning, everyone! Sorry I'm late."

"Have you seen Stacy, by any chance?" he asked, trying to ignore the way his gut clenched at the sight of her. "I don't want her wandering off. She's not familiar with the area and might get lost."

"Yes, we spoke a few minutes ago." She explained about Stacy taking the dog for a walk. "Don't worry. She'll be fine. I used to roam all over this place when I was young."

"Dr. Donovan's been inquiring after his father," Iris informed her niece. "We didn't tell him very much. We couldn't."

"I'm sure you were as helpful as you could be," Beth said, silently thanking God that her aunts had the presence of mind to keep quiet.

"Yes, some of your aunts' comments were very enlightening."

Brad's comment gave her pause. She sensed a change in his demeanor from last night. He seemed a tad more reserved, not quite as friendly. Or maybe it was just her imagination, which had been in overdrive lately. And after Stacy's cruel comments, she was admittedly feeling a bit sensitive about things.

"My aunts can be quite talkative when they put their minds to it. Can't you, dears?"

The two women burst into giggles, then stood. "We'll leave you to entertain Dr. Donovan, dear," Ivy stated, casting her sister a meaningful look.

"Iris is anxious to try another incantation. She's trying to raise the dead," the older woman explained to Brad, who nearly tipped his rocker backward into the front window but caught himself just in time.

Feeling her cheeks warm, Beth told her aunts, "You'd better go upstairs and rest. It wouldn't be good to overtire yourselves." She smiled apologetically at the handsome doctor, wondering what he must be thinking.

Her aunts sounded like a couple of nuts.

They are a couple of nuts!

She had no sooner formed that thought when out of the corner of her eye she spotted Buster dragging a large bone onto the front lawn. "Holy hell!" She covered her mouth when she realized she'd spoken her thoughts aloud and glanced at Brad to see that he had heard her.

Damn! She was really having a bad day...make that *year*.

"I beg your pardon," Brad said, staring at her strangely.

"Nothing. I've…I've got to see about my dog. He's gotten into…something…the garbage…yes… the garbage. Buster, shame on you!" The cellar doors were warped and didn't always shut properly. What if Buster had gotten back in?

Good grief! What if Stacy had seen Buster dig up the bones? What if she told her father about them?

Vaulting over the porch railing effortlessly, as if she'd been doing it most of her life—which, of course, she had—Beth rushed toward the dog, knowing something had to be done about the bones buried in the cellar. Right now! Before Dr. Bradley Donovan insisted on having them all committed to the hospital for the—*criminally?*—insane.

CHAPTER FIVE

BRAD HAD BEEN THINKING about Beth all day. Though her strange behavior that morning had given him pause, he knew his obsession was much more than that.

He was attracted to her—to her crooked smile, the way her nose crinkled when she laughed, the way her butt looked so damned appealing in a pair of tight jeans. He was attracted and that confused the hell out of him—his father's disappearance and her possible involvement in it, notwithstanding.

They really had very little in common. She was his total opposite, in every way imaginable. She seemed to live for the moment, while he planned everything out to the last detail. He'd already purchased the funeral plot next to Carol's and had begun saving for Stacy's college education. He was a stickler about his clothes; she seemed indifferent to what she was wearing. She always looked nice, just not coordinated.

So what did he find so compelling about her?

Beth was passionate about what she loved—the inn, her aunts and her desire to make something of herself. And he admired that about her, made him wonder if she'd be just as passionate with him in bed. He thought so. There was a lot of untapped desire in Beth; he could feel it.

She wasn't afraid of hard work. He'd seen her up at dawn, helping out in the kitchen or readying guest rooms when the hired help needed assistance. And she was kind. The times he'd seen her interact with Stacy she'd shown patience and caring, even when his daughter didn't respond in kind.

The back screen door banged, and he glanced over to find Beth hauling bags out to the garbage cans.

"Need some help?" he asked as he approached.

She gasped loudly and clasped her throat. "You startled me. You shouldn't sneak up on someone like that. I could have had a heart attack."

"I'm sorry. I just thought you could use some help." He nodded at the plastic garbage bags and shook his head. "Shouldn't you use some ties at the ends? You're going to spill whatever's in there into your cans. It'll make a disgusting mess." He couldn't hide his abhorrence, which made her smile.

"I let the garbageman worry about that. What are you, the garbage police? And what are you doing out here? It's cold, in case you haven't noticed."

"I was going to walk down to the pond before turning in. Care to join me?"

She hesitated. "I don't know. I—"

"Come on," he urged, taking her hand. "Looks like you could use a break. You work too hard."

Her hand fit perfectly in his and he squeezed it. She didn't object and followed his lead. "There's no one else to do the work, if I don't," she explained. "There are some days I wonder why I bit off so much, then others when the very idea of owning this place energizes me and makes me happy."

"I feel the same way about my practice. It's tiring as hell sometimes, but yet so rewarding."

"I can't even imagine what it must be like to save someone's life."

He smiled and pulled her down beside him onto a fallen log. "It's like no other feeling in the world. And it makes all the years of study and hard work worth it."

"I know what you mean. This place is everything to me. I never thought I could do it. My self-esteem was pretty much shot after my marriage ended. And I'm not really sure I had much to begin with."

"You don't seem insecure at all."

"My mother was very strong-willed and made me feel as if I could never do anything right. I met Greg Randall in college, and his attention bolstered my flagging ego, so when he finally asked me to marry him, I jumped at the chance to defy Mother and get out from under her thumb."

He nodded. "I take it things didn't work out the way you expected."

She sighed. "Marrying Greg didn't solve any of my problems. If anything, it made them worse. Rather than stepping out from behind my mother's shadow, I was swallowed up by my husband's life-style and overbearing personality.

"When his infidelities surfaced, my insecurities and self-doubts magnified. And it took years for me to realize that I had married Greg for all the wrong reasons and that I wasn't as stupid and worthless as I'd been led to believe.

"For the first time in my life, I feel like I'm succeeding, doing something important with my life. I'm not an extension of anyone else, but my own person, and I like the person I've become."

"I like the person you've become, too, Beth." He wrapped his arm about her and this time she didn't pull away. "Thanks for sharing your story with me."

"I'm sorry. I don't know what made me go on like that. Maybe I'm more tired than I thought."

"Or maybe you just needed someone to talk to. I've found myself in that same boat many times."

Beth turned in his embrace and looked up at him. There was yearning in her eyes, but also fear. He wanted to kiss her, to take her burdens away, but he knew she would never allow any man to do that. She was proud, and he was still confused, more now than ever.

PHINNEAS PICKENS HAD BEEN the loan officer for Mediocrity's only bank for over twenty years and was a well-respected member of the community.

He was meticulous, almost persnickety about his dress, and it was his habit to wear three-piece suits to work. In the front pocket of his vest he carried a gold watch with a long gold chain that had once belonged to his grandfather. It was his habit to check that watch every fifteen minutes to make certain he remained on schedule.

Punctuality was a virtue. Phinneas's mother had impressed that upon him at the tender age of six when he'd arrived home late for dinner one evening and had his backside thrashed as a result. He'd never been late again.

The banker had many routines, and he followed them without exception, almost religiously, in fact. On that sunny afternoon he found himself dining at Emma's Café on Main Street, where it was his habit to eat lunch five out of seven days a week without fail.

Tuesday was meat loaf day and Phinneas loved Emma's meat loaf. In fact, he loved everything Emma Harris cooked. His wife's cooking left a lot to be desired, and that was putting it mildly. Finnola couldn't boil water without burning it. He loved his wife, but he hated her cooking.

Across the table from the loan officer sat Seth Murdock, the town's sheriff and one of Phinneas's closest friends. He was a tall man, almost six foot three inches, with an appetite for food that equaled his passion for fishing. His uniforms were specially made for him by Mrs. Murdock to accommodate his large girth, which increased on a weekly basis, due to his fondness for beer and beer nuts.

"Had to inspect the old Swindel house yesterday," Phinneas informed the sheriff between bites of mashed potato, savoring the lumpless creation beneath his tongue and sighing in appreciation. Finnola's potatoes had lumps the size of small boulders. "Beth's applied for a loan to finish up the repairs on the inn. She's got her work cut out for her, that's for certain."

The sheriff shook his head. "Throwing away good money after bad, if you ask me. Never could abide those two old gals. My daddy never trusted them, and I don't either." He forked a Brussels sprout and continued, "If you ask me, they did away with Iris's fiancé all those years ago. The man just up and disappeared, and I'd bet money the old witch and her sister did him in. They probably boiled him in oil and cast some spell on the poor guy. Daddy was sure of it, but he didn't have any evidence that could prove their guilt beyond a reasonable doubt. Maybe one day I will."

Phinneas nodded. "I feel uncomfortable around those two, and that's a fact. Why, just the other day I saw Ivy Swindel at the bank. I did my best to avoid her, but, of course, that's like trying to avoid getting wet when it rains. That woman is always flapping her jaw about my schooldays, saying what a terrible student I was. It's very annoying, not to mention totally untrue. I was an excellent student." His indignant expression softened when he added, "But I don't hold anything against their niece. Beth's a good woman and has worked hard to make something of herself, after that miserable episode with Coach Randall." He shook his head. "Such a shame. The man was a fool."

"I hear what you're saying, but I've always subscribed to the adage, the apple doesn't fall far from the tree. I'd bet money that Beth knows more than she's saying. After all, she's lived with those two old hags for years."

"But how could she? Beth wasn't even alive when Lyle McMurtry disappeared."

The sheriff shook his head. "Don't know. I just feel it in my gut." He patted his protruding belly. "Damn good meat loaf."

At the next table, Brad sat quietly eating his turkey sandwich. He had dropped Stacy off at the movie theater an hour ago to catch a matinee and had come into the café to grab a bite to eat, though the food at the café wasn't nearly as good as the inn's, he'd discovered.

He hadn't meant to eavesdrop, but when the sheriff had mentioned the Swindel sisters and Iris Swindel's missing fiancé, his interest, as well as several red flags went up. Someone by the name of Lyle McMurtry was missing; so was Brad's father. Was there a connection, or was it merely coincidence? He decided to find out.

Turning in his chair, Brad tapped the burly sheriff on the shoulder. "Excuse me, Sheriff. I'm Dr. Bradley Donovan from Charlottesville, Virginia. I couldn't help overhearing your conversation about the Swindel sisters."

The sheriff smiled in greeting, holding out his hand to shake Brad's. "Always nice to meet a visitor to Mediocrity. I'm Seth Murdock. How can I help you?"

"I'm not on vacation, Sheriff. I'm staying at the Two Sisters Ordinary. It's the last known whereabouts of my elderly father, who is missing."

The man's dark eyes widened, and then he said something to Phinneas and joined Brad at his table. "You say your father's missing?" Sheriff Murdock asked. "For how long?" He kept his voice purposely low and looked about the room to make certain none of the other diners had overheard their conversation.

Spreading gossip in Mediocrity was as commonplace as spreading manure.

"My father's been gone about six weeks." Brad

explained about Robert Donovan's trip and the post-card he'd received from the Ordinary.

"Did you notify the authorities in Charlottesville?"

Brad shook his head. "No. I thought perhaps I was overreacting. But now I'm worried, especially after hearing what you said about the two old ladies and the missing fiancé." His *Arsenic & Old Lace* theory might not be that far-fetched after all.

"There's something strange about those two old ladies. I'd bet my career on it."

His expression grave, Brad replied, "I've spoken to them about my father. They claim not to know anything, but I have a feeling they're lying or trying to mislead me."

Seth's eyes lit with purpose. "What makes you think so?"

"They seemed pretty uncomfortable when I brought up my dad. It was obvious they didn't want to talk about him or answer any of my questions concerning his stay at the inn."

"And Beth?"

Brad shrugged, wondering how much he should say. He didn't want to implicate the woman if she was innocent. But if she was hiding something—and it certainly seemed she was—the matter needed to be investigated. His father's life might depend on it. "Ms. Randall was uncomfortable and a bit evasive, too.

"I don't mind telling you, Sheriff, that I'm worried. My father isn't the type to just disappear. He always calls or sends a note to let me know where he is and when he's coming home. But I've checked my home answering machine numerous times, checked in with my service to see if he's called, and there have been no messages."

"And you think there's more to his disappearance this time?"

Brad rubbed the back of his neck. "To tell you the truth I don't know what to think. I'm just worried that something's happened to my dad."

Murdock leaned on his beefy forearms and stared intently at the doctor. "Do you think the Swindel sisters are somehow involved in his disappearance?"

"Maybe." He sighed deeply. "But more importantly, what do you think? Do you have any information you could relate? I've only heard bits and pieces of the story."

"Lyle McMurtry and Iris Swindel had been engaged at the time of his disappearance," the sheriff began. "Those two were madly in love, or so my daddy told me. But something happened. Nobody knows what. I figure McMurtry cheated on her and she found out.

"Anyway, Iris must have gotten really angry, because Lyle suddenly disappeared. Then she dropped out of sight, and no one saw her again for a good long while. I figure she murdered him in a jealous rage, got rid of the body somehow, probably with the help of her sister, and then went into hiding until things cooled off.

"My daddy never found McMurtry's body, so he didn't have sufficient evidence to arrest the old witch when she came back to Mediocrity."

"That doesn't bode well for my father. I guess I should ask a lot more questions of those two old ladies, press them harder until they talk."

"First off, Dr. Donovan, I think you should come by my office and fill out a missing person's report. That'll make things official and I'll be able to start investigating your father's disappearance. These kinds of matters are better left in the hands of professionals like myself."

The sheriff handed Brad his card. "I'll be heading back to the office as soon as I finish my lunch. Come by and we'll get started. I want to get a written statement, description, that sort of thing. With any luck, your dad's just lost track of time, but we need to be certain."

"I will, and thanks, Sheriff Murdock. I appreciate your willingness to help."

"My daddy, God rest his soul, held this position before me, and I'd like to put that Swindel mystery to rest, one way or another. Besides, I know what it's like to lose a father. It's not easy. I still miss mine."

Brad prayed that he hadn't lost his father, just

misplaced him. "I'll be by your office in a little while. Thanks again, Sheriff. Enjoy the rest of your lunch."

The man nodded, then headed back to his table. Brad resumed eating his meal, but he didn't have much of an appetite, not after hearing what Murdock had to say about the Swindel sisters and their niece.

LOCKING THE DOOR TO her bedroom, Beth plopped down in the middle of her tester bed and dialed Ellen Golden's Philadelphia phone number.

Ellen was an investigative journalist for the *Inquirer,* the city's largest newspaper. She was smart, maintained excellent business connections, and had been Beth's best friend since childhood.

Beth hadn't had a lot of friends while growing up, thanks to her mother's overprotectiveness. The one exception had been Ellen, a skinny, timid child who apparently hadn't posed much of a threat to Margaret's sensibilities or active imagination.

Ellen and Beth had been misfits all through junior high and high school. They were never part of the sacred inner circle, which was okay with them, because they'd always had each other.

"Ellen Golden," said the familiar voice over the other end of the line.

"Hi! It's me," Beth said, barely above a whisper. "I need your help."

"I'm packing, so I can't talk long. What's up? You sound awful. Has something happened to one of your aunts? I hope not. I adore those two old delinquents."

Heaving a sigh, Beth wondered how much she should confide. She and Ellen rarely kept secrets from each other. At twelve, when Beth had gotten her period, Ellen had been the first person she'd told; and when Ellen had lost her virginity the summer after high-school graduation in the backseat of Kevin Taylor's car, she and Beth had stayed up all night discussing the finer aspects of doing *it*.

"I'm worried about my aunts, but it doesn't have anything to do with their health," she said finally. "They're fine. I'm the one having the nervous breakdown."

"Really?" Her friend sounded surprised. "What's happened?"

"Remember the rumors surrounding the disappearance of Lyle McMurtry, the guy who disappeared all those years ago?"

"How could I forget? Everyone in town suspected your aunts were involved in his disappearance and that Iris might have murdered him. Of course, they also believe the inn's haunted, which is a crock of you know what. Why?"

"I'm not sure she didn't… murder him, I mean." Beth felt horrid and disloyal even thinking such a thing, let alone voicing it aloud.

There was a long silence, and then Ellen's voice filled with incredulity. "What are you saying? That your aunt Iris is a murderer? Are you crazy? You've always been such a staunch believer in her innocence. You don't really believe that she or that other sweet old lady had anything to do with McMurtry's disappearance. Do you?"

"I'm...I'm not sure. I went down to the basement yesterday to get some jam, and I...I found some bones. Well, to be more accurate, Buster found them."

Ellen gasped. "What kind of bones?"

"I'm not sure. They look human to me."

"Holy hell! I can see why you're worried. Does anyone else know about this?"

"No! Are you kidding? I didn't even tell my aunts what I'd discovered. They'd probably blab it all over town. And besides, I'm not one hundred percent certain what it means, so how can I accuse them of something like that?"

"I see your point. You're in a tough spot. How can I help?"

A knock sounded at the door, and Beth's voice dropped even lower. "Someone's here. Hang on a minute."

"Beth, are you okay?" Aunt Ivy's voice floated through the closed door. "I thought I heard voices."

Beth took a deep breath. "I'm fine, just talking to Ellen."

"All right, dear. Say hello to her for me. She's such a lovely girl."

"I will, Aunt Ivy."

"Sorry to disturb you. I just wanted to let you know that I'm off to town to meet Louise Wilson for lunch. We're going to talk about that Red Hat Club idea of mine."

"Sounds like fun. Thanks for letting me know. I want to hear all about it when you get back."

"Have a good chat, dear."

Listening to her aunt's retreating footsteps, Beth breathed a sigh of relief. "Sorry," she said to Ellen. "It was my aunt."

"So I gathered. Now, getting back to our conversation—you mentioned needing my help."

"I'm going to ship you one of the bones." It was the one Buster had dragged onto the lawn this morning—the one she presently had hiding in her closet, right next to her Barbie doll collection. "Could you use your contacts to get it analyzed somewhere, to see if it's human."

Ellen's voice filled with dismay. "But I'm leaving this afternoon for my college reunion cruise. I won't be back for at least ten days, maybe more."

"Oh, no!"

"I'm sorry. I can't get out of it."

Realizing she was being selfish, Beth said, "Go and enjoy your cruise. It sounds like fun. I hope you have a good time. Maybe you'll meet your Prince Charming."

"Doubtful. I'm on assignment. Can't talk about it now. But go ahead and send the bone. I'll take care of it as soon as I get back."

"And you won't mention this to anyone? Promise me, Ellen. My aunts' lives could be at stake."

"I promise. But what if Iris is guilty? Have you considered the possibility? You can't keep something like that hidden. You'll be an accessory, and—"

Beth's voice filled with frustration. "I know all that. But I can't think about it now. I just need to take this one step at a time, pray for the best and hope it doesn't all blow up in my face."

"All right—we'll cross that bridge if and when we come to it. Besides, we really won't know what we're dealing with until after we have the bone analyzed by a medical examiner. I have a friend in the field who owes me a favor. But it could take a while. Philadelphia's murder rate keeps Grant pretty busy."

"I've got another problem."

"Worse than the one you just told me about? I find that hard to believe."

"Well, believe it. One of my former guests is missing—an elderly gentleman. His son is here looking for him. I'm worried sick the old guy might be buried in my basement. I haven't had the guts to find out."

"Quit overreacting. I admit things look suspicious

right now, but you've got to keep clearheaded. Your aunts are old, not vicious or insane. Why would they want to kill off a guest? That doesn't make any sense."

"No, they're not vicious. I'm not sure about the insane part." Beth paused, and then took another deep breath, adding, "Aunt Iris is trying to raise the dead."

"Holy hell! Did she say why? And who's she trying to raise? You don't think—?"

"I'm not going to ask. What I don't know can't hurt either one of us."

"Send the bone. I'll get to it as quickly as I can."

Beth breathed a sigh of relief. "Thanks, El. You're a good friend."

"So what does the old guy's son look like? Is he handsome? Employed?"

"Brad Donovan is very nice looking. He's a pediatrician, lives in Virginia, and has a teenage daughter who hates me."

"Too bad he's not a gynecologist."

Beth smiled into the phone. "You're warped, you know that, Ellen?"

Her friend laughed. "And you're the Virgin Married. It's time you got out of your cave and started living again. Greg is history. All men aren't bastards."

"If that's true, why are you still single?" Though Beth knew the reason. Ellen was still smarting over her ex-boyfriend, Randy, who was supposed to have been the *one,* but instead had turned out to be a big fat *zero*.

"I have a career. And I haven't met anyone I want to marry."

"Me neither. So get off my back. You're worse than my aunts."

"Speaking of which, has Ivy checked out the doctor yet?"

"Of course, and she thinks he's hot. But I'm not interested. I've got enough to deal with at the moment."

"That's true, which is why I'm cutting you some slack. We'll talk more about this hunky doctor of yours when I get back."

"He's not *my* hunky doctor. And it's doubtful he'd be interested in a woman whose aunts may have whacked his father and buried him six feet under."

"Good point. Well, just hang tough till I get back. And don't make yourself nuts over this. You know how you get?"

"Too late for that, I'm afraid."

AFTER PROVIDING SHERIFF MURDOCK with the pertinent information he needed to begin the investigation into his father's disappearance, and then picking up his daughter at the movie theater, Brad returned to the inn.

When Stacy announced she was going to take a nap, he decided to use his free time taking a walk around the grounds. He needed to clear his head and try to make sense of everything Seth Murdock had told him during their meeting.

Brad had a hard time reconciling the Iris Swindel he knew with the one the sheriff suspected of murder. She was a sweet old lady. Of course, she hadn't been that old when the murder allegedly happened, and people tended to change for the better as they matured. For all he knew, she could have been a wild hellcat when she was young. God knows he had no doubt about her sister. Ivy was still a pistol.

A dog barked loudly, catching Brad's attention. Gazing in the direction of the barn, he found Beth tossing a ball for Buster. She was laughing at the animal's antics and Brad felt his heart constrict at the sight of her.

He chided himself at his reaction. No matter how he might feel about Beth, he had to keep things in perspective. She might know more about his father's disappearance than she admitted. And even if she didn't, even if she was innocent in the entire matter, they would never suit.

His position in the medical community and on the board at the hospital dictated that he find a competent, emotionally well balanced woman who could perform the duties of a doctor's wife, should he decide to marry again. Lonely as he had been these past four years, the thought had crossed his mind more than once. And Stacy needed the calming influence that a woman in the house would bring.

But marriage meant getting close to someone, taking the risk that whomever he fell in love with could leave him again, as Carol had done. He didn't think his heart could take that kind of pain again.

Why in hell am I even thinking about this? I hardly know the woman, Stacy dislikes her intensely, and Dad is still missing.

Shaking his head, Brad walked toward the barn, as if pulled by a force he couldn't control.

When Beth spotted Brad, her first instinct was to run into the barn and hide in the hayloft. But he called out to her and waved, and she knew escape was impossible.

Pasting on a smile, Beth asked when he approached, "Did you enjoy your trip into town?"

"Yes, it was interesting, to say the least. I learned a great deal about Mediocrity's history and some of the town's inhabitants."

"Really? That's nice." Feeling uncomfortable at his nearness, the intensity of his gaze, she stepped back to put distance between them, but he closed the gap once again. "I've...I've got to fetch some hay bales for my autumn decoration, so—"

"We need to talk, Beth. I ran into Sheriff Murdock in town."

Her stomach churned acid. "I'm busy right now. Perhaps we can discuss this another—"

"Now, Beth! I want to talk now. I need to know about Lyle McMurtry. I understand he was engaged to your aunt Iris before he disappeared. Why didn't you tell me?"

"I don't know much about him. My aunt's never spoken to me about him or the reasons for their breakup. And it's really none of my business, anyway."

"Why didn't you tell me there was another missing person in this town besides my father?"

"I didn't think a fifty-year-old matter had anything to do with your father. And I'm not in the habit of discussing my aunt's personal business with strangers. She's suffered enough over the years."

"Why does everyone in this town, including the sheriff, think your aunts are involved in McMurtry's disappearance?"

"I have no idea. But there are people in this town who like to gossip and spread malicious rumors. They speculate when they have no basis for their unkind suspicions."

"Do you know what happened to Lyle McMurtry?"

Beth thought of the bones buried in her basement and her cheeks grew hot, but she shook her head. "No, of course not. Why would I? I wasn't even born when he disappeared."

"And my father? Do you know where he is?"

"I told you, I have no idea what happened to your father. I'm sorry he is missing, but—"

"I think you're hiding something."

Eyes flashing fire, she clenched her fists. "How dare you accuse me of such a thing? You don't even know me."

"You're not a very good liar, Ms. Randall. I know that much."

"And you're no gentleman, Dr. Donovan. Now, if you'll excuse me." She tried to walk past him, but he clasped her arm.

"Not so fast. I have more questions."

She gasped at his audacity. "How dare you lay a hand on me? Let me go."

"Or what?"

"Or I'll scream down this barn, that's what. Now let go." She tried to yank free, but he merely tightened his hold. She opened her mouth to make good on her threat, and he pulled her to him, crushing her lips beneath his own.

Beth was so shocked she couldn't think, only feel. Though Brad's hold was rigid, his lips were warm and soft. He knew how to kiss, that was for damn certain, and how to make a woman forget that her life was in chaos at the moment. But she couldn't allow herself to forget, couldn't allow any warm, fuzzy feelings to develop, just because his lips felt like liquid fire beneath her own.

Pushing hard against his chest, she drew back her hand and slapped him soundly across the cheek, for his impertinence and for making her feel things she didn't want to feel. The awful sound reverberated against the cold stillness of the afternoon, against her heart, which wasn't nearly as immune as she'd professed.

"Don't touch me! You have no right."

Brad observed the way she hugged her arms around her middle, nibbled her lower lip, even as she stood indignant and accusing. She'd felt something; he was sure her response mirrored his own.

"I apologize for losing my temper, but not for kissing you. That I enjoyed. It was worth the slap." He rubbed his cheek, wondering if the woman lifted weights. She sure did pack a wallop.

Without another word, she stalked off in the direction of the inn, head held high, stride purposeful.

Brad sighed as he watched her walk away. Beth was wonderful. And he was too damn attracted to her. He knew nothing could come of it. As much as he liked kissing Beth, wanted to make love to her, he couldn't lose sight of the fact that she was duplicitous and mysterious.

If he allowed himself to get involved with the captivating woman, he was just asking for trouble.

CHAPTER SIX

"But I don't understand. What kind of club has no rules?"

"The kind that's just for fun, dear," Ivy explained to Louise Wilson, her former pupil and dearest friend, over lunch at Myra Fletcher's tearoom, The Silver Teapot.

Louise had been an excellent student and first in Ivy's English Literature class. They had found much in common—their love of Shakespeare, for one—and their bond had continued after the younger woman began teaching at the high school, following, in some respect, in Ivy's footsteps. She was sweet-natured and kind, but lacked the self-confidence one needed to be an independent thinker and true leader, which is how Ivy viewed herself.

"The Red Hat Society was formed for having fun, being silly and doing whatever we older women damn well feel like. There are no rules, except that each member of the group has to wear purple dresses and red hats. The idea for the club came from a wonderful poem. In it, the author states that when she gets old she's going to wear purple. It goes on to talk about brandy and satin sandals. And the best part— learning to spit." Ivy clapped her hands, her enthusiasm evident by the sparkle in her eyes. "When I read it, and then researched the Red Hat Society online, I knew it was perfect for me."

Louise pulled a face. "Red and purple? Oh dear, Ivy. That sounds just awful. Everyone will look at us as if we've lost our minds. I might be getting old, but I like to think I have some fashion sense."

When one was a traditionalist like Louise, one didn't need fashion sense, only a charge account at a department store that specialized in conservative clothing.

Sipping her tea, Ivy took a bite of egg-salad sandwich, one of Myra's specialties, and smiled widely. "Yes, dear, that's the whole point of it. We will live our lives outrageously. I think at our age we deserve to, don't you? I've never been much of a conformist, you know that."

The woman rolled her eyes at the understatement. "You've never given a whit about what others think about you, Ivy Swindel. Even your teaching methods were a bit unorthodox. I remember the time you came to class dressed as Kate from *The Taming of the Shrew*. I thought Principal Andrews was going to fire you on the spot for wearing such a low-cut bodice."

The older woman smiled at the memory. "Harvey Andrews was anal-retentive, as the younger people say. He was just upset because I wouldn't let him sample the wares."

Eyes wide, Louise shook her head. "I'm not sure I'm as brave as you are."

"Of course, you are, dear. I realize you're younger, and may still be a slave to the dictates of society, but you'll come to realize one day, as I have, that it's just not worth it. You have to be your own person, Louise, live life on your own terms. As they say, life's short."

"But who will want to join such an unconventional group? You know Finnola Pickens has that gardening club she's always flaunting in everyone's face. As if we really wanted to belong to such a boring thing. I hear they actually discussed aphids. Can you imagine?" She rubbed her arms against the chill that suddenly prickled her skin.

"When the women of this town see how much fun our group's having, they will flock to join us, leaving Finnola to her aphids and rosebushes. You'll see."

Louise, who had never quite gotten over the fact that her high-school sweetheart, Phinneas Pickens, had chosen Finnola Lockheart to be his lawfully wedded wife, thus rendering her a spinster, smiled delightedly. "Do you really think so?"

Ivy nodded. "Without a doubt. But, of course, the

women who join have to be fifty or older, in order to wear purple dresses and red hats. The younger ones will have to settle for lavender and pink. Experience and age should count for something. The hats will signify our red badge of courage, so to speak, for living so long and surviving society's dictates."

The younger woman, an avid swimmer who was almost as wrinkled as Ivy from too much sun exposure over the years, poured milk into her cup of orange pekoe tea. "But what will we do in our club? I mean, we just can't sit around staring at one another for a whole meeting, can we?"

"From what I've read, most of the groups meet over lunch in restaurants. So yes, we'll be staring at each other, chatting, and eating calorie-rich foods. And if we desire, we can plan trips to New York City to see plays, or maybe even visit a nudist colony. But only if everyone agrees, of course," she added quickly when her friend's brows nearly hit her hairline.

"I wonder if we could persuade the group to go to Philadelphia. I hear the Chippendales perform at a club there," Louise ventured.

Eyes bright with anticipation, Ivy clapped her hands. "I'll insist on it. And if some don't want to go, that'll be their loss. We'll go just the same. Quite honestly, Louise, I don't think those men are ever coming to Mediocrity. This town's just too provincial."

There were some things in life that never changed, and Mediocrity was one of them. Even though the town had grown over the years and now sported a movie theater and public swimming pool—despite a lot of dissension over the latter—the residents remained as conservative and narrow-minded as they'd been when Ivy was growing up.

Back in high school, she had enjoyed shocking her classmates by being the first female to smoke cigarettes in public. And it had done her heart good to defy her rigid, puritanical parents every chance she got by flaunting convention, dressing as she damn well pleased—sometimes in trousers—swearing in public, and keeping company with men her father never approved of.

Iris had been the obedient daughter, the one who could do no wrong, and the apple of her parents' eyes until she'd dared to exhibit human frailty and had fallen off the pedestal on which they'd placed her. It had been a rude awakening for her sister, but not nearly as traumatic as it had been for her minister father, who had accused Ivy of leading Iris astray with her wild, wicked ways.

According to the Reverend Josiah Swindel, the Devil had taken up residence in Ivy.

Louise cast her friend a doubtful look. "But what about Iris? You know she doesn't approve of some of your more, shall we say, outlandish ideas."

"Oh, pooh!" Ivy shook her head. "Iris is a stick-in-the-mud, always has been. Besides, right now she's preoccupied with her potions and spells. Trying to raise the dead isn't all that easy, you know."

Eyes wide, Louise leaned across the table in conspiratorial fashion. "Do you think she's trying to raise—" her brows lifted "—you know?"

Stiffening in her seat, Ivy cast her companion an annoyed look. "I have no idea what you're talking about, Louise Wilson, and neither do you. Remember, Iris is my younger sister and I'll not allow idle gossip and speculation to touch her. I've protected her all these years, and I'll continue to do so."

"Protected her from what?"

From herself, their parents, the ugliness that had touched her life.

"Why, from life, of course. Now, what do you say we go shopping and look for some red hats and purple dresses? I bet the used-clothing store will have something we can use."

"But what will we call our group? Surely, we have to have a name for it."

Ivy thought a moment, sipped her tea and then smiled in satisfaction. "I have the perfect name for our new group: *Red Hats and Roses.* What do you think?"

"Why roses? What does that have to do with anything? The ladies might think it's another gardening club."

Ivy's sigh was full of impatience. "That's possible, Louise, but I doubt it. Roses are beautiful, just like us women. Why can't we pay homage to that fact? And besides, the name has a nice ring to it. I don't know anyone who doesn't love roses, do you?"

"Well, no. But—"

"We don't have to have a reason for everything we decide to do. That'll be part of our mystique. Now let's go shopping before your practical nature brings on a bout of dyspepsia."

BETH'S HEART WAS STILL racing by the time she arrived back at the inn. She couldn't believe Brad had had the audacity to kiss her. She couldn't believe how much she had enjoyed it.

"Damn it all to hell!" she muttered, switching on her computer to check e-mails to see if she'd received any new reservations. The one thing she'd been smart enough to do after opening the inn was to invest in an online-reservation system. It had already paid for itself.

"Excuse me!"

She looked up to find a middle-aged couple speaking to her through her open office window and felt her cheeks heat, praying they hadn't heard her outburst. The slender man was tall with dark hair, his wife thin and very attractive. Together they made a handsome couple.

"Hello." She pasted on a smile. "Welcome to the Two Sisters Ordinary. Can I help you?"

"We're Joan and Charles Murray. We have a reservation," the man said, and his wife looked up at him adoringly, making Beth wonder how long that look would last. Of course, not everyone married a philandering idiot.

"You're the newlyweds from Virginia, right?" The Murrays were older than she'd anticipated. She'd been expecting twenty-somethings for some reason and had no idea why. And what did age have to do with happiness anyway? Not a damn thing, as she knew only too well.

Moving out of her office to the entry hall, she greeted her guests properly. "I have your room all ready. It's the nicest one we have, with a working fireplace and Jacuzzi tub."

Joan Murray's face lit with pleasure. "That sounds wonderful! Can we see it?"

"Of course, I just need you to fill out a registration form while I take an imprint of your credit card, and then we'll be all set." She took care of the business details in a matter of moments, grabbed the key to the room she used as a bridal suite, and instructed them to follow.

"We're very happy you chose to spend your honeymoon with us. If there's anything you need, just let me know." The way the couple was devouring each other with their eyes, Beth doubted they'd be leaving their room anytime soon.

"The inn's not open to the public for meals yet, so you shouldn't have any problem finding a table this evening." She explained the various meal times and location of the dining room. "The menu for this evening and every evening is posted near the dining area."

Charles nodded. "Are there TVs in the rooms? Joan's a big fan of *24*. We'd hate to miss it."

"Yes." Beth opened the door to their room and invited them in. "As addicted as I am to movies, I didn't have the heart to deprive my guests of entertainment."

"Oh, this is lovely. Isn't it, Charles?" Joan gushed with pleasure. "I just love the brass bed. It's so authentic looking." She turned to Beth. "Is it very old? And are these Laura Ashley fabrics?" She ran her hand over the peach-and-green checked comforter.

"Yes, to both questions. The bed once belonged to my aunts' parents."

"I just love what you've done with this room."

Pleased by the compliment, Beth returned Joan's smile and thanked her. She had worked very hard to get the furnishings and interior design just right. "Redoing this historic house has been a labor of love."

"Well, you've done a great job. I'm sure we'll be very comfortable. And look! There's an ice bucket with champagne." She smiled widely at her hostess.

"How very thoughtful of you, Beth. Thank you! I'm sure we'll put that to good use."

"And the tub, sweets," Charles said, winking at his wife, who blushed a charming shade of pink. "Don't forget the big tub."

The Murrays looked very much in love, and Beth experienced a twinge of envy. Making her excuses, she quit the room, feeling more depressed than ever about her own failed marriage, even though none of it had been her fault.

Or had it?

Everyone had warned her that she and Greg were too different and wouldn't suit, but she'd refused to listen. At the time, which she thought of as her naive years, Beth had thought Greg to be perfect mate material and the panacea for all of her problems. Little had she known that what little self-esteem she had would soon go flying right out the window. It wasn't easy being passed over by your husband for another woman.

Greg had been far more adventurous and experienced in sexual matters than she could ever hope to be. He had liked things kinky—bondage, porn, erotic lingerie—while her preferences had run to the more conventional—lights off, button-down pajamas and underpants that actually had a crotch. Not that there was anything wrong with the other. It just wasn't who she was.

But apparently it was Penelope Miller's persona. Prior to her divorce from Greg, she'd found a pair of red crotchless panties stuffed in the glove box of their Mazda. Knowing they weren't hers, Beth had formed the only conclusion she could—her husband had been cheating on her. When she'd confronted him, he didn't even try to deny it, telling her that he'd found someone who pleased him, in and out of bed, and who wasn't afraid to experiment.

Beth had shied away from sexual encounters after that, feeling as if she was somehow lacking. Though she had to admit that Brad had made her feel things she hadn't felt in years, if ever.

Brad Donovan had made her want again and that scared the heck out of her.

"THIS PLACE IS SO LAME. When are we getting outta here? I'm bored. There's, like, nothing to do."

Brad heaved a sigh at his daughter's dramatics. Stacy's opinion was nothing new. She'd voiced it a hundred times over since they'd arrived, and it was getting tiresome. "You're just going to have to tough it out, Stace. Grandpa's whereabouts are what's important right now." He cut into his filet mignon. It was rare, just the way he'd ordered it.

"But—"

Savoring the taste of the juicy meat, he said, "I'd like to enjoy my meal, but I can see that's going to be impossible. Now lower your voice." He glanced around the dining room, to find the honeymooning Murrays sequestered at a table in the far corner. They were absorbed in each other, and he doubted they'd heard his daughter's outburst.

Brad sighed as he watched them. One of the things he missed most about being part of a couple was sharing intimate dinners and a great bottle of wine with someone you cared about. He envied the newlyweds.

"I wasn't yelling."

"I didn't raise you to be rude, especially in public. And I don't want you hurting Beth's feelings with your comments."

The young girl's lips thinned. "She told you, didn't she? Even after she promised she wouldn't. I knew she wouldn't keep her word."

Setting down his fork, he stared intently at her. "Told me what? Are you and Beth having a problem that I should know about?"

Cheeks reddening, Stacy shook her head emphatically. "No! Absolutely not! Honest. Everything's fine."

"Then why don't I believe you?" His daughter had always been a terrible liar, which was a blessing. She hadn't been able to put one over on him yet.

"This chicken's really good. Do you want a bite?"

He almost smiled at her transparent tactics. "No, thanks. I'm glad you found something to your liking."

"The food's good. And I guess the two aunts are okay. They're nice for old people." She lowered her voice. "But I think Beth's aunt Iris is a witch." Her eyes grew round. "I mean, she makes up potions and stuff and has books on the occult."

A witch was one thing, but a murderess was quite something else. "You shouldn't be bothering the Swindel sisters." Though he knew in his heart that the old ladies would never harm a child, even if they had allegedly offed Lyle McMurtry.

"I'm not," she insisted. "They asked me to visit. I guess they're lonely or something. Anyway, tomorrow I'm going to surf the Net with Ivy. She buys and sells stuff on eBay. That's pretty cool."

"Just don't wear out your welcome."

"I won't. I get bored being with them after a while anyway. There's only so much you can talk to old people about."

"Grandpa doesn't bore you. You talk to him all the time." Stacy and his dad had a terrific relationship, one he was almost envious of. She confided things to her grandfather that she would never tell Brad.

When Stacy had gotten her first period and thought she was bleeding to death, it had been his dad she'd gone to for help. And though taken aback by the nature of the emergency, Robert had kept his cool, piled both of them into the car, and had driven his granddaughter to the drugstore to pick up the items she needed.

Brad remembered being very grateful that he hadn't been home at the time and had been spared the ordeal. His daughter was growing up, and he felt somewhat sad about that. Even though he was a doctor, he often-times felt ill equipped to handle delicate female matters. That's when he missed Carol the most.

"That's different. He tells neat stories and makes me laugh. Gramps is totally cool. He doesn't get upset about stupid stuff, like you do."

Brad wouldn't mention that his dad had been a loving but tough taskmaster when he was growing up. Stacy would never believe it anyway. As far as she was concerned, the man walked on water.

"Has either of the Swindel sisters mentioned Grandpa or said where he might be?"

She shook her head. "No. Why?"

"Just curious."

"Do you like Beth?" The change of subject came out of nowhere. "Are you going to kiss her?" The follow-up question had his mouth gaping open.

Guilty heat rose up his neck, landing squarely on his cheeks. "Yes, of course I like Beth. She's very nice. And you shouldn't ask personal questions. What I do is none of your business—I'm the parent, not you. You'd do well to remember that, young lady."

"Then why is your face getting all red? I knew it. You like her! Well, I don't, so you can't marry her!

Beth's not as nice as Mom, and she doesn't like kids."

"What makes you say that?"

"Because she was married and doesn't have any. That should tell you something."

"Not every marriage produces children, you know that."

"Promise you won't marry her. I'll run away if you do. I mean it."

Brad studied the anguish on his daughter's face, saw the fear in her eyes and felt badly for her. Stacy still hadn't adjusted to her mother's death or the fact that life had to go on without her. "I hardly know the woman. And I won't have you dictating to me or making threats, do you understand?"

She nodded, despite the look of defiance on her face.

"What's gotten into you, anyway? You've been acting strange ever since we arrived."

Sipping her Coke, she shrugged. "This place creeps me out. It's so old, and the town's even older. The movie I watched was, like, ancient. Have you ever heard of *The King and I?* People sang and it was weird."

Yul Brynner was probably rolling over in his grave right about now. "I believe most film critics would consider the movie a classic." He smiled indulgently. "Of course, no one blows up in it."

"How much longer are we staying, Dad? I want to go home and see my friends. I'm missing out on everything."

"Not until we have word on Grandpa." And Brad had no idea when that would be.

WHILE BRAD AND STACY finished dessert, Beth made the rounds of the dining room, greeting her guests, as was her custom. She dreaded having to face Brad after what had happened between them, but to ignore him outright would make her look inhospitable and might raise questions she had no answers for.

Pausing by their table, she forced a smile. "Good evening. Are you enjoying your dinner?"

"This apple pie is really good," Stacy said without looking up. "So's the vanilla ice cream."

"Glad you like it. The pie was made from one of Aunt Iris's recipes that my chef adapted."

"Give Lori kudos from us," Brad said with a sweet smile that Beth chose to ignore. Well, at least outwardly ignore. Inside she was churning like a cement mixer. "The meal was excellent."

"I will. Now if you'll excuse me, I need to check on my aunts. They didn't come down for dinner this evening, and I need to find out why." Usually if Iris and Ivy decided to eat in their rooms, they would let her know so she could bring food up for them.

"I'm thinking of taking a walk around the lake after dinner. Would you like to come, Beth?"

Beth's cheeks flamed, despite her intention not to show any emotion. There was no way she was going to be alone with Brad again. And she sure as heck wasn't going out in the dark with him! "I can't. I have several important matters to take care of this evening."

"Yeah, Dad. You shouldn't bother Beth. She's busy," Stacy chimed in, surprising the innkeeper, who wondered why the girl was coming to her aid.

Brad shot his daughter an annoyed look and Beth almost smiled at the idea that Stacy aggravated her father as much as he annoyed Beth. "Well, enjoy the rest of your evening. I'll see you both in the morning."

"Beth—?"

She turned back, arching an eyebrow. "Yes?" It was clear Brad didn't want her to leave. No doubt he'd reconsidered and wanted to apologize for kissing her. Well, he was several hours too late for that.

His smile was downright lascivious, considering his young daughter was sitting across from him. "Sweet dreams."

Sucking in her breath, Beth turned on her heel and stalked away without commenting. The man was infuriating, to say the least.

If she had wanted to be aggravated, she could have invited her mother for the Thanksgiving holiday!

Eager to put Brad out of sight and out of mind, Beth hurried to the kitchen, plated up two dishes with roasted chicken, wild rice, green beans and a hefty portion of apple pie, to soothe Aunt Ivy's sweet tooth, and headed up the stairs.

LORI WATCHED BETH EXIT the kitchen, and then began cleaning up from dinner. With only a few in-house guests to prepare for, the kitchen wasn't that messy and she knew it wouldn't take her long.

When Lori had loaded the last dish in the dishwasher, she grew anxious about what was waiting for her in her room. She'd checked her e-mail right before dinner and had found a note from Bill. She had put off reading it, not wanting anything to distract her from preparing the evening meal. The other day when she'd thought of Bill she'd lost her concentration and burned the chocolate-chip cookies she was preparing for afternoon tea. She'd had to remake the entire batch.

Lori knew she should have changed her e-mail account and address after she'd moved. But her parents kept in touch with her through e-mail, which was less expensive than calling, and she didn't want to make it difficult for them to reach her. At their age, any abrupt change in routine set them into panic mode.

She hoped the decision wouldn't prove costly for her. Bill was clever and smart. She wouldn't put it past him to try and trace her e-mail account, he was that resourceful. Lori had no intention of underestimating his ability to find her.

Hurrying to her suite of rooms, which was located just off the kitchen at the back of the house, Lori sat down at the computer keyboard, kicking off her shoes in the process.

It took a moment for her computer to boot up. The familiar "You've Got Mail" set her heart to racing, and she clicked open the e-mail from Bill, her mouth going dry when she read:

Lori, I don't understand why you left. Did I do something wrong? And where the hell are my knives and recipes? Come back so we can talk and get this situation worked out. I can't find anyone who's the least bit competent to replace you.

Well, that was something anyway. She'd never thought to see the day when Bill Thackery admitted he needed her.

Write and let me know you're okay. I've been worried. Bill.

Lori felt guilty about worrying Bill, but she had no intention of writing back and giving him the chance to find her. It was better this way, she decided, deleting the missive and then heading into the bathroom to take a shower and wash away all memories of Bill, once and for all.

CHAPTER SEVEN

"IRIS, MERCIFUL HEAVENS, you're as white as a ghost!" Ivy placed a gentle hand on her sister's forehead. "And you're warm. I think I should call the doctor."

"No!" Iris wagged her head emphatically. "Dr. Porter is out of town and I won't have that young pipsqueak who's taking his calls treat me. I don't like the looks of him. He has shifty eyes. And I heard from Sarah Johnston that he nearly flunked out of medical school."

"Oh, for heaven's sake, sister, you are too bullheaded for your own good! The man wouldn't have graduated if he wasn't qualified," she said, tucking the blanket more securely around her. "You need to drink fluids and lots of them. I'll get you some water."

"Quit fussing over me, Ivy. You're worse than a mother hen. I'm fine. I'm sure I'll be right as rain come morning."

The door to their suite opened, and then they

heard Beth call out, "Aunt Iris? Aunt Ivy? Are you here?"

"In the bedroom, dear. Iris is feeling a bit under the weather, I'm afraid. And she won't let me call the doctor. Maybe you can talk some sense into her."

"Tattletale," Iris whispered, pasting on a wan smile when her niece walked in, in an effort to ease her troubled expression.

Beth set the heavy tray down on the bedside table. "I was worried when you didn't come down for dinner, so I brought you both something to eat."

Iris shook her head. "Oh, I couldn't eat a thing right now, dear, but that was very thoughtful of you."

Peering closely at her aunt, Beth grew even more concerned. Iris was hardly ever sick and she didn't like the looks of her pasty complexion. "You look awful. Are you sure you don't want the doctor to examine you?"

"That's what I've been telling her. She's as white as chicken flesh."

"It's probably nothing more than a twenty-four-hour virus. Ivy is just an alarmist."

"Do you have a fever?" Beth asked.

"She does," Ivy answered for her sister. "I just felt her skin and it was warm."

"Be right back." Beth fetched the digital thermometer from the bathroom medicine cabinet and, when she returned, placed it in her aunt's mouth. Iris tried to protest, but Beth would have none of it, saying, "Be a good aunt and keep quiet for a few minutes, while I take your temperature."

"At least Iris listens to you, dear," Ivy told Beth. "I'm so glad you came up when you did. I've been at wit's end trying to care for her, but she's as stubborn as a mule. Iris never could abide being sick."

When Iris grimaced Ivy smiled widely. "Ha! About time you had to shut up and listen."

The thermometer beeped done. "One hundred point nine. Not too high." Beth felt a measure of relief. "But I think you should take a couple of aspirin. They'll make you feel better and bring down your fever."

"I can't abide the stuff. It makes me sick to my stomach."

She then turned to her other aunt. "Aunt Ivy, would you mind going to my room for the Tylenol? It's in my medicine cabinet."

"I will. And I'll even help you sit on Iris while you pour them down her throat."

After Ivy disappeared out the door, Iris shook her head. "Good heavens, but that woman can be irritating. She's been mothering me for years. Even when we were children she bossed me around."

Taking her aunt's clammy hand in her own, Beth replied with an understanding smile, "Because she loves you and cares about you. We both do and want you to get well."

The ailing woman sighed. "I know that, dear, but I've never been a good patient. What Ivy said was true. I used to drive my parents to distraction whenever I got sick."

"Well, isn't that God's honest truth?" Ivy walked into the room with the Tylenol and handed the bottle to her niece. "You were horrid as a child. I remember the time Mama summoned the doctor to the house to examine you for chicken pox and you made that poor man chase you around the room. For a goody-two-shoes, you did have your moments of defiance, sister." The two women exchanged a weighted look.

"Why don't you go ahead and eat, Ivy dear? The food is getting cold. And it'll keep your mouth occupied and give my ears a chance to rest."

Ivy smiled. "Wonderful idea! And I'm going to eat your pie as well as my own."

Listening to the exchange, Beth smiled to herself, thankful that some things in life never changed.

BEHIND THE WHEEL OF HIS Lincoln Navigator, a car almost as large as his ego, Aubrey Fontaine drove directly to Mediocrity's only hotel, The Excelsior. It was a tall brick building located in the middle of Main Street and looked as if it hadn't seen any major renovation since its construction at the turn of the century.

He parked his vehicle in front of the hotel in a space designated Handicapped, deciding he'd rather pay the fine than lug his suitcase two blocks. His back wasn't what it used to be, and Aubrey felt the parking ordinance was discriminatory and unfair, at any rate. Why should he be deprived of a parking space just because some poor unfortunate had problems? He had his share of problems, too; not that anyone gave a good goddamn about them.

Strolling into the building as if he owned it, he was surprised to find the interior newly decorated, though a bit garish for his taste. Red-flocked wallpaper that would have been better suited in a bordello covered what walls weren't paneled in black walnut, and a massive crystal chandelier hung in the center of the lobby. The hardwood floors were covered in expensive Oriental rugs that were authentic and of very good quality. Aubrey had discerning taste and could spot a fake a mile away.

Leaning on the front desk, also fashioned out of black walnut, he drummed his fingers impatiently, waiting to be recognized. If the talkative young woman had been an employee in one of his establishments, he would have fired her on the spot.

Efficient and polite customer service was paramount in his business and he didn't tolerate anything less. Plus, he hated to be kept waiting. Time was money and his was always in short supply.

The young red-haired woman finally turned and

smiled in greeting, earning a scowl from Aubrey for her trouble. "I'm Aubrey Fontaine. My secretary reserved a room for me."

Appearing a bit disconcerted, she punched his name into the computer and nodded a few moments later. "Yes, Mr. Fontaine. We have you in the General Meade Suite. I trust the room will be satisfactory. It's one of our nicest suites."

"What's the nicest?"

"That would be our Presidential Suite, the Ulysses S. Grant. But as I told your secretary, it's been booked for months. We have an older couple who reserves it every year for their anniversary, and—"

He held up his hand to cut her off. "Does this hotel offer room service? I'm starving and will need to order dinner as soon as I unpack."

"Yes, sir, this is a full-service hotel. You'll find a room-service menu in the drawer of your room desk. The food here is very good."

"I'll be the judge of that, young woman. Where can I find information about the town? I'm researching the history."

"I would recommend trying the Mediocrity Historical Society. It's located on Branch Street. They have records going back over a hundred years or more. And there's also the public library. They have a great deal of historical documents on microfilm."

"Excellent! And the newspaper, *The Mediocrity Messenger,* where might that be?"

"Two blocks down on your left. You can't miss it. A big silver eagle is perched over the *Messenger's* doorway."

Aubrey had seen the monstrosity coming into town and knew just where the newspaper was located. If Mediocrity got any quainter, he might have to throw up.

He found his suite of rooms on the eighth floor. Aubrey never booked a regular room—they were too damn small and he liked to spread out. Plus, suites usually had oversize bathtubs. Aubrey showered in the mornings to save time, but at night he liked relaxing in a tub of soothing hot water, where he would formulate his plans for the following day.

He wasn't sure when he would visit his birth mother. He didn't feel ready for a confrontation just yet. Besides, he needed to find out everything he could about the town, the Swindel family, and the man known as Lyle McMurtry before paying her a visit.

Knowledge was power. Aubrey had made his fortune based on that premise.

Come morning he would head over to the local barbershop. It was the best place to glean gossip and information in a small town. He'd never met a barber who didn't like to flap his gums and talk a blue streak, and Aubrey was ready to listen…and plan.

THE SOFT KNOCK WOKE BETH out of a restless sleep, and she bolted out of bed. Opening the door, she found Ivy standing in the hallway wringing her hands nervously.

"What's wrong? Has something happened?"

"It's Iris. She's taken a turn for the worse. She's been moaning and carrying on something awful. I checked her forehead, and she's burning up with fever."

Beth grew alarmed. "Did you take her temperature?"

"What on earth for? I know a fever when I feel one."

Grabbing her robe and donning it, Beth followed her aunt up the stairs. When she examined Iris her conclusion was the same as Ivy's: her aunt had a very high fever. Iris's eyes were glazed, her lips dry, and she was moaning and thrashing about on the bed.

"I'd like you to take her temperature—" Beth handed her aunt the digital thermometer "—so we can tell the doctor how high it is. I'm going to ask Dr. Donovan to examine Aunt Iris. I won't rest easy until we've had a medical opinion."

"Excellent idea! Too bad you couldn't put on something a bit more—"

"Really, Aunt Ivy!" Tossing her aunt an exasperated look, Beth went directly to the Donovans' room and knocked on the door as quietly as she could, hoping not to waken Brad's daughter or any of the other guests.

He answered the door wearing only his pajama bottoms. His eyes widened in surprise when he saw her, and hers widened in appreciation. In spite of the fact she was concerned for her aunt's welfare, Beth couldn't help noticing that Brad had a very muscular chest for a doctor. Not that she was interested, of course.

"Beth, what's wrong? You look upset."

"I'm sorry to wake you, but Aunt Iris is very ill. I was hoping you could come upstairs and check on her. She's running a very high fever, and I'm worried about her."

"I'll toss on some clothes and be right with you." True to his word, he came back in a matter of moments, carrying his black medical bag, which he carted with him wherever he went.

Leading him up to her aunts' suite of rooms, Beth explained, "Iris hasn't been feeling well all day. Ivy wanted to call the doctor, but my aunt wouldn't allow it. Her own physician is out of town, and she doesn't trust the new one."

"You did the right thing by coming to get me. It's best not to take chances with the elderly. A simple cold can lead into pneumonia quite easily."

Ivy smiled in relief when Brad entered the room. "Thank you for coming, Dr. Donovan. My sister is in a bad way. I just took her temperature and it's one hundred two."

His expression somber, he nodded and retrieved the stethoscope from his bag, then listened to the woman's heart and lungs carefully. He was relieved to find that Iris had a regular heartbeat and that her lungs were clear. "Your aunt is strong, Beth. I don't hear any congestion in her lungs, but I'd like to get that fever down. What have you given her?"

"Just Tylenol. Iris won't take aspirin," she replied, feeling better now that Brad had taken charge of the situation. Her medical knowledge was limited.

"Is your aunt allergic to any medications?"

Beth looked at Ivy, who responded, "Not that I know of. Iris just doesn't like the taste of aspirin, says it upsets her stomach."

He removed the blood pressure cuff from his bag and affixed it to her aunt's arm. "Has she vomited?"

"Once. She tried to eat some of the dinner Beth brought up, but the poor thing couldn't keep it down."

Checking Iris's blood pressure, then her pulse, Brad turned to look at the two worried women. "I think she's got a virus. Hopefully it'll run its course in twenty-four to forty-eight hours, but I'm going to stay with her, just to make certain she doesn't develop any complications."

"That's very good of you, Doctor," Ivy said with a grateful smile. "Beth and I appreciate your being here more than I can say. And since my sister is in such capable hands I'm going back to bed. If I don't get some rest, I'll be useless in the morning. But I'm sure my niece will stay and keep you company, in case you need any assistance."

Beth knew very well what her aunt was up to and flashed the woman a disgusted look that said she wasn't at all pleased with her meddling. "I was intending to," she remarked, receiving a smile of satisfaction from Ivy before she retired to the bedroom.

"I'm going down to the kitchen to get some coffee," Beth informed Brad, hoping he hadn't noticed her aunt's odd behavior. "Would you like some?"

"That'd be great. No telling how long this vigil is going to last. The caffeine will help to keep me awake."

Beth placed her hand on his shoulder and he turned his head to look up at her. "I appreciate your doing this, Brad. Thank you."

He smiled. "No need to thank me. It's what I do."

"I know, but still—"

"It's fine, Beth, now go."

Returning a few minutes later with two mugs of steaming coffee and a freshly brewed pot, Beth placed the tray on the table, turning toward her aunt. The sight of Brad seated next to the bed, holding Iris's hand, touched her more than words could say. It was a very kind gesture, but then, she already knew he was a kind man.

If she was looking to get involved again, if things had been different concerning his dad, if he wasn't so city and she so country, than Brad would have been the perfect candidate. But Beth didn't want to get involved again. The pain of a failed marriage was still fresh in her mind and heart. And failing again was the one thing she could not do, in any aspect of her life.

"Has there been any change?" she asked.

"Your aunt's been mumbling under her breath." She handed him the coffee mug and he thanked her, adding, "I gave her some more Tylenol. I'm sure she vomited up what you gave her. Let's hope she can keep this down. We need to get that fever reduced."

Taking the chair next to Brad, Beth sipped her coffee thoughtfully. Only a few short hours ago his kisses had driven her wild with yearning. Now she was sitting next to him, trying to pretend that his nearness had no effect on her.

Had Brad been affected, too?

Suddenly her aunt cried out, and she nearly burned her mouth on the coffee. "Ouch!"

"Lyle, Lyle. I'm so sorry. Please forgive me, Lyle."

Beth and Brad exchanged a look of surprise, before Iris squeezed Brad's hand tightly and declared, "I love you, Lyle. I've always loved you. Why didn't you love me as much as I loved you?"

Her aunt's voice was full of such pain and sorrow,

Beth's throat and chest tightened. But she couldn't help wondering what her aunt was apologizing for.

What had Iris done to Lyle McMurtry to warrant such anguish?

"It's all right, Iris. I'm here," Brad whispered, playing the role of McMurtry.

Beth sucked in her breath at the compassion he showed her aunt.

"Lyle, Lyle. I should never have—" Then she quieted, leaving Brad and Beth to wonder what she would have said had she continued.

"I've never heard her talk about Lyle McMurtry before. Her voice sounds so pained. I wish I knew what had happened between them."

"Then you really don't know?" Brad searched her face, which was guileless.

"No, I really don't."

"Lyle, I'm so sorry," Iris cried out again, and Brad squeezed the old woman's hand to comfort her.

"It's all right, Iris. There's nothing to be sorry for."

She sat straight up in bed, looking him squarely in the eye, as if she were perfectly lucid. "You know there is! Why do you deny it?"

Beth sucked in her breath but said nothing.

"I didn't want things to end the way they did. Why did you deceive me so? I thought you loved me."

Tears streamed down her face as she listened to

her aunt's conversation with her dead fiancé. Iris still grieved for the man, still loved him, even after all the years that had passed.

"I do, Iris. You must believe me." Brad's admission had the power to quiet the woman and she fell into a fitful sleep.

"I think she'll rest for a while now." Noting the beads of perspiration dotting Iris's forehead, the way her damp nightgown clung to her skin, Brad knew her fever had broken. "I think the worst is over. The fever's lost its grip on her. She'll rest more naturally now."

"Oh, thank God!" Beth took the handkerchief he offered and blew her nose. About to hand it back, she thought better of it, smiled self-consciously and stuffed it into her pocket. "You're very kind. I appreciate the way you offered solace to my aunt. It went above and beyond your role as a doctor."

"I told you, it's—"

She shook her head. "What you did was a lot more than a doctor caring for a patient. It was extremely compassionate and unselfish, especially considering that you believe my aunt had something to do with your father's disappearance."

"Let's move into the other room and let your aunt rest for a bit," he suggested, taking Beth's hand and leading her into the front room.

"I don't know what role, if any, your aunt played

in my father's disappearance. I hope none. I like those two old gals."

Beth smiled. "They like you, too."

"What about you, Beth? Do you like me, just a little?"

At the question, her palms started to sweat, and she pulled her hand out of his. "I think you're very nice."

"That's not what I asked. Do you like me?"

Their gazes held, and Beth could feel her pulse quicken. Trusting someone was difficult for her, but she liked Brad very much, more than she should, in fact. "Yes, I like you. But I wouldn't read too much into that. I like a lot of people. And until your father returns—"

His eyes filled with regret, and Beth knew the truth of her words had hit home. "Dammit! Where is he? Why doesn't he call and let me know he's all right? I keep calling the house, checking for messages, but so far there's been no word."

"Perhaps he's had some kind of mishap and has developed amnesia. That would explain his lack of contact."

Brad shook his head. "He's got plenty of identification on him. They would have found it, if he'd been taken to a hospital." *Or the morgue.*

"Well, then, maybe he's just got some things to work out for himself. All of us need space, from time to time. Maybe he needed to get away, to sort things out and come to terms with whatever might be bothering him."

"Or maybe he's dead," Brad said, his voice choked with emotion.

Beth placed a comforting hand on his arm. "You mustn't talk like that. I'm sure he'll turn up."

He heaved a deep sigh. "The sheriff is looking into Dad's disappearance. Perhaps he'll be able to find something out."

"I'm sure he will." Just as she was sure that Seth Murdock would be paying her a visit sooner than later, and she was dreading the confrontation.

BETH ENTERED HER AUNTS' suite the next morning to find Iris much improved. She was sitting up in bed, allowing Ivy to fuss over her while she ate her oatmeal.

"I've been thinking about damson plum jam ever since Beth gave some to Phinneas Pickens. I'd love to have some for my toast," Iris told Ivy. "Would you mind going down to the cellar and fetching me some, sister?"

"No!" Beth forced a smile as she moved toward the bed and the old ladies stared strangely at her. "I mean, I'll go. There's no need for Aunt Ivy to make the long trek down to the basement. It's so cold down there this time of year."

Ivy's brow wrinkled in puzzlement, then she

shook her head. "I'm perfectly capable of getting the jam, dear. There's no need to concern your—"

"I'll get it. I have to go down there anyway, to—" she thought a moment "—to bring up some apple-sauce for dinner. Lori's making pork tenderloin and wants to serve your homemade applesauce. You know how all the guests rave about it."

"Well, isn't that nice," Iris said, quite pleased by the compliment. She turned to her sister. "We'll need to go down to the cellar soon, Ivy, and can more vegetables and fruits. I've been getting the urge to can again, haven't you?"

The one thing Beth didn't need was for her aunts to go snooping around the basement. Not with those damn bones buried down there. It would be just like them to blab their discovery to the world, forgetting that they were responsible for putting them there in the first place. "This is the wrong season for canning," she reminded them. "Why not wait till spring?"

"Is there some reason you don't want us going down to the basement, dear?" Ivy asked, looking suspicious all of a sudden and turning the tables on Beth, who had wondered that very thing not so long ago.

She shook her head emphatically and laughed. "No, of course not! I just thought I'd save you the trouble. And it is winter. You usually don't put up fruits and vegetables in the winter months. There's not much to choose from."

"Well, Hank planted a patch of pumpkins, so I thought we might put up some pumpkin for pies," Iris said, "and there's also apples stored in the cellar, so we can put up more applesauce."

Beth nodded absently, knowing she had to do something about those bones. She couldn't keep Iris and Ivy out of the basement forever. She had to find a new hiding place, and soon.

CHAPTER EIGHT

SHERIFF MURDOCK COOLED his heels in the front parlor of the Two Sisters Ordinary, waiting for Beth Randall to return from checking on her ailing aunt. She'd already been gone fifteen minutes, so he'd taken the opportunity to study his surroundings, and he liked what he saw.

Seth hadn't stepped foot in the inn since its opening, but he could tell that Beth had done a fine job of remodeling and decorating the old place. Everything matched, even the yellow-and-green hooked rug beneath his feet. It was hard not to be impressed.

Ethel had been begging him to book an overnight "romantic" stay at the Two Sisters to rekindle their passion, or some such nonsense, but he had a perfectly good room at home and didn't see any sense in wasting money. Besides, if he'd wanted to make love to his wife, he could do it in his own bed.

His romantic nature had pretty much buried itself after Ethel began tipping the scales at over two hundred pounds. Patting his stomach, he sighed, knowing he wasn't much to look at these days, either. Damn beer nuts! But Christ! She weighed nearly as much as he did. Of course, he still loved her, but he just wasn't very interested in sexual things these days. Not like when they were first married; then he and Ethel couldn't keep their hands off each other. He shook his head and mumbled, "Damn beer nuts!"

"Sorry to keep you waiting, Sheriff," Beth said upon entering the sunlit room. She smiled politely, offering him a seat in the wing chair, while she perched on the sofa. He couldn't help but notice that she seemed anxious about something, and he was curious to know what that *something* was.

"Hope your aunt's doing okay," he said to be polite, placing his hat on the table next to him and thinking that Iris Swindel was too mean to die. He'd get that old hag, if it was the last thing he ever did.

"Aunt Iris is doing much better, thanks. She had some sort of virus, so I've made her stay put for a couple of extra days." He noted how she kept rubbing her palms on her pants. She was sweating. But why?

"Bet she hates that. I'm not much for lying abed myself. Ethel says I'm the worst patient there is."

Beth's smile was strained. "Aunt Iris dislikes it intensely. But it's for her own good." She folded her hands in her lap. "Now, what is it you need to talk to me about?"

"Dr. Donovan's filed a missing person's report

on his father. I'm investigating the man's disappearance. Since your inn was Robert Donovan's last known whereabouts, I figured this is where I should start my investigation."

If he had something concrete he could use as probable cause and could get a search warrant from old Judge Havarty to tear the inn apart, Seth was certain he would find a missing link or clue that would lead him straight to the old ladies' involvement in the disappearance of the two men.

"I'm afraid I don't have much to add to what I've already told Brad…uh…Dr. Donovan. His father stayed here a few days, paid his bill and left."

Seth scribbled in his notepad, observing the woman's face for any sign of deception. Aside from her nervousness, she seemed to be telling the truth, but then it was often difficult to know when it came to women—they were a devious bunch. "How did he pay?"

"I rechecked the records this morning, and Mr. Donovan paid cash. I remember at the time thinking it was odd because most of my guests pay by credit card."

"And were your aunts acquainted with Robert Donovan?"

Seth looked for signs of panic in Beth's eyes. He saw none. But that didn't mean she wasn't hiding something, only that she was an accomplished liar. "They spoke to him a few times, and I think they may have played a hand or two of bridge, but other than that, they know nothing about his whereabouts."

"I'll be the judge of that when I speak to them."

Her face filled with alarm and she paled. Finally, the reaction he'd been expecting.

"Is that really necessary, Sheriff? I told you—"

"A man is missing, Beth. It's very necessary. But I'll wait until your aunt is feeling better before discussing the matter with her. I'll need to talk to Ivy as well. Those two are a matched set."

"All right, but please keep your questioning brief. My aunts tire easily. I'm sure you understand."

Though he nodded, Seth knew both of the old ladies had more energy than he did. They were always volunteering for one thing or another; church functions were of particular interest to them, most likely because of their father. And Iris never drove anywhere when she could walk, which was lucky for the town's residents since the diminutive woman could barely see above the steering wheel.

"Can you tell me why Dr. Donovan feels your aunts are holding back information about his father?"

Beth stiffened, her eyes darkening. "I have no idea. You'll have to ask Dr. Donovan. All I know is that he's very anguished over what might have happened to his father. Perhaps he's grasping at straws. I'm sure at this point any answer, even an incorrect one, is better than none."

"Donovan knows about McMurtry's disappearance, Beth. I think it's made him even more suspicious of your aunts. You have to admit that two men of the Swindel sisters' acquaintance turning up missing, even fifty years apart, is mighty peculiar, to say the least."

"It's coincidence. Why can't you see that? My aunts are elderly women and rather frail. They wouldn't have the strength to harm a fly."

Seth rubbed the back of his neck. "Don't take much strength to poison a man."

Anger flared in Beth's eyes as she clenched her fists and shoved them between her knees. "I don't like what you're implying, Sheriff."

"I didn't mean to upset you. I'm just doing my job."

She rose to her feet. "Well then, you're probably anxious to be on your way so you can continue your investigation."

He remained seated. "One more question before I leave. Have you discovered anything unusual or out of place, something you would deem as not being an ordinary occurrence?"

She shook her head. "No! Nothing," she replied, almost too emphatically, making Seth wonder what the young woman was hiding...and why.

GAZING OUT THE WINDOW, Beth watched Sheriff Murdock walk down the front walkway toward his police cruiser and breathed a sigh of relief. Thank God the interrogation was finally over, she thought. Not only had she been forced to answer his insulting questions, but she was still worried that her aunts would venture down to the cellar and start nosing around.

Answering Sheriff Murdock's questions and maintaining her composure had been difficult. She felt bruised by the inferences he'd made, not to mention dishonest that she hadn't been totally forthcoming. It just wasn't in her nature to be deceitful, though unfortunately she was getting pretty good at it.

The sheriff was like a dog with a buried bone— poor choice of words! He wasn't likely to give up until he found what he was looking for, and that scared the hell out of her.

Beth had no idea what would happen when her aunts were questioned. They wouldn't be able to stand up to close scrutiny. They would become confused, frightened. She sighed, wishing she could ask them about the bones and find out what they knew. But she couldn't risk it. If Iris and Ivy were to blab to Murdock about the bones, he'd arrest them on suspicion of murder. And she couldn't allow that to happen.

Why oh why did everything have to be so damn complicated? She thought she'd had it bad when she had a cheating husband to contend with, but that was nothing compared to what she was dealing with now: an ongoing murder investigation right under her nose, all thanks to Dr. Donovan. And the worst part was she couldn't really blame him. She would have done the same thing, if the shoe had been on the other foot and her family had been at risk.

Last night Beth had felt a very deep connection to Brad. His compassion in dealing with her aunt had touched her deeply. If only things had been different. If only they had met under different circumstances, they might have become good friends, maybe even more than friends. Brad was the kind of decent man she had always hoped to meet.

But, of course, there was too much between them now—his father's mysterious vanishing act being the biggest obstacle. He would never trust her; he would never believe that she had nothing to do with Robert Donovan's disappearance. It was guilt by association. His suspicions had colored all of them with the same crayon.

He had driven upstate early this morning, in the hope of searching out information about his father from other towns' sheriff departments, and was due back in a little while. She hoped he found out something concrete, something that would finally convince him that she and her aunts were innocent. Even if nothing could ever be between them romantically, they could still be friends.

LATE IN THE AFTERNOON of the same day, Beth gazed out the front parlor window to see Brad getting out of his car and strolling toward the inn. He was accompanied by a gorgeous blonde with a body that could have made a dead man pant. She'd never seen the woman before and had no idea who she was, but Beth already knew that she didn't like her.

And where had Brad met her? Certainly not on his quest for information about his father.

The sight of them laughing together and sharing an intimate moment stirred something inside Beth that she hadn't felt in years: jealousy. Perhaps because the woman looked very much like her ex-husband's girlfriend, only taller and more refined. This woman had the kind of polish that would suit the handsome doctor to a tee. Her clothing was expensive, her makeup done just so. She obviously wasn't the type to hang around in jeans and sweaters with her hair blowing every which way.

As they approached the front door, Beth stepped back from the window, but she was still able to hear their conversation, and she wasn't above eavesdropping.

"You're very funny. Do you know that, Brad? Thank you for sharing such amusing anecdotes about your medical practice."

Beth could hear Brad's laughter, imagine the way his eyes twinkled when he grinned, like a naughty schoolboy who'd just found buried treasure in his backyard. Her mouth tightened. Brad had never shared any information about his practice with her, amusing or otherwise.

Men were all the same—attracted by flash, not substance. She'd thought Brad would be different, but apparently he wasn't.

Hurrying into the foyer, she made great pretense of rearranging the flower arrangement of mums she'd created only an hour before and waited for them to enter.

Brad smiled when he saw her. "Hello, Beth! I was hoping to catch you in. This is Karen Richards. We met at the pharmacy today, and she happened to mention that she was looking for a nice place to stay, so I recommended your inn."

How about hell? Beth silently suggested, holding out her hand. "I'm Beth Randall. I have a vacancy, if you're interested, Ms. Richards." Unfortunately, her money situation being what it was didn't allow her to turn away customers.

Karen Richards perused her surroundings, then looked Beth over from top to bottom, as if she were judging an adversary. "Your inn looks very…respectable. What kind of rooms do you have left? I'd prefer a suite, if one is available."

"I'm sorry. The suites are booked. The only room I have vacant at the moment is on the first floor, near the kitchen," she lied. "It has one twin bed and its own bathroom." It was the worst room in the inn—the one she offered when she was full—only the inn wasn't full at the moment.

The woman's smile was condescending. "How very fortunate for me—indoor plumbing. I'm impressed."

Cheeks reddening, Beth wondered if the money was going to be worth it, after all. She thought not.

Brad appeared embarrassed by the woman's remark. "Uh, the rooms are very nice, Karen. And you certainly can't beat the inn's food," he replied, looking confused by her rudeness. "It's the best in town."

Beth smiled her thanks between gritted teeth. "How many nights do you intend to stay, Ms. Richards? The room will only be available for a few nights." Money or no money, she couldn't tolerate Ms. Queen Bitch for longer than that.

The blonde smiled at Brad. "That should give me plenty of time."

Beth took care of the paperwork in a matter of moments, handing the woman the room key. "It's room one-oh-two. Just follow this hallway toward the back of the house. It's the last door on the right. You can't miss it. I hope you find your accommodations comfortable."

"Well, if you ladies will excuse me, I've got to go find Stacy."

"Stacy?" Karen asked, and Beth went in for the kill.

"Stacy is Brad's twelve-year-old daughter. She's very sweet and he's totally devoted to her. It's refreshing to see a father and daughter who are so close."

"Thanks, Beth!" Brad was obviously pleased by her remark. "Stacy's roped me into taking her fishing. I haven't been in years, and I'm not very good at it. Tennis is more my game."

"Fishing?" Karen's eyes widened and Beth almost laughed out loud at the horror on the woman's face.

"Yes. Would you like to go?" Brad offered. "I'm sure my daughter won't mind."

Beth's amusement faded quickly, until the blonde shook her head. "No, thanks! Tempting offer, but I've got to unpack and freshen up." She hurried to her room, leaving the doctor staring after her.

Poor Brad. Didn't he realize that the only thing Karen Richards was hoping to hook was a well-to-do doctor? Why were men always taken in by such obvious creatures?

Because men didn't think with their brains.

"Do you like to fish, Beth?"

"I'm crazy about fishing, but I'm not sure I can get away right now. I've got to—"

"Oh, come on," he coaxed, his smile dimpling,

which always made her toes curl. "It's your duty to entertain your guests, isn't it?"

"Well—"

"You could consider it payment for medical services rendered."

She knew she owed him a great deal for last night. Plus, if she got the chance, she'd be able to pump him for information about his conversation with Seth Murdock and maybe find out exactly what and how much the nosy sheriff knew.

"All right, I'll come. I'll meet you down by the pond in fifteen minutes. The fishing gear's in the barn. Just ask my handyman, Hank, to fix you and Stacy up with whatever you need."

"Great. I'll see you there."

Right brow arched, she crossed her arms over her chest. "Really, even though I wasn't your first choice?"

"I was merely being polite. I knew Karen wasn't the kind of woman who would enjoy fishing. She's much too refined."

Cheeks reddening, Beth fought hard to keep her temper in check. "Yes, I suppose you're right, while I'm just a country bumpkin who wouldn't know a designer dud if it came up and bit me on the ass."

"I didn't mean that. What I meant to say is that you're fun, while Karen is—"

"Perfect?"

He shook his head. "Karen is preoccupied with her appearance." And Beth wasn't, was the inference.

"I see. Well, perhaps you should look to your own preoccupation, Dr. Donovan. It's not every man who irons his jeans."

Rather than being insulted as she'd intended, Brad tossed back his head and laughed, and the booming sound skittered right up her arms, raising gooseflesh. "My jeans are ironed because I send all of my laundry out. My dad's ruined too many of my garments over the years, and I don't trust him with the wash anymore."

"Oh. Well, they look very nice. I just thought that you being a doctor and all—"

"That I iron my jeans and was born with a silver spoon in my mouth? Now who's prejudging whom?"

Beth didn't know what to say. She had prejudged him, and had been neatly and nicely put in her place. "I guess I owe you an apology."

He shook his head. "No, you don't. All I ask is that you show up on time for our date."

Before she could protest that it wasn't a date, that she didn't date anyone, especially smart-aleck doctors who were much too good looking for their own good and knew how to give mouth-to-mouth resuscitation to unsuspecting females, he had disappeared.

It would serve Brad right if she didn't show up at the pond. He was too presumptuous by far. But, of course, she would. And it wasn't because she liked fishing, but because she liked smart-aleck, good-looking doctors who were well-versed in mouth-to-mouth!

STACY WAS STANDING ALONE at the edge of the pond when Beth approached. The wind was blowing, and she was happy to see that the girl had worn a parka. Buster ran to greet her, nearly knocking Stacy down in his enthusiasm to lick her face, which made her giggle uncontrollably.

"Hello, Stacy," she said. "Are you having fun?"

The girl sobered instantly. "I was till you got here. Why'd you have to come and spoil things?"

Beth did her best not to feel insulted. "Your dad invited me. Where is he, by the way?"

"He ran back to the barn to get some worms." She pulled a face, which told Beth quite a lot about Stacy's experience with fishing.

"Do you know how to bait your own hook?" she asked.

"You mean with worms?" Stacy shook her head. "Gross! I'm not touching those icky things. They're slimy."

"Well then, I think you'll find me handy to have around. I'm very good at baiting hooks."

Eyes widening, the young woman took a moment to decide. "I guess you can stay, but only if you bait my hook and don't go flirting with my dad, like that stuck-up woman I saw out of Ivy's bedroom window earlier today. I could tell right away she's hot for my dad."

Beth thought she'd been the only one to notice. "How can you tell?"

"I saw her press her boobs into his arm, that's how. Aunt Ivy saw it, too, and she said it was shameful the way she was behaving, like some hussy on the prowl."

Swallowing her grin, Beth said, "I'm surprised to hear Ivy said that. My aunt enjoys public spectacles, especially if she's involved." At Stacy's pointed look, Beth realized she'd said too much. "Never mind."

"Aunt Ivy says what she thinks. I like that about her. Gramps is the same way."

There was wistfulness about Stacy when she spoke of her grandfather. "Do you miss him?"

She plopped down on the cold ground next to Beth, who had her arms wrapped around bent knees. "I hope he comes back soon. Don't tell Dad, but I'm starting to think that maybe he won't."

"Why would you think that? I'm sure he'll be back soon."

"Because Aunt Ivy said that old people are sometimes like dogs—they go away to die, and we don't know if we'll ever get to see them again."

Alarmed by the older woman's comment and wondering what she'd based it on, Beth felt doubts start to creep in again, but she didn't have time to question Stacy further because her father walked up just then.

"Hey, you two, I've got the night crawlers. Guess we can get our fishing tournament started."

Beth eyed the man's inappropriate clothing, and shook her head. Brad was still dressed in the same slacks and sweater that he'd worn when he'd left this morning. His shoes were leather, very expensive, and she didn't think they'd stand up to getting wet. "Don't you want to change before you go fishing?" she asked.

"No, why?" He looked down at himself. "This is what I always wear to sporting events."

"This is not a sporting event. We're going fishing. And I hear we're having a fishing tournament. Is that correct?"

Stacy nodded, smiling enthusiastically. "Dad says whoever catches the most fish in an hour gets an ice-cream sundae tomorrow. I'm gonna win because I love hot-fudge sundaes with lots of whipped cream and nuts."

"So I take it my aunts have told you about Claymore's Ice Cream parlor? It's very good. But I should warn you, I'm very good at catching fish, and I love caramel sundaes."

"Hey, aren't you two forgetting that I might just beat you both?" Brad said. "Fishing is a man's sport, after all."

"Nah," Beth and Stacy replied in unison, shaking their heads.

"Everyone knows girls are better than boys, Dad."

"Yeah, Dr. Know-it-all, everyone knows that." And no one dressed the way Brad was dressed could possibly catch any fish. Most likely he'd scare them all.

"I guess you blowhards better prove it then."

An hour later they had. Beth had six bluegills flapping in her basket, Stacy had five, while Brad had come up empty-handed.

"The hour's almost up, Moby Doc. It doesn't look like you'll be winning this fishing tournament, after all." Beth laughed at his forlorn expression.

"I don't know what happened," he said, scratching his head.

"I think it's the way Beth baits the hooks, Dad. You should have had her do yours."

"Or maybe it's those fancy clothes you're wearing," Beth said, and Stacy laughed and covered her mouth.

"I guess I should have changed."

"I'm going for a jog around the pond with Buster, Dad. Beth said it was okay." Without waiting for his permission, the girl and dog took off at a trot.

"Well, I guess I'd better get back to the inn. My aunts will be waiting for their tea." Beth decided not to question Brad about his conversation with Murdock. They'd been having a good time, and she didn't want to spoil things by bringing up his father again.

"I had fun today, Beth. It's nice to find a woman who enjoys sports."

Her cheeks colored. "I've been fishing for quite a while," she said. "And don't fool yourself. I hate sports. Just ask my ex-husband, the jock. It was one of the reasons we weren't compatible."

He moved toward her and she backed away. "Why are you so afraid to be alone with me?" he asked. "I won't kiss you again, if that's what you're worried about."

"I have my reasons for being wary of men, Brad, same as you have your reasons for being wary of me. You have to admit it doesn't make for a very good beginning to a relationship."

"I like you, Beth. You've made me feel things that I haven't felt in a very long time. I know this isn't the time to say this, what with my dad's disappearance and all, but I wish there could be more between us." He drew her into his arms and she didn't resist when he lowered his head and kissed her.

The kiss was sweet and heated her blood to an uncomfortable degree. When she felt herself weakening, she pulled back. "You shouldn't have done that. It's not going to change our present set of circumstances, or the fact that your daughter dislikes me, or the fact that you don't trust me. And I don't blame you for that, because I don't trust many people either, most especially men."

"Not all men are like your ex-husband. Some of us value our wives and respect our marriage vows. You can't just close yourself off from life. At some point, you have to take a risk and learn to trust again."

"Why? Risk involves getting hurt. I've already been down that road. Why would I want to go there again? And I'm quite content to be alone. I have no one to answer to but myself."

"Everyone needs someone. It's the way God intended for things to be."

"You're a romantic. I used to be that way once. Careful you don't get blindsided one of these days." She was thinking of women like Karen, who pounced, mated and went in for the kill before their unsuspecting mates even knew what they were about.

"I've already been blindsided. It always happens when you're least expecting it."

Thinking that he was referring to Karen, she touched his arm. "Be careful, Brad. I'd hate to see you get hurt."

His sweet smile touched her heart. "It would be worth it, I'm thinking." Then he clasped her face between his hands, taking her by surprise, and kissed her again, gently, almost reverently, before walking away.

Beth watched him go and heaved a deep sigh of yearning. If only things were different, she thought.

But they weren't. The cards were stacked against them, in more ways than one.

She wished she could confide in Brad, tell him about the bones in her basement and hear him say that he believed and supported her one hundred percent.

But to do that meant she'd have to trust him implicitly. And trust was a luxury she couldn't afford.

CHAPTER NINE

EARLY THE NEXT MORNING, Beth hung up the phone and darted from the hallway into the kitchen, shouting for her chef. Lori, who was in the midst of preparing banana French toast for the guests, looked up when the innkeeper burst into the room. Beth had a huge smile on her face and looked ready to pop a blood vessel.

"Guess what? *The Messenger* wants to do a feature article on the Two Sisters. Poppy Woodcock is on her way over as we speak to interview us. Isn't that exciting?"

Apprehension skittered along Lori's spine, but she forced a smile, pretending to be delighted while trying to figure out how to avoid being interviewed.

If there was one thing she didn't need right now it was her name publicized in the newspaper. Even though she needed publicity and good reviews to establish herself as a talented chef, Lori couldn't risk the exposure and having Bill find her. Success would come eventually. She believed in her talent and just needed to be patient and wait it out.

"I think you should do the interview, Beth. I'm not very good at that sort of thing, and you're the owner, after all." She had no idea if articles from small local newspapers, like *The Messenger,* would be picked up by the wire services, but she couldn't take that chance.

Beth waved away her objection with a flick of the wrist. "Don't be silly! You'll be fabulous. And you are the genius behind all those delicious recipes you've created. Without your expertise, the restaurant would be nothing. I insist you receive equal coverage, and I won't hear another word about it."

Knowing exactly where those recipes came from, Lori blushed at the generous offer. Normally, she would have jumped at the chance to further her career, but not when Bill was hot on her trail. "I'm not… I don't feel comfortable talking about myself. I'd probably mess everything up."

Filling two mugs with coffee, Beth motioned for her chef to join her at the table. "I'm more than happy to brag about your incredible talent, Lori, so don't worry. I'm sure Poppy is just looking for a bit of background information, like your training at the Culinary Institute, or where you worked before coming here—stuff like that."

And that was exactly what Lori feared. Trying not to sound overly interested, she asked, "Do you think the article will be picked up by the wire services?"

"I can't imagine why it would be. Mediocrity is

such a small town and there are plenty of inns in Pennsylvania much more impressive than mine. But wouldn't it be great to make it into the big city papers? Just think of the publicity we'd get. It could put the Two Sisters Ordinary on the map."

Chastising herself silently for opening her big mouth, Lori replied, "That's true. It would be quite a coup."

Beth reached for a freshly baked blueberry muffin and bit into it. "Maybe I should call my friend Ellen at the *Philadelphia Inquirer.* I wonder if she can get a cell phone signal while at sea." She went on to explain, "Ellen's on a college-reunion cruise at the moment. She's an investigative reporter and apparently is on the trail of some big story."

"I wouldn't bother your friend, Beth, especially if she's on a cruise. There's nothing worse than having a vacation interrupted. And she'll probably be unable to help anyway. The *Inquirer i*s a tough nut to crack."

The innkeeper's eyes widened. "That's right! You lived in Philadelphia. Do you have a contact that could help us? I'd be forever grateful."

Lori shook her head emphatically. "No! I didn't know many people there. I worked at the restaurant from early morning till late at night, which didn't leave much time for socializing. You know how reclusive we chefs are." She smiled, hoping to make light of her comments and get Beth off her present course.

Though her employer nodded absently, Lori could see the wheels turning in her head, the determination lighting her eyes. She knew Beth well enough to realize that the innkeeper would continue to look until she found a way to make them all famous, or infamous, as the case may be.

Heaving a sigh, she hoped selfishly that the local newspaper was too small for any wire service to bother with. Bill read the *Inquirer* religiously, and if he found out her location… She didn't want to think about that.

Bill could have her arrested for theft, sue her for breaching her employment contract and make her life miserable for years to come. Seeing him again would also force her to admit feelings she'd denied for too long.

"What's wrong? Why are you looking so glum? I thought you'd be happy that we're going to get this great opportunity."

Lori forced a smile. "I'm very happy. I was just thinking over what I would say to the reporter. Nerves, I guess."

"Well, have another cup of coffee and calm down. Poppy's been at the newspaper for years. She's old, but very nice. We'll get through this, you'll see."

"I sure hope you're right." The alternative would

not be good for anybody, but it would be particularly devastating for Beth. Once word got out that her chef was a thief the inn would become notorious, and that would not be good for business.

AS EXPECTED, AUBREY HAD received an earful from the local barber the previous afternoon, and a pretty decent haircut as well.

He'd learned from Max Greeley that there were two Swindel sisters; both were former school-teachers who had a reputation in the community for being eccentric. His birth mother and her sister lived in a huge Victorian mansion at the south end of town. The Swindel family home had been turned into an inn and was presently presided over by their great-niece, Elizabeth Randall.

News of the property had piqued Aubrey's interest immediately, and he was now in his car, driving toward the Two Sisters Ordinary. Being a business-man with foresight, he'd already researched the property records at the local courthouse and knew the house sat on fifty acres of land, sported a decent-sized pond, many fruit trees and a couple of outbuild-ings, including a barn.

Slowing down when he saw the inn's wooden sign hanging from a post near the road's edge, he pulled over, observing the impressive four-story structure with the wide wraparound front porch, which, of course, he would tear down when he bought the place. The barn and pond were barely visible from the road, but he was able to pull forward a bit to get a better view. And he liked what he saw. He liked it a lot.

The setting was bucolic as hell, but Aubrey was astute enough to know that the inn's location made it a prime piece of real estate, which would be ripe for development. In fact, he'd already decided that the property would make an excellent upscale condominium resort.

Mediocrity and the surrounding area was already a minor tourist destination. With the right advertising and promotion, he could put the place on the map and make a fortune off of it.

Of course, if he did buy the place, the old ladies and their niece would have to go. And though he might experience a momentary twinge of regret for tossing his mother onto the street, he'd get over it. It was no more than she deserved, no more than she'd done to him when she abandoned him, like a bundle of unwanted garbage, all those years ago.

His father was presumed dead. He'd learned that much from reading old newspapers at the library. Lyle McMurtry had disappeared over fifty years ago under very mysterious circumstances. Apparently, Iris Swindel had been the one suspected of foul play, though it had never been proved.

It looked to him like the old lady had a ruthless

streak, and Aubrey had little doubt from whom he'd inherited his. Like mother, like son.

Taking away the old woman's ancestral home would be sweet revenge, he couldn't deny it. And if she had offed his father, then it would be a fitting punishment, as well.

Before Aubrey made his intentions to buy the property known to anyone, he wanted to conduct more research, to determine what kind of offer he'd make and see if he could discover what skeletons, if any, were in Elizabeth Randall's closet.

Everyone had weaknesses and he was a master at ferreting them out. Vulnerable people made great victims. It was the truth of the world—his world, anyway. The strong survived.

There were few who could beat him at the game of real-estate acquisition. He knew what it took to come out on top: smarts, money and a desire to win at any cost.

And Aubrey intended to win.

BETH WAS FOLDING LAUNDRY and thinking about the morning's newspaper interview. It had gone quite well, or so the reporter had claimed. And since Poppy Woodcock was the expert and editor of the social pages, Beth figured she knew what she was talking about.

Lori had seemed apprehensive during the entire hour it had taken to finish the interview and Beth wondered why her chef had been so reluctant to have her name in the newspaper. She was obviously troubled about something, but Beth didn't know what. She'd asked Lori if she had been having financial or work-related problems and had offered to help, but the woman insisted that everything was fine.

Instinct told Beth that Lori wasn't telling her the truth. But short of calling her chef a liar, there wasn't much she could do about it. She sure as heck couldn't afford to have the woman quit a week before Thanksgiving and ruin the opening of the restaurant.

Smoothing the peach guest towel and placing it on top of the existing pile, Beth was reminded of the conversation she'd had with Karen Richards just a short while ago. The woman had complained that the towels in her room were rough and had scratched her delicate skin, which was a pile of horse-doody, as far as Beth was concerned, because she took special care with all of the inn's linens. Beth did the laundry herself, and her towels were always sweet smelling and fluffy.

Anyway, who cared if Ms. Queen Bitch was unhappy with her towels? Karen was leaving tomorrow to take a room at the hotel, where the accommodations would be more "suitable to her sensibilities." But Beth figured the husband-hunting creature was leaving because there were more men and better pickings at the Excelsior.

"Well, good riddance!" Actually, she felt relieved

that Brad wouldn't be one of Karen's targets any longer. She had done everything to entice him to bed, but he hadn't fallen into her trap. Smart man!

The heat from the dryers made Beth's forehead sweat and she wiped away the perspiration with the back of her sleeve. She looked a mess and was grateful that she was alone in the laundry area. Her hair was frizzing from the high heat and humidity, her shirt had torn at the hem, and her faded jeans had seen better days. In short, she looked like the aftermath of a tornado.

"Here you are. I've been looking all over for you."

At the sound of Brad's voice, the first thing Beth thought was *Damn!* She turned to face him and could see by his surprised expression that he wasn't used to seeing slovenly females. Fighting the urge to reach up and calm her wild mane, she asked, "You have? Why? Is there a problem?"

He shook his head. "No problem. Stacy has just reminded me that I owe both of you a trip to the ice-cream parlor today. I was hoping you could join us after lunch. I noticed things quiet down around here just about then."

"That's true, but it's not necessary for you to buy me a sundae just because you were the big loser of the fishing tournament," she quipped, thinking of her weakness for all things caramel and how she would love a sundae right now.

His grin matched hers. "Stacy insists that you come. She said it wouldn't be fair to leave you out of the celebration since you baited all of the hooks for her."

Beth could hardly believe her ears. "What did you have to do, bribe her with a new car?"

Brad's laughter was as rich and smooth as warm caramel, making her weak in the knees. "We both want you to come, and if Stacy's had a change of heart where you're concerned then I'm happy. I've learned over the last few years that trying to make sense of a teenager's mind is a futile proposition. Perhaps your expertise with worms overwhelmed her."

Grinning, Beth said, "Well, in that case, I'll be happy to join you. I'll meet you in the foyer around one. Does that sound good?" Brad shuffled his feet, looking rather nervous and making her wonder if he'd already reconsidered the offer. "If you've changed your mind and would rather not include me, that's fine. I won't be upset."

"It's not that! It's quite the opposite, in fact. I'm trying to find a way to invite you out to dinner this evening without sounding like an ass. Guess it's too late for that. I'm a little out of practice."

She stared at him in disbelief. "You're asking me out on a date?" Good Lord! She hadn't been on one of those in a while. The idea sent her stomach fluttering and heat rising to her cheeks.

"Yes, though I guess I'm not doing it very well. I

found a nice restaurant on the outskirts of town, and I thought we could try it."

Beth figured he was talking about the Brookside. New chef owners had taken it over about a month ago and had totally refurbished the place. And she knew when she'd read in the newspaper about their extensive menu that it could prove serious competition for the Two Sisters.

She hadn't eaten there as yet. There was something rather dismal about eating at a nice restaurant alone, though she'd been dying to try the food, to see if she and Lori had anything to worry about.

Brad was offering her that chance. But as tempting as his invitation was, it was on the tip of her tongue to refuse. A trip to an ice-cream parlor, chaperoned by a moody adolescent, in the middle of the afternoon was one thing, but dinner alone with Brad was something else. And Beth wasn't certain whose virtue would be more at risk.

Not good, Beth! Very bad, in fact!

"Come on," he urged at her hesitation. "I promise to be a perfect gentleman." He held up three fingers. "Scouts' honor. And I don't make the sign lightly."

She found his action endearing. "I'm not at all surprised to find out you're a Boy Scout, Dr. Donovan. And you're usually, but not always, a gentleman. But I guess any man who has the courage to invite me out the way I presently look deserves a yes."

His smile widened. "Great! I made the reservation for seven-thirty."

"You made a reservation not knowing if I'd go?" She shook her head, knowing she should be annoyed by his presumption. But the truth was she was flattered. "Now that's what I call confidence."

"I was hoping," he said, looking sheepish.

"What about Stacy? Won't she be upset that we're going out together?"

"My daughter doesn't dictate to me, Beth. And besides, I've already spoken to her about it and she said it was fine because she'd already made plans with your aunts. Apparently, they've invited Stacy to a pajama party this evening. From what I've been told, Iris is going to perform a bit of witchcraft." He smiled. "When my daughter heard that, nothing else mattered."

Beth was positive that once her aunts got wind of Brad's intention to ask her out, they did everything in their power to convince the young girl to stay with them. "Did Aunt Ivy offer to buy Stacy something on eBay, by any chance?"

"Now that you mention it, I believe she did."

"Those two old ladies can be pretty persuasive when they put their minds to it. When I was Stacy's age I loved hanging out with them. They were a lot more fun than my mother."

"Is your mother still alive? I've never heard you mention her."

"Oh, yes. She's too mean to die." Beth grinned at Brad's shocked expression. "We don't get along very well, in case you haven't figured that out."

"Maybe you're too much alike. My dad and I butt heads all the time because we're so similar in nature."

She looked horrified. "God, I hope not! I'd have to have a personality transplant, if that were the case."

"Is your mother coming to spend the Thanksgiving holiday with you?"

"Bite your tongue, Doc! I've got enough on my plate without Margaret Shaw coming to visit."

He smiled and said, "Consider the subject dropped," then glanced at his watch. "I've got to go. I told Stacy I'd meet her at the car at ten o'clock, and I'm late. She's taking me shopping, for underwear. Hers, not mine." He rolled his eyes. "Wish me luck. I'll see you later."

Beth smiled as she watched him depart, but her pleasure quickly faded when she began to wonder if she was making a big mistake by becoming more involved with the handsome doctor. After all, nothing had been resolved, and she had a lot to lose.

Her heart, for one thing.

"I'LL GET A CHECK OUT to you as soon as I can, Mr. Weathers. I realize I promised you full payment last week, and I fully intend to pay you for the windows you've replaced, but I've had some unexpected expenses and I'm a bit short at the moment." Beth's face paled as she listened to the window installer's diatribe, then she hung up the phone, looking dejected and depressed.

"Is there a problem, Beth?" her aunt asked. "I'd be happy to help if there is."

Beth heaved a sigh. "It's nothing, Aunt Iris, just another creditor calling to be paid. I wish I'd hear something from Mr. Pickens about the loan I've applied for. How long does it take to approve a loan anyway?"

Iris patted her niece's hand. "Be patient, Beth. Good things come to those who wait, and I'm sure you're going to get that loan."

"I hope you're right, because I'm not sure what I'll do if I don't."

Karen Richards's smile was filled with delight as she pressed herself against the wall and listened to the inn's proprietor moan to her aunt about her financial troubles.

An inn as lousy as the Two Sisters had no right to be open and duping the unsuspecting public, forcing them to find other, more expensive places to stay. And a woman as homely and unsophisticated as Beth Randall had no right to entice good-looking, wealthy doctors like Bradley Donovan, either.

Karen had a hard time believing that Brad preferred the country bumpkin to her. And she wouldn't soon forget it. She wasn't a woman who liked to lose.

"I CAN'T BELIEVE I'M actually having dessert after pigging out on that huge caramel sundae earlier." Beth forked a piece of cheesecake into her mouth and made appreciative sounds. "I'm going to get as fat as a pig, but this cheesecake is so heavenly, it's worth it."

Watching her tongue flick out to lick the tines of the fork, then dip down to her lips, made his throat constrict. Beth eating cheesecake was a singularly erotic experience.

"How come you're not eating your pecan pie?" she asked. "It looks so good."

"Would you like a bite?"

"Definitely!" She grinned. "You should know better than to offer me anything that smacks of dessert. I'm totally addicted to sweets." Leaning closer, she licked the gooey substance off his fork, and he could smell the clean fresh scent of her, making him harden.

"*Mmm*. That's yummy," she said, "though it would have been better with vanilla ice cream, like we serve it."

He smiled at her enthusiasm for all things sugary. "I know I've already told you, but you look very nice tonight. I like your dress." It was black, short and formfitting, showing off her body to perfection. Beth looked damn sexy and certainly not anyone's idea of a country innkeeper.

Her cheeks filled with color. "Thank you. I rarely

dress up anymore. As you know, things are pretty casual at the inn. To be perfectly honest, I haven't worn this dress in years. It's a wonder it still fits."

He perused her thoroughly. "It fits very well."

His comment made her uncomfortable. Beth reached for her water glass and gulped down the cold liquid. "My dinner was very good," she said, trying to change the subject. "Though I think the marinade they used for the rack of lamb was a bit overpowering. Lori's is better."

"I don't think this place is going to be much competition for your new restaurant, Beth. Don't get me wrong, the food's fine and the owners have done a terrific job with the decor—French country, I guess you'd call it—but the food isn't in the same class or as good as the Two Sisters'. Your chef is extraordinary, very creative."

Her smile filled with thanks. "That's very nice of you to say, though you may be a bit prejudiced since you're a guest of the inn."

"I'm a predictable Boy Scout, right?"

"I don't think *predictable* is the right word. Your invitation to dinner was certainly unexpected, though very much appreciated. I just think you're a very nice man and like to make people feel good. It's part of your bedside manner, I suspect."

He reached for her hand and was pleased when she didn't pull back. "I'd like to show you more of my bedside manner, Beth. What do you say to a little ride after we're done here?"

"But where would we go?" She glanced out the double-hung window they were seated near. "It's getting rather late, and there's not much sight-seeing to be done in the dark."

He squeezed her hand. "I was thinking more of finding a nice secluded spot and parking for a while, rather than going sight-seeing."

Her eyes widened. "You were? I mean, I'm not sure about that. What kind of a Boy Scout makes out on the first date?"

He grinned. "A smart one? Actually, I was thinking of just parking and doing some talking, getting to know each other better." Was that disappointment flashing across her face? "But I'm game, if you'd rather do the other?"

Her cheeks reddened. "Don't be ridiculous! We're adults, and adults don't park and neck. That's for teenagers."

He was feeling as randy as a teenager tonight, that was for damn certain! "We won't do anything you don't want to do. What do you say?"

"I guess talking would be okay. I mean, what's the harm in that, right?"

"Exactly. What could possibly be the harm?"

CHAPTER TEN

THE WIND WAS HOWLING, the moon full, and it seemed like the perfect night for romance. Beth felt as if she were sixteen again and out on her first date. Her palms were sweating, her heart racing, and Brad hadn't done anything except park the car under a stand of pine trees and turn off the ignition.

She'd actually felt disappointed when he'd first mentioned parking and then had gone on to explain how they were merely going to talk, not make out. How stupid was that? He was a gentleman and in charge of his emotions, unlike her, and she should be grateful for that.

What the hell had happened to her self-restraint?

Apparently it had flown out the window at the idea of hitting it hot and heavy with the good doctor. Well, thank God one of them had some self-control, though it was a bit disconcerting to discover that he wasn't quite as enamored with her as she was with him.

Brad had definitely been aroused by the sight of

her in the black dress. She'd seen undeniable evidence of that earlier that evening when he'd met her in the front hallway for their date. And she'd been flattered to no end. It had been a long time since a man had gotten up a head of steam over her.

"Are you cold?" he asked. "I can keep the car's heater running, if you are."

Was he kidding? She was hot, uncomfortably so, and had considered asking him to roll down the windows, to let some of the cold night air in. "No, not at all."

"That's too bad. I was going to suggest climbing into the backseat, where it would be warmer."

She glanced back, caught his teasing grin and shook her head. "Really, Dr. Donovan, I'm shocked! You lured me out here on the pretense of talking, remember?"

"I lied. What I really want is to kiss you senseless. I was hoping you wanted that, too."

Her eyes widened. "If you ask, I'll probably say no."

He sighed with disappointment. "That's what I figured."

"So don't ask." Beth couldn't believe she'd just said that. She was about to open her mouth and rescind the suggestion when he reached for her.

"You're incredibly sexy, do you know that? You and that little black dress are driving me wild. And

I usually have a firm grip on my emotions. I never do or say anything impetuous. You can ask anyone who knows me."

She had already figured that out, which made his admission even more astonishing. No one, including her stupid ex-husband, had ever accused her of being sexy, and not just sexy, but *incredibly* sexy. "I—"

Not giving her a chance to respond, Brad covered Beth's lips with his own, dragging her across the padded console that divided the BMW's bucket seats, until she was sitting full on his lap, providing her with a very good indicator of his present state of mind, which was very similar to, if not exactly, her own.

Wrapping her arms around his neck, she boldly deepened the kiss. His lips were warm and soft, and she felt herself melting. She wished she could stay in Brad's arms forever so she could experience, over and over, the joy that was rushing through her at that very moment.

When he groaned, Beth figured she wasn't the only one dissolving into a puddle of yearning. She also decided she must be doing something right and was definitely not frigid, as her ex-husband had led her to believe. Of course, Greg had never kissed her like this, never made her feel cherished, safe or sexy as hell. He'd always been too wrapped up in his own pleasure.

Suddenly, Brad pulled back, looking flushed and

very pained. "You keep wiggling your butt like that and I won't be held responsible for what could happen next."

She gazed into eyes filled with desire that matched her own and sighed. "You're good for my ego, Doc."

He shook his head, and she could see in that moment the uncertainty that was beginning to replace passion. "I'm sorry for coming on so strong. Like I said, I don't usually behave like this. You make me forget all the rules I live by."

"That's okay."

"No, it's not." He helped her get back to her own seat. "You're driving me crazy, Beth. I want you, very badly, and I have no right to expect anything more than friendship from you, especially with everything that's been going on."

With quick, nervous strokes she smoothed down the skirt of her dress, wishing it was longer, and tucked her hands between her knees. Knowing that what he said made perfectly good sense, she felt sad. It would be foolish to give her heart to a man who would soon pack up and return to his real world—a world totally alien to her.

"Friendship's important," she finally said. "And if that's all we ever have, I'll cherish it. I'm not anxious to get hurt again. And if things keep on as they are, I'm afraid that's what's going to happen."

"I'll never hurt you. You have my word on that."

"Scouts' honor?" she couldn't resist saying, and he nodded somberly. "You won't mean to hurt me, but it'll happen just the same. It's the way of things."

He reached out his hand to toy with the hairs at the nape of her neck and gooseflesh broke out over her arms. "I care about you a great deal. I hope you know that. I haven't felt this way about a woman in a very long time. Four years, to be exact."

"I care about you, too. More than I should. But as we've already discussed, nothing can come of it. You're wise to realize that now before it's too late."

"Dammit!" He palmed the back of his neck. "I feel like I'm treading water, that my life's been forced into limbo because of my dad's disappearance."

"Be realistic, Doc. You and I are two very different people. We would never suit in a million years. You're a pediatrician who loves children. I don't ever want to have a child." He seemed surprised by her admission, but she didn't stop to explain. "You're polished and successful. You need someone in your life who knows all the correct things to say and do. I just sort of bumble through life and hope for the best."

"What makes you think I care about appearances?"

Her mouth dropped open. "You're kidding, right? You're always dressed so meticulously, not a hair out of place, not a crease left to sag. You probably have the cleanest garbage cans in Virginia." She sighed.

"You're a planner. I've seen you make list after list while trying to figure out the best way to find your father. And I know what's expected of a man in your position. Charlottesville is very Southern, very proper. I had a friend who went to UVA and she said the doctors' wives were the most perfect and organized creatures she had ever seen. You need someone who epitomizes that, and it's certainly not me."

He smiled, caressing her cheek with his fingertip. "Don't sell yourself short. You've accomplished a lot and should be proud of yourself."

Beth thought about the bones in her basement, the lies she had told, the secrets she still held, and knew she had very little to be proud of. "Your bedside manner is as impeccable as always, Doc, but I think we should be getting back to the inn now. I wouldn't want my aunts to send out a search-and-rescue team."

"All right, but I have a feeling that whatever's between us isn't over—and I don't want it to be."

She smiled at the earnestness she heard in his voice. Brad was honest and forthright, a real Boy Scout. Too bad she couldn't say the same thing about herself.

"I WONDER WHY DAD and Beth aren't back from having dinner?" Stacy asked, looking out the upstairs window, a worried expression covering her face.

Ivy and Iris exchanged weighted looks, then Ivy said, "They probably had to wait for a table. Sometimes new restaurants can be crowded. Isn't that right, sister?"

"That's very true," Iris concurred, hoping her niece was having a good time and opening herself up to new possibilities. She wanted Beth to marry again, have children, even though the woman insisted she never would.

It was unnatural for a woman not to want a child of her own. Those who were lucky enough to have them didn't realize what a special gift they'd been given. Not everyone was as fortunate or deserving.

"What's wrong, Iris? You look rather odd."

Iris flushed at where her thoughts had taken her. "It's nothing, just a bit of indigestion."

"You ate a whole lot of popcorn, Aunt Iris, and six of Lori's chocolate-chip cookies, too."

Ivy's eyes twinkled at the child's honesty. "Looks like we can't get away with much these days, sister," she said, and the young girl smiled.

"I ate my share, too. They were really good. I like Lori's cooking, though sometimes it's pretty fancy." Placing her hands on her hips, she asked the two women, "So, what are we going to do now? Do you have any more magic spells to weave?"

Iris shook her head. "I'm afraid not. I only know a few, but I'm going to practice some more for the next time we get together."

"That would be cool. I had a good time tonight. I

wasn't sure I would, because you guys are old and everything, but you were like some of my friends at school. You know, easy to talk to and hang out with."

"Why, thank you, dear." Iris smiled happily. "Ivy and I try to stay up on things. We taught school for many years and it was always necessary to know what the kids were thinking, so they couldn't put one over on us."

Her sister chuckled. "Yes, but they always managed to anyway, sister."

Seated on the sofa, Stacy pulled her knees up under her chin and heaved a sigh much too world-weary for a child her age. "I hate school. The only reason I go is to hang out with my friends."

"Why is that, dear?" Ivy asked, her brows drawing together. "You should be enjoying the experience of educating yourself. Everything you learn now will be put to good use later in life."

"That's what my dad says, but I don't believe it. I hate history. It's, like, totally boring. Who cares what happened hundreds of years ago? I don't."

"Have you talked this over with your father?" Stacy's views on receiving an education were mirrored by many of the young people these days and that worried Iris.

Stacy shook her head. "Dad was a brain in school. He'd be ashamed if he found out I was stupid."

"You're not stupid! And I don't want to hear you

say that again, do you understand?" Iris's tone softened. "I wasn't a very good student of geometry, but I managed to squeak through with the help of my sister, who tutored me. Perhaps all you need is a little extra help with your difficult subjects."

"Do you think you guys could help me? I haven't a clue about algebra."

"Oh, merciful heavens," Iris declared, "I'm not sure! I haven't done mathematics in years and years. And it's changed so much."

Stacy heaved a sigh. "See, I'm doomed. You guys are teachers and you don't even know how to do this stuff."

"Well, sister and I would be more than happy to tutor you in history and English," Ivy offered. "Beth might be willing to help you with math, though I think that was her worst subject."

The girl's eyes widened. "Really? I thought I was the only one."

"Oh, no, dear, we had an awful time convincing our niece to stay in school. Beth disliked it for the same reasons you do."

The young girl seemed pleased by the revelation. "There's another reason I don't like school. Billy Carson makes fun of me because I'm flat-chested. All the kids say mean things now. I asked my dad to buy me a padded bra, but he said no, that I was too young to worry about stuff like that."

"Well..."

Ivy leaned forward. "Now men—that's a subject I know a little something about. And I also know how to find bras on the Victoria's Secret Web site."

"Oh, wow! I hadn't thought of that."

"That's because you're not as devious as my sister, Stacy."

Iris shook her finger at Ivy. "Going behind Dr. Donovan's back is not a good idea, sister."

"Yes, it is! Dad shouldn't be involved with my choice of underwear, anyway, but since there's no woman in our house and Gramps is gone—"

Ivy and Iris exchanged a same-wavelength look: Beth would make an excellent mother for Stacy and a wonderful wife for Brad.

If only that unfortunate incident with Robert Donovan hadn't occurred, Iris thought, heaving a sigh.

"If I go along with this plan to buy underwear on the Internet, will you promise to keep an open mind about history? It was my favorite subject to teach, and I'd like to share what I know with you."

"Listen to Iris, dear. She knows about everything old."

"Will you teach me some of that witch stuff, too? I want to learn how to make Billy's dick fall off."

Ivy clamped her hand over her mouth to keep from laughing out loud.

Iris gasped. "Merciful heavens, I certainly will

not! Wherever did you get such a horrible idea? You young children continue to astound me."

Stacy shared a conspiratorial smile with Ivy that had Iris gritting her teeth and saying, "You shouldn't listen to anything my sister tells you. She's quite unorthodox when it comes to men."

"Iris is just jealous, Stacy dear. Men have always flocked around me instead of her."

Stacy listened to the exchange, and then burst out laughing. "You two remind me of my dad and grandpa. They're always arguing over silly stuff."

"We don't argue, dear. We're merely having a grown-up difference of opinion," Ivy said. "Iris and I are very devoted to each other."

Stacy rolled her eyes, shortly after Iris did. "Whatever. Why don't we watch another movie? The TV guide said that *Vampires from Hell* is on Showtime, and I've been dying to see it."

Iris made a face. "That sounds dreadful."

"I'll make more popcorn," Ivy offered, clapping her hands at the prospect.

THE SATURDAY MORNING before Thanksgiving, Brad made his way down the crowded sidewalk and headed straight for the sheriff's office, hoping to get a definitive answer regarding his father's whereabouts and ignoring the swell of Christmas shoppers intent on getting a jump on the upcoming holiday.

For a small town, Mediocrity's retail establishments seemed to be thriving, which was refreshing to see. So many towns of similar size were drying up from the likes of shopping malls and Wal-Marts, but not this one.

The merchants of Mediocrity had obviously banded together to stimulate the locals' interest. Their shop doors were similarly decorated with greenery and lighting. Carols poured out of open doorways onto the street and the smell of fir and pine scented the air.

The holiday feeling was infectious, and Brad wished he didn't have such a serious subject on his mind. Hopefully, his dad would be found before Christmas, and the three of them could celebrate together as they always did. He worried that Stacy wouldn't be able to accept any other alternative. Outwardly she pretended that she wasn't overly concerned, but he knew better. She'd behaved in a similar fashion right after her mother died, and it had taken Stacy a while to release the emotions she was hiding inside.

Reaching the sheriff's office, he entered the dimly lit room and found Murdock leaning back in his swivel chair, eyes closed, and feet propped up on the desk. If the man spent his days doing this, then it was no wonder he hadn't found his father yet.

"I'm not sleeping, if that's what you're thinking," the sheriff said, as if he could read Brad's mind. "I do some of my best ruminating with my eyes closed."

Finally opening his eyes, Seth Murdock stared up at his visitor and smiled. "Good morning, Dr. Donovan. I figured I'd be hearing from you right about now. Shut the door behind you and have a seat here in front of the desk." The sheriff straightened himself and his desktop.

"Do you have anything new to report, Sheriff Murdock? You said you'd stay in touch during your investigation, but it's been several days since we spoke last and almost two weeks since I first arrived. I was hoping for some progress by now."

Seth reached for the beer nuts he always kept in a tin on his desk and popped a few in his mouth, despite the early hour. "Care for some? I'm addicted to the damn things." When Brad shook his head, he continued, "Don't have much to tell, that's why I haven't been in touch. I spoke to Beth and her aunts, and they've told me nothing I didn't already know. If those three women are privy to any information concerning your dad, they aren't saying."

"So it was a dead end?"

Murdock nodded. "'Fraid so. The old gals were guarded when I questioned them. I get the feeling Beth had tipped them off about my visit and told them not to say anything."

Brad suspected the sheriff might be right. Beth

was very protective of her aunts. But why? What were the old ladies hiding? "What about the APB you were going to put out? Any results from that?"

"It's been instituted. But so far, there's been nothing solid to investigate. I had one promising call from a chief of police up in Allentown, but that proved to be a false alarm. Seems the Allentown PD found a dead drifter alongside the interstate, but the man they discovered was in his early forties and didn't match the description of your daddy. Sorry."

Brad breathed a sigh of relief. "Hell, don't be sorry. I'm just glad my father hasn't turned up dead." *Yet.*

Murdock nodded. "I hear ya. And I don't envy the position you're in. I wish I could do more, have something new to report, but I don't. These kinds of investigations are slow going."

"How slow? Are we talking weeks, months, years? Are you saying I might never find out what's happened to my father?"

"Depends on how productive the leads we get turn out to be. So far, we haven't got much to go on. And yes, oftentimes missing folks just stay missing."

"What the hell could have happened to him?"

"Hard to say, son, but if I were you, I'd try to wheedle more information out of Beth. My gut—" he patted his protruding stomach "—tells me she knows something."

"I'm not sure I can do that, Sheriff. Beth says she

doesn't know anything." And after last night, after the way she kissed him, he was inclined to believe her. Her response couldn't have been faked. But he still had niggling doubts about her aunts.

"Listen, Dr. Donovan, if you want to have a friendship or whatever with Beth Randall, that's your business. But if you're intent on finding out about your dad, then you should do whatever's necessary, even if that means romancing the information out of her."

Brad bolted to his feet. "What are you implying, Sheriff? You shouldn't cast aspersions on Ms. Randall's reputation by assuming things you know nothing about."

"The way I figure it, you wouldn't be so protective of Beth if you didn't have feelings for her. She's an attractive woman, you're a healthy man—that's all I'm saying."

Brad felt heat rise up his neck at the man's accurate assumption. "You have no right to say anything about me or Beth. And I sure as hell don't like it."

"A neighbor of mine dined at the Brookside last evening, said you and Beth looked pretty chummy, eating off each other's forks and all that."

"We're friends, nothing more. And since when is it a crime to take a friend out to dinner?" Beth had been right about the gossip network in town.

"It would only be a crime if that friend turned out

to be implicated in your father's murder. Think about what I'm saying, Dr. Donovan, and tread carefully. Your father's life could be at stake, and I know you don't want that on your conscience."

Storming out of the office before he said something he might regret, Brad thought about little else on his way back to the inn.

He'd always lived his life honorably and above reproach. How then could he do what the sheriff suggested? It went against who he was, what he believed, not to mention his gut instinct. And he was usually a pretty good judge of character.

Brad shook his head. He couldn't deceive Beth. He cared too much. At some point he needed to trust her and he figured now was as good a time as any.

CHAPTER ELEVEN

BETH HAD JUST ESCORTED the seventh and eighth guests of the day upstairs and reseated herself at her desk when the front door opened again.

Saturdays were usually busy, so she hadn't been overly surprised by the steady influx of people that had arrived earlier that morning, though she was half tempted to hide under her desk to avoid another interruption. She'd been trying without much success to double-check Lori's extensive grocery list for the restaurant's opening, to make certain her chef hadn't forgotten anything. She knew Lori was waiting anxiously for the go-ahead to place the order.

"Hello? Is anyone here?"

At the sound of the familiar voice, chills skittered against Beth's backbone like icy fingers, and her mouth suddenly went dry.

It couldn't be! Please, God, don't let it be!

Bolting to her feet, she caught a glimpse of the woman she dreaded seeing most in the world—her mother. "Mother, what on earth—" She needed this right now like she needed another crisis to avert.

Hell, who am I kidding? This is *a crisis!*

"Surprise, Beth! Are you happy to see me?" Margaret Shaw's smile was filled with a touch of uncertainty, which surprised Beth. Margaret was nothing if not audacious, presumptuous and insensitive. "I've come to spend the Thanksgiving holiday with you and maybe Christmas, too." Honestly, the woman had more chutzpah than a rabbi trying to convert a Christian to Judaism.

"Beth? Won't that be fun?" Was she kidding? Since when had her mother ever been fun? Fun and Margaret uttered in the same breath was oxymoronic at its finest. "But I wasn't expecting you. You didn't call to let me know that you were coming. I'm not sure I can accommodate you. The inn is booked solid."

"Don't worry about that, sweetie. I've already reserved a room. My friend Elise Little called on my behalf and reserved a room under her name, so I could make this visit a complete surprise. I see by your expression that I've succeeded."

Forcing a smile, Beth moved forward to hug her mother, who enveloped her tightly, and then asked, "Have you gained weight, Beth? Those jeans look rather tight on you."

Counting to ten, twenty, and then finally thirty, Beth extricated herself from her mother's hold. "I don't really know. I haven't weighed myself in years. I don't even own a scale." Owning a scale was an exercise in depression, and if Beth wanted to be depressed, she had only to talk to her mother or ex-husband.

"Isn't that unusual? I weigh every morning without fail. If I gain even a pound, I diet until I lose it. That's how I've kept myself looking so trim all these years. A woman alone has to—"

"Since when have you ever been alone, Mother?" Margaret Shaw was the kind of woman who didn't do alone very well. Her mother needed someone—anyone—to harass or she couldn't be happy. "What happened to Herb? I thought you two had gotten serious. At least, that's what you said in your last letter."

Brushing away from her face tendrils of graying hair that had obviously escaped the hair dye she used religiously, Margaret sighed dramatically. "I am well rid of Herb. He proved to be a major disappointment."

But then, didn't everyone who came in contact with Margaret prove disappointing?

"He was cheap, and I just can't abide a man who's cheap. I wanted to vacation in Florida this winter, and Herb refused to pay for it. What else are men good for if they can't foot the bill every once in a while? I certainly held up my end of the relationship, listening to his stupid war stories, supporting him in those asinine investment fiascoes—" Margaret shook her head. "I always give too much. It's my greatest flaw."

Beth was about to—*gag violently, throw up, hurl*—respond, when the door opened and Brad entered the house. She knew there was no way to avoid introducing him to her mother, though she dreaded it, especially after seeing the predatory look Margaret cast his way.

"Hello, Brad," she said with a wan smile. "Come and meet my mother. Dr. Donovan is staying at the inn with his daughter," Beth explained before making the introductions.

Brad shot her a surprised look, and then held out his hand, smiling graciously. "It's nice to meet you, Mrs. Shaw."

"Thank you, Dr. Donovan. A doctor, now that's impressive. What kind of a doctor are you, if you don't mind my asking?"

"Brad's a pediatrician, Mother," Beth blurted before he could respond, hoping to avoid the kind of inquisition her mother was famous for. Doctors were at the top of her mother's "eligible husbands" list because they were wealthy, well respected and had the kind of social standing Margaret Shaw had always craved for herself and Beth. "Dr. Donovan lives and practices in Virginia." *And is therefore unavailable,* she added silently.

Margaret's smile was full of unabashed interest. "It's so nice to meet a man who loves children. I've despaired of my daughter ever presenting me with any grandchildren. Since her husband divorced her—"

Beth clenched her fists. "*I* divorced Greg, Mother, not the other way around."

"Whatever. The details aren't really all that important, only the fact that your marriage failed, and in such a short time."

"Yes, that's true. And to think yours failed, too— it just took a bit longer."

Looking increasingly uncomfortable at the hostile exchange between mother and daughter, Brad smiled apologetically and said, "If you ladies will excuse me, I've got to go upstairs and check on Stacy." He quit their company quickly, hitting the stairs two at a time and looking every inch a man who had just escaped the executioner's ax.

Beth could hardly blame him. She'd tried running from her mother, too, but the woman seemed intent on following.

"Now see what you've done with your smart comments? I'm sure that nice doctor thinks we do nothing but fight all the time," Margaret said.

"We do, Mother, which makes me wonder why you've decided to come here." *And ruin my holiday, not to mention my life.* Beth folded her arms across her chest, waiting for her response.

"Can't a mother visit her daughter without a reason?"

Beth wasn't buying that explanation, not for one damn minute. "You haven't visited me since the divorce, so I doubt you've been dying to see me."

Margaret reached out her hand and caressed her daughter's cheek, which totally surprised Beth. The affectionate moments between them were few and far between, if they actually existed at all. She couldn't really remember.

"I've been worried about you, sweetheart, living here all alone with those two incorrigible old ladies. How are your aunts doing, by the way? Have they been staying out of trouble? I don't know why you didn't put them in a nursing home years ago. I should have done it myself and taken the burden of that decision from you."

Biting the inside of her cheek to keep from shouting invectives at the insensitive woman, she replied, "Aunt Ivy and Aunt Iris are both fine. They don't need a nursing home, only someone to look after them. And I'm quite willing to do that, so you needn't interfere, Mother. They're upstairs in their suite, if you want to visit them."

"I will later. I need to get settled in and rest first. The flight from San Francisco was a nightmare. I hate flying those red-eyes. I always wake up feeling like I've been drugged. But they're cheaper, and I must watch my pennies now that I've retired from the bank."

"I'll check the computer to see what room I've put you, or should I say Elise Little, in? Be right back."

"Take your time. I'll just wander the front room and see what you've done with the place since my last visit."

"Great," Beth said with fake enthusiasm, knowing her mother would be filled with criticism upon her return. That had always been her way. As far as Margaret was concerned, Beth could do nothing right.

Switching on the computer, she cursed silently under her breath. The one thing she hadn't counted on during this hectic week before Thanksgiving was putting up with her mother. But she couldn't very well toss the woman out on the street. She was, after all, her mother.

Biology was the pits!

And there was still that pesky problem about the bones buried in the basement. If Margaret Shaw got wind of them... Beth shook her head, unable to bear the thought of what a hideous circumstance that would be.

It seemed the woman could ferret out information by way of osmosis. And she wasn't what one could call circumspect. She liked drawing attention to herself, and if she had to use a bunch of bones to achieve that result, she would, consequences and everyone else be damned.

"WELL, WELL, AS I LIVE and breathe. Look what the cat's dragged in, sister."

Stepping into her aunts' suite of rooms, Margaret forced a smile, wondering why the old women took such delight in annoying her. "Nice to see you, too, Aunt Ivy. I see you're still as charming as ever." Ivy was the more outspoken of the two women and they'd never gotten along very well.

The older woman's smile didn't quite reach her eyes. "Does Beth know you're here, Margaret?"

"Of course. She was thrilled to see me."

Iris set down the book she'd been reading. "I can only imagine," she said, leveling a look that indicated she knew her niece was lying.

"If you two hadn't poisoned my daughter against me, she—"

Ivy's laugh was caustic. "Ha! The relationship you share with Beth is your own doing, Margaret, and you know it. Neither Iris nor I have ever uttered a harsh word against you in all these years."

"Though we've certainly felt like it," Iris blurted, earning a proud smile from Ivy.

"Thank you, sister! I couldn't have said it better myself."

"I know I haven't always been the best mother," Margaret admitted, "but I love Beth."

"Well, you have a damn peculiar way of showing it." Ivy shook her head, her face a mask of disapproval. "You're always criticizing that girl over every little thing. Between you and that idiot she married it's a wonder she has any self-esteem left."

"I do not always criticize Beth."

"You mean to tell me that you haven't made one unkind remark to her since you've arrived or offered up one of your famous suggestions? Pardon me for saying so, Margaret, but I find that very difficult to believe."

"I—" The younger woman's cheeks flushed.

"I knew it."

"I may have mentioned to Beth that she'd put on some weight, but it was merely an observation, not a criticism."

"Margaret, you didn't?" Iris cast the woman a condemning look. "Why can't you support your child and love her for who she is, instead of always trying to change her? If you knew Beth as we do, you'd be so proud of the woman she's become."

"Beth has single-handedly turned this dilapidated old relic into a charming, highly sought after inn," Ivy informed her niece. "Why, her new restaurant is already getting rave reviews from the customers who've eaten there."

"I noticed some of the changes she's made. They're very nice."

"Did you bother to tell Beth that?" Iris wanted to know.

"Not yet, but I will."

Choosing to ignore the warning look her sister flashed her, Ivy said, "Old age has provided me with the courage to speak my mind, Margaret, and so I will. You, my dear, need to mend fences with your daughter. If you don't, you'll regret it for the rest of your life. You'll end up miserable and alone, with no one to love and care for you."

Margaret burst into tears, taking the two older women by surprise. "I know that. Why do you think I've come all this way?" She rose to her feet and began to pace. "I want to be part of Beth's life. I hate the life I've been living. It's dreary and boring and—"

"If you've come because you're lonely, Margaret, then that's not a good enough reason. Beth doesn't need any more burdens. She has enough on her plate, running this inn and taking care of us." Prepared to do battle, Iris crossed her arms over her chest.

Halting in front of the two women, Margaret replied, "I won't lie. I am lonely and very alone. I woke up one morning a few weeks ago after Herb and I had broken up and realized my life was empty and that everything I loved was gone."

"Because you pushed them all away," Ivy reminded her. "Even your husband never felt he measured up to your high expectations. Surely you knew that."

"Melvin was weak."

"Yes, he was. But there aren't many men who can measure up to a strong woman such as you. I know, because I'm the same way. Why do you think I've never married?"

"Men are not worth the aggravation and heartache they've caused me over the years. I'm done with them. I just want my daughter back."

"That, my dear, is easier said than done. Beth's been hurt, over and over again—first by her father, then you, and finally by that philandering ex-husband of hers. She trusts very few people now. It won't be easy winning her over, I'm afraid."

Iris rose to her feet and looked Margaret squarely in the eye. "And I won't stand idly by and allow you to hurt her again, do I make myself clear? Ivy and I owe that girl a great deal. We love her more than words can express."

"I have no intention of hurting Beth. I love her, too."

"Then you'd better start showing it. And you'd better keep your viperous tongue sheathed and learn to hand out something other than criticism," Ivy warned.

"I do tend to speak before thinking."

Iris and Ivy gazed at each other and then rolled their eyes in disbelief at the understatement.

"What do you think of Dr. Donovan?" Margaret asked, hoping to change the subject. "He seems very nice. And I got the feeling that Beth liked him."

"He is very nice. But Beth doesn't want anyone

to interfere where Dr. Donovan is concerned. The situation is…is complicated."

Ivy nodded. "Yes, complicated."

Margaret's brows drew together. "In what way? I don't understand."

The old ladies knew better than to confide anything that their niece would be able to use against Beth. "Dr. Donovan's daughter, Stacy, hasn't warmed up to Beth very much," Iris explained. "She hasn't gotten over the death of her mother. The poor child is protective of her father and very afraid that he'll marry again."

"Well, she needs to get over it."

"Yes, that's true. And she will, in her own time," Ivy said, adding, "I can see the wheels turning in your head, Margaret, and I wouldn't go there, if I were you, not if you want to make amends with Beth. She won't appreciate or tolerate any matchmaking where Bradley Donovan is concerned. She's said as much."

"I intend to be very discreet, just like always."

Before Ivy could reply, her niece walked into the room, carrying a large silver tea tray.

Beth was surprised to find her mother and aunts chatting away like a bunch of magpies. The three women had never been what you would call close. Actually, Iris and Ivy had always kept their distance from her mother, not that she could blame them.

Setting the tray on the table, she said, "I've brought tea and sandwiches. I thought you might be hungry." She looked at her mother. "Did you have a nice nap?"

Margaret smiled. "Why, yes. The bed is very comfortable. In fact, the entire room is just lovely, Beth. You've done such a wonderful job of decorating."

Beth's mouth unhinged at the unexpected compliment, waiting for the criticism she knew would be forthcoming. "But…?"

"But what…?"

"You usually add a but. Weren't you going to say *But you need to do this or that?*"

"Well—"

Iris and Ivy, who were standing behind Beth, wagged their heads in warning.

"Well, of course not, sweetheart. Everything is just perfect. I couldn't be more pleased with my accommodations. Your guests are very lucky."

Forehead crinkling in confusion, Beth wondered who this woman was masquerading as her mother. Perhaps Elise Little had come to visit, after all. This Margaret Shaw, with all the smiles and compliments, was a total stranger, an imposter, an alien being from another world.

Maybe Aunt Iris had cast a spell over her mother and turned her into someone more palatable and pleasant to be around. After all, it happened to frogs all the time.

"I'm looking forward to dinner, Beth. Your aunts tell me that the food here is quite good."

"We start serving at six. Just let me know what time you'd like me to make your reservation."

"I'll do that."

"Well, I'd better get back downstairs. With all the new guests who've arrived, I'll be running around like the proverbial chicken."

"Is there anything I can do to help?" Margaret asked, taking Beth by surprise once again. "Since I'm here you may as well put me to work."

Was the woman kidding? Beth had done most of the housework and cooking when she'd lived at home. Her mother was in no way, shape or form domestic-goddess material. "I don't make my guests work, Mother, and there's nothing I need help with, at any rate." At the hurt she saw flaring in her eyes, she softened her tone and added, "But thank you."

"Did I tell you, dear, that Louise and I will be holding our first meeting of the Red Hat and Roses Club tomorrow?" Ivy grinned. "We're very excited."

"I've heard of them," Margaret said, looking almost envious.

"Isn't it rather close to Thanksgiving to be holding your meeting, Aunt Ivy? I'm surprised anyone will be able to attend."

"Many of our members are widowed or unmarried, dear, and therefore have nothing to celebrate on Thursday. Of course, I intend to suggest to all of them that they attend the grand opening of your restaurant. I may propose it as a field trip, in fact."

Beth grinned. "Stacking the deck, are we?"

"I also intend to spread the word," Iris said. "I'm going to town first thing Monday morning and visit every shopkeeper and business I've frequented over the years. Since I've been kind enough to spend my money in their establishments I expect them to return the favor."

"Perhaps I'll come with you, Aunt Iris," Margaret offered. "I'd like to see what changes have occurred since my last visit."

Iris considered the request for a moment. "Very well, Margaret, but I don't want you insulting any of the business owners, like you did the last time. Frieda Thompson wouldn't allow me back in her dress shop for six months after you called her merchandise tacky and out of fashion."

The woman's cheeks crimsoned and Beth swallowed her smile. "I'll make it a point to keep my opinions to myself," Margaret said.

Beth was tempted to reply that would be a first, but held her tongue, interested to see how long her mother's newly found niceness would last.

Beth gave Margaret another twenty-four hours, max.

LATER THAT AFTERNOON, Beth got a rather unpleasant surprise when she opened the front door. "Mr. Pickens, what a nice surprise." *Not!* "What are you doing here? Do you have word about my loan?" She crossed her fingers behind her back, inviting the man to step inside.

The banker shook his head, and Beth's hopes plummeted. "I'm afraid not yet. These things take time. I'm here to make another inspection of the basement."

Her eyes widened. "The basement? But I thought you already inspected the basement the first time you were here."

"Just wanted to make sure there's been no water leakage or damage. It looked sound, at first glance, but I didn't really take a close enough look and I need to do that now. If it's a problem I can come back another time."

Hell, yes, it's a problem! A rather major problem, Beth thought. "No, no problem at all. I'll just run ahead and make sure everything's as it should be." She didn't trust Buster one bit. Just yesterday she'd caught him pawing and whining at the cellar doors, trying to get them open.

"Don't bother. I know the way. And I'm sure you've got plenty to do."

"It's really no bother," she said quickly. "We can go out the back door. I'll just grab my coat."

Mr. Pickens followed her down the hallway and

into the kitchen. Lori was busy preparing the evening meal and didn't look up when they entered, which was just as well. Beth wanted to get Mr. Pickens's visit over with as quickly as possible.

Beth and the banker had no sooner stepped out of the house when Stacy called out to them, making Beth cringe. "Hey, what's going on? Where are you guys going?"

Stopping in her tracks, Beth introduced Mr. Pickens to Stacy. "I need to show Mr. Pickens the basement, Stacy. We won't be long."

"Cool. Can I come? I've never seen an old basement before?"

"I don't think so, this is business and—"

"It's okay with me," Mr. Pickens said, and Beth could have kicked him right then and there.

"Can I, Beth? Mr. Pickens said it was okay. Please."

She heaved a deep sigh. If she argued with the stubborn young woman, Mr. Pickens might get suspicious, thinking Beth was hiding something, like a couple of dead bodies! She tried once again to dissuade the child. "It's awfully dark and damp down there, Stacy, really spooky. I always hated going down when I was your age. There are spiders and mice and—"

"I don't get scared. I want to go."

"All right then, but don't say I didn't warn you."

As they approached the cellar doors, Beth caught sight of something white and calcified lying directly in front of them. It looked suspiciously like a bone and her heart leaped into her mouth.

Oh, hell! What am I going to do now?

"Well, will you look at that?" Mr. Pickens said, bending down to retrieve the bone and examining it carefully. "Wonder where this old thing came from?"

Beth had no intention of telling him that Lyle McMurtry had been down there for over fifty years.

"What is it? Can I see?" Stacy asked.

The banker held out the artifact. "I think it's the jawbone of a bear cub." Beth let out the breath she was holding and silently thanked the Lord. "Wonder how it got here? I haven't seen a bear in these parts in years."

She thought quickly. "Most likely Buster dragged it here from the field. He's always bringing in trophies for me to praise."

He tossed it aside. "My dog used to do the same thing. I sure do miss that old hound."

"Are we going down in the cellar now?" Stacy wanted to know.

Beth felt like strangling the inquisitive child. "That's up to Mr. Pickens, Stacy."

"I'm going to inspect the foundation first, Beth. I can do that from outside. Then we can go in."

Beth nearly hugged the man. One person snooping around was bad enough, but a nosy kid like Stacy could ruin everything.

"Oh, shoot! My dad's waiting for me. I gotta go and get cleaned up for dinner. He told me not to be late."

"Well, then you'd better scoot. It wouldn't be good to keep your dad waiting." Beth made a mental note to kiss Brad when she saw him, not that she needed that much encouragement. Kissing Brad had become one of her favorite pastimes.

"Can we go down there some other time, Beth?" Stacy asked.

Beth nodded. "Yes. We'll do it another day. Now run along. And if you see my aunts, tell them I'll be in shortly."

Beth breathed a sigh of relief as she watched the young girl turn on her heel and head back. Now if she could just think of a way to get rid of Mr. Pickens…

CHAPTER TWELVE

BETH STEPPED ONTO the front porch later that same evening and found Brad seated on one of the rockers. He looked lost in thought, and she wondered if she should tiptoe back inside and leave him to his musings. But he seemed sad and curiosity got the better of her, along with a strong desire to talk to him again.

"What are you doing out here all alone?" she asked. "You're not inside enjoying dessert? I thought you were looking forward to the chocolate cheese-cake tonight."

He looked up at her and smiled, and Beth's heart did a little tap dance. "Stacy and I finished dinner a while ago. The cheesecake was wonderful. Stacy wanted to watch some music videos, so I decided to come out here and think for a bit."

"I hope I'm not intruding. I was just going to take a walk down by the pond. I should be inside catering to my guests, but I felt the need to escape for a while."

Rising to his feet, he approached her. "I assume

this has something to do with your mother's arrival this morning?"

His concern touched Beth. "As I'm sure you noticed we don't get along very well. And her unexpected arrival has really thrown me for a loop." Seeing her mother again, after such a long time, brought forth all sorts of conflicting feelings: anger, hurt, need, sadness. She was confused by the tangle of emotions surging through her.

Beth thought she'd had everything figured out when it came to her mother, but after seeing Margaret this afternoon and noting the effort she'd made to get along and be generous with her praise, she wasn't entirely sure.

Of course, that didn't excuse this morning.

"Maybe your mom just needed to see you, to reassure herself that you were okay. Mothers are instinctive when it comes to their kids, and you said you were her only child."

She sighed. "Maybe yours was that way, but my mother cares only about herself. I'm certain nothing's changed, despite her attempt at civility." Still, she had been awfully convincing.

Dammit! I don't need this right now. And I certainly don't need my mother back in my life.

Taking her hand, Brad led her off the porch toward the rear yard. They walked in silence as they made their way down to the pond, the wet grass dampening their shoes. The night air was frigid, making Beth's cheeks cold and she huddled deeper into her parka, wondering if Brad would be warm enough in his green cable-knit sweater.

"Maybe you should try meeting your mom halfway and see what happens," he suggested. "Children often think their parents will live forever and when they find out they don't, it makes it more difficult to accept their death, especially if there's been animosity between them."

"I understand what you're saying, but I don't think that applies to my mother. We've been estranged for years, and she's as healthy as a horse." Although she *had* aged a great deal since Beth had last seen her. Her once-smooth skin now bore wrinkles and her eyes didn't sparkle as they usually did. Perhaps Brad was right. Maybe she should try to be more receptive to the woman's overtures.

"I still miss my mom," Brad went on. "I wish I could talk to her about even the most mundane things, like Stacy's schoolwork or a troublesome patient. She was always a good listener."

Beth heard the sadness in his voice and envied the relationship he'd had with his mom. "I'm sorry your mom's not with you anymore. I'm sure she was a lovely person. My mom never listened, never really heard anything I said. She was too wrapped up in her own problems to care about mine." Even the day

Beth had called to tell Margaret about Greg's affair, thinking she might offer advice and support since she'd been in a similar circumstance, her mother had been anxious to get off the phone.

When Beth and Brad reached the pond, they seated themselves on the old wooden glider situated near the water's edge and began swinging slowly back and forth as they talked.

"Mom and Dad had one of those fairy-tale marriages you always hear about. They were so in tune with each other they could finish each other's sentences."

Brad's arm came up to wrap around her shoulders. Beth welcomed the warmth and closeness of the gesture. "I'm sorry about your dad. I know you miss him very much. Hopefully, he'll turn up soon."

He sighed in resignation. "I spoke to Sheriff Murdock this morning. He had nothing new to report. All his leads have turned out to be dead ends."

"But in a way that's good. Isn't it? I mean, if they had found your dad it might not be under the best of circumstances. And if he were in a hospital or something, I'm sure they'd know that by now. Though, like I said before, he could have amnesia and not have any identification with him."

"I pray you're right. I'm not sure Stacy can take any more bad news. She's just now recovering from Carol's death. If she has to face my dad's as well—"

She squeezed his hand. "Don't talk like that. He'll

turn up. You'll see. Just don't give up." She felt guilty at the tortured look on his face, guilty that she hadn't been a hundred percent honest with him.

"I'm not so sure about that. Murdock said missing persons often stay missing and family members never find out what's happened to them."

Beth thought about the bones in her basement. And though she was almost positive that they had nothing to do with Robert Donovan, she couldn't be certain. The Lyle McMurtry disappearance still hung over her head, an ax ready to fall.

Needing to cleanse her soul, to tell him everything she knew, she said, "Brad, I—"

"*Shh!* Let's not talk about this anymore. Just let me kiss you."

His lips were warm despite the cold—and very persuasive. Beth allowed herself to fall under their magic once again. Kissing Brad was like coming home, like being where you knew you'd be safe and cared for. It was a wonderful place and she never wanted to leave.

When Brad unzipped her parka she didn't object. She wanted to feel, to lose herself in the passion. It was so much easier thinking about making love with Brad than all the other horrible things she had to consider.

"I want you, Beth," he whispered, cupping her breast through her blouse, grazing the hardened nipple with his thumb until she wanted to scream for mercy. When his kiss deepened and he thrust his tongue into her mouth, she forgot about everything except the glorious way he made her feel. "I want you so bad it hurts."

The anguish in his voice touched her, for it mirrored her own need and desire. "I want you, too, but not here. Someone might come looking for me."

Raising his head, he looked into her eyes and smiled. "I was thinking of the barn. I noticed some fresh hay up in the loft the last time I borrowed a pole to go fishing. And your handyman's left for the day, so there'd be no one to bother us."

Could she do it? Could she make love with Brad, despite all of her misgivings and the fact that nothing permanent could ever be between them?

"I care about you deeply, Beth," he said, caressing her cheek. "This isn't just about sex, though I won't deny I've wanted you from the first moment we met."

"All right," she finally whispered. "Let's go to the barn." Beth knew it was totally irresponsible of her to ignore her guests, not to mention her better judgment where Brad was concerned, but she didn't care anymore. For once in her life she was going to do something totally selfish, something just for her, and the consequences be damned.

"EXCUSE ME, BUT I noticed you were sitting alone and wondered if you might like some company. I'm alone this evening, too, and would love to join you, if it wouldn't be an imposition."

Aubrey had spotted the attractive blonde as soon as he stepped into the hotel's dining room. She was exactly his type: classy, desperate and built like a brick shithouse. He had observed her anxious looks, the way her eyes darted from table to table, as if she were looking for someone—anyone—and knew she wasn't the type of woman who enjoyed eating alone.

Aubrey wasn't obsessed by sex. He went weeks, often months without it. Sex, he'd discovered early on, zapped a man's energy and his ability to focus on matters of importance, like the business of making money. Women were distractions he couldn't afford most of the time, but he'd decided to make an exception this evening, mostly because he was bored out of his skull.

"That would be lovely," she said. "Please sit down and join me. I haven't ordered yet." She widened her smile to reveal even white teeth. Aubrey couldn't abide bad teeth or gum disease. That's why the first thing he'd done after starting his company was to institute an employee dental plan.

"I'm Karen Richards," she said.

"Aubrey Fontaine. It's nice to meet you." He held out his hand to shake hers, noting how she zeroed in on his gold Rolex.

Women were so transparent. Thank God he'd

never desired marriage or children. Distractions and burdens were not his thing. Neither were gold diggers.

"So what brings you to Mediocrity, Mr. Fontaine?"

"Aubrey, please."

"All right, Aubrey. And you may call me Karen. I guess since we're dining together we may as well forgo the formalities."

"Excellent." Though he had no intention of revealing anything but the most superficial details of his reason for coming to Mediocrity. Deals were often lost because of careless remarks. "I'm looking into buying some investment property, but so far haven't found anything worth taking another look at."

"That doesn't surprise me. I haven't found anything even remotely interesting to spend my money on in this town. The shops are a joke and the last inn I stayed at was horrific."

Aubrey's attention piqued. "What inn was that, if you don't mind my asking? I've seen only one, but it looked nice enough from a distance."

"I'm talking about the Two Sisters Ordinary. I stayed there a few nights upon my arrival, but it didn't meet my standards, not by a long shot. To be perfectly honest, it was a horrible experience. The food was okay, but the linens were ghastly, my room microscopic, and I didn't like the innkeeper at all. She was quite rude. It came as no surprise when I overheard the innkeeper say that she was having financial problems. The place was poorly furnished, the amenities sadly lacking."

Aubrey's eyes lit with purpose. "That's a shame. I'm a man who values good service and comfort, which is why I have a suite here at the Excelsior."

She continued as if he hadn't spoken, which Aubrey found annoying. Most people hung on his every word. "I could hardly use the bath towels the inn provided—they were rough and scratched my tender skin. When I complained, nothing was done about it."

"I can see how that would be a problem for a woman with such lovely skin as yours." She ate up his praise with relish and Aubrey wanted to laugh. The lovely Karen was a husband-hunting opportunist; he'd bet his last dollar on that.

"Thank you, Aubrey. How sweet of you to notice. I always use a moisturizer before bedtime."

The waiter arrived just then, preventing him from telling the woman that he didn't give a rat's ass what she used on her middle-aged face.

Needing fortification for what was shaping up to be a very long night, he ordered a bottle of Bordeaux for the table. "I hope you like French wine. It's the only kind I drink." When she nodded, he motioned for the waiter to fill their glasses.

"So what brings you to this area? Are you on vacation?"

She shook her head. "Not exactly a vacation. I just needed a few days away by myself. Sometimes the rat race of the city gets to me and I need a little downtime."

He assumed she was speaking of Philadelphia, but he didn't intend to ask. She was going to be a one-night stand, nothing more. He didn't want to know any more about her than he had to. Sex was all he wanted, and if the woman expected more, she was in for a rude awakening.

"It's a shame about your experience at the inn. I wonder how the innkeeper intends to make any money, treating her guests in such a fashion," he remarked.

"Just between you and me, I think the place is haunted. There were strange noises at night. And I've heard rumors about those two wacky old ladies who live on the top floor. One is supposed to be a witch."

Ah, she was speaking about dear old Mom.

Aubrey sipped his wine, noting the way Karen had leaned forward to give him an ample view of lush breasts spilling over her low-cut bodice. "How very perfect," he murmured in appreciation, and she smiled seductively.

"I'm looking forward to getting to know you much better, Aubrey. I think we have a lot in common."

Sex was always a good common denominator, and a woman like Karen Richards used it to achieve her own ends.

"Shall we have dessert in my suite and plumb the depths of this relationship?"

Dipping her index finger into her wine, she slowly sucked off the liquid. Always-in-control Aubrey squirmed in his seat and worried that his erection might levitate the table.

"GOD, BETH, YOU DRIVE me wild. I want you so much I ache with it." Brad deepened his kiss, laying her down on the soft, sweet hay. The barn smelled of leather, old timbers and earth, but the woman beneath him masked the pungent odors with the lavender fragrance she wore.

Lavender was an old-fashioned scent, and he loved it. Beth was like that in many ways—old-fashioned, sweet and honest to a fault. It was what had attracted him to her in the first place.

"Oh, Brad, you make me feel things I haven't felt in years." Smiling softly, she caressed his cheek.

"That's good, because I feel exactly the same way about you," he replied, making short work of the buttons on her blouse and then opening it to reveal a black lacy bra, which surprised him. Even though Beth was all woman, she didn't come across as the girly, frilly type.

Unhooking the front clasp, he heard her sharp intake of breath as the cold air puckered her nipples, making them harden instantly. "You're beautiful," he said, covering the soft mounds with his hands and then his lips. He suckled until she moaned in pleasure.

"I'm not sure how much of this torture I can take," she admitted. "It's been a very long time since I've done anything like this."

"Me, too, honey. But I want us to take our time and relish every moment of being together." He wanted to remember their first time and he wanted it to be special, especially for Beth.

Removing the remainder of her clothing and undergarments, then his own, until they were naked and facing each other, Brad devoured Beth with his eyes. "You're absolutely beautiful."

She gasped when her attention fell on his erection. "Oh, my!" Her eyes widened. "I had no idea."

"You'd better quit looking at me like that, woman, or this little get-together will be over before we get started."

With a shy smile he found quite endearing, she ran exploring fingers over his chest and stomach. Her touch excited the hell out of him. "*You're* beautiful," she said, making him chuckle.

"Men aren't beautiful. God reserved that privilege for the fairer sex. But thank you."

"You make me feel beautiful. I think you're the first man who's ever done that."

"Because you are. Never doubt it."

They kissed then, long, lingering kisses that had

them both panting with desire, then Beth whispered, "Make love to me, Brad. I want you."

Not needing a second invitation, Brad covered Beth's body with his own, caressing every inch of her warm flesh with his lips and tongue, until she squirmed restlessly beneath him. When he inserted his tongue inside her, she sucked in her breath, blurting, "Oh, God! You're torturing me."

"Not for much longer, honey." He made sure she was wet and ready for him and then entered her slowly, moving deeper into the tight orifice until her breath quickened with increased desire. "Are you doing okay?"

"I'm perfect. But I should warn you, I've never been able to have an orgasm this way, so don't be disappointed if I don't."

Her honesty touched him and he kissed her lips gently. "Not every woman can, but I'll do my best."

He tilted her hips and pumped into her, using short then long strokes, until she was writhing beneath him in mindless passion.

"Brad, oh, Brad," she cried out. "This feels so good, *soooo* very *goood!*"

Brad used every ounce of self-control to prolong the encounter. He wanted Beth to feel everything, experience untold pleasure, and he wanted her to orgasm while he was still in her, so they would be one.

Her breathing grew shallow as he took her higher

and higher. Her head lolled back and forth, her eyes squeezed tight as she fought to reach the pinnacle of her passion. Brad urged her on, holding her hips as he rode her deeply while she bucked wildly against him.

Finally, with one last, hard thrust, he took her over the edge and she screamed, making him climax instantly.

Her face bathed in sweat, Beth opened her eyes slowly and the smile she wore took his breath away. He knew in that instant that he was in love with her.

"I love you, Beth. I think I have from the first moment I laid eyes on you."

Palming his face, she whispered, "I love you, too. Making love with you was wonderful. Thank you for making me feel like a woman."

"You're every inch that, honey. We're perfectly suited for each other. You know that, don't you?"

Her smile suddenly faded, her eyes filling with regret. "Let's get dressed. There's something we need to discuss."

Worry creased his brow. "All right, but I'd rather make love to you again."

"There are some things I need to explain before we take this relationship any further. You may change your mind and regret what just happened, but I want you to know that I never will."

Brushing stray hairs away from her face, he kissed

the tip of her nose. "Nothing you could tell me will make me want you any less."

A tear trickled down her face. "You're a wonderful man, but I think you should reserve judgment until after you hear what I have to say."

"Let's get dressed," he said, handing Beth her underwear. "I can't think straight when you're naked."

Her smile filled with sadness as she began to dress.

CHAPTER THIRTEEN

"ALL RIGHT," Brad said, leaning against the wooden ladder that led up to the hayloft, arms crossed over his chest. "What is it you want to tell me?"

Seating herself on a hay bale, Beth wondered how to tell someone you loved, someone you'd just been intimate with, that you'd been deceiving him. Since there was no easy way to do that, she cleared her throat and said, "This is going to be difficult for you to hear, but I hope you'll keep in mind that I was only trying to protect two people I love very much."

Instantly suspicious, Brad's brows drew together and his tone sharpened. "Do you know what's happened to my father? Is that what this is all about? Did your aunts do away with him?"

She shook her head. "I don't think so. I mean, of course not! I'm sure my aunts are innocent where your dad is concerned, but—" She swallowed with some difficulty.

Agitation filled his voice. "But what, Beth? What are you trying to tell me?"

It was difficult to look into his eyes, but she forced herself to maintain contact. "I found bones—or I should say, Buster found some bones buried in my basement. It happened shortly before you arrived."

"What?" He sprang away from the ladder, his look incredulous and condemning, making her heart sink. "What kind of bones?"

"I don't know. They looked human to me, but I'm not an expert. I've sent one of them off to be analyzed." If only Ellen would call with some answers, but Beth wasn't sure when her friend would be back.

He moved toward her then, reaching out to clutch her shoulders and drawing her to her feet. The angry look in his eyes gave her pause. "Why didn't you tell me this before? Why have you been lying to me all this time? You knew how upset I was about my dad, yet you said nothing."

"Until the medical examiner's report comes back there's nothing to tell. And I couldn't risk putting my aunts in jeopardy."

"Your aunts? What about my father? He might be buried down there."

"Those bones couldn't belong to your father. He hasn't been missing long enough for his body to decompose."

"But they could belong to Lyle McMurtry. In fact, they probably do."

She clenched her fists. "You don't know that! There's no proof whatsoever that my aunts are involved with those bones in any way." Which was why she hadn't told them about her find—she refused to hurl accusations until she was positive Ivy and Iris were involved.

"The fact that the bones are buried is proof enough. And what if my father has met the same fate as McMurtry? God, Beth! Do you realize what you've done?"

"Yes. I've protected two old ladies from vicious attacks and possible imprisonment. And I would do it all over again if I had to. I love them just as much as you love your father."

His lips thinned. "I trusted you. When you said you knew nothing about my father's whereabouts I believed you. Not at first, but you lied so well. You duped me completely. I feel like such a fool."

Her face grew hot. She wanted to lash out at him for implying she was a liar, but knew she had deceived him, hadn't been totally honest and felt his anger was somewhat justified. But only somewhat! "I had no choice. And I still know nothing about your father's whereabouts. How many times do I have to tell you that?"

"So you say."

She counted to ten, then asked, "What do you intend to do?"

"What else can I do? I'll tell Murdock everything you've just told me first thing in the morning."

Panic surged through Beth and she clutched his arm. "You can't! He'll arrest my aunts on suspicion of murder. They're old ladies—they won't survive the ordeal. Please, Brad, you must reconsider."

"And what if they're guilty? What if those sweet old ladies killed my father? What then?"

"They didn't. I'm sure of it. It's not in their nature to be mean. I've known them all my life. You've met them. How can you even think they'd be capable of such a horrific thing?"

"And are you as convinced where McMurtry is concerned? Can you say without a doubt that he's not currently residing in your basement? You didn't know your aunts fifty years ago, Beth. You have no idea what they were like or capable of back then. A scorned woman will do anything for revenge, even murder."

"No!" She shook her head in denial. "It's not true."

"You heard Iris the night she was ill, apologizing and begging for McMurtry's forgiveness. What reason would she have to do that, if she hadn't harmed him in some way?"

"I don't know. I only know in my heart that neither one of my aunts is capable of murder."

But what about the locket and the shirt material she'd found? What did they have to do with any of this? She didn't know, but she was relieved that at least she hadn't told Brad about that incriminating discovery. So far, honesty hadn't been the best policy.

"I'm sorry, but if there's the least chance, the remotest possibility, that my father is buried down in your basement I have to know. I can't live my life wondering. And I have a daughter to consider. Stacy is owed an explanation regarding her grandfather's sudden disappearance. I don't want her growing up thinking that he abandoned her."

Beth thought quickly. She needed time to figure out what to do. "Will you at least give me until tomorrow morning before going to the sheriff? I'd like to prepare my aunts for what might happen." When she saw the indecision on his face, she pressed harder, adding, "You said you loved me. Please, Brad!"

"That's not fair, Beth, and you know it. You told me the same thing, knowing all along that you'd lied, over and over again."

"I'm sorry. Truly I am. I never meant for any of this to happen. I tried to tell you there was too much standing between us for a relationship to ever work."

"Looks like you were right," he said.

There was a bitter edge to his words that knifed into her heart. She'd finally found a man she could love and respect, and now she would never have him.

"Okay. I'll wait until tomorrow, but no longer."

"Thank you!" Beth breathed a sigh of relief, and then began to formulate her next move.

MONDAY MORNING CAME AND with it, Sheriff Murdock. He arrived at the inn shortly after nine, which meant Brad had kept his promise about contacting him first thing that morning. She hoped he'd gotten Murdock out of bed.

Well, the sheriff could search all he wanted, but he wasn't going to find anything. Beth had made sure of that. The bones were hidden where no one would think to look for them. She had moved them late last night, after everyone had gone to bed and they now resided beneath Buster's doghouse.

She was actually starting to think that she and Nancy Drew had more in common that she'd originally believed.

"Morning, Beth," the sheriff said, removing his hat before stepping into the front hallway, which was empty. Most of the inn's guests still remained in their beds or were seated in the dining room having breakfast.

"I received a call from Dr. Donovan early this morning. He claims you've got bones buried in your basement. Is that true?"

In the grand tradition of every woman who had ever lied to save her neck, her mouth dropped open and eyes widened in astonishment. "You're joking?

Brad said that? I realize we had a little—" she blushed "—*disagreement* last evening, but I never thought he would stoop so low, just because he didn't get his way."

Now it was the sheriff's turn to look embarrassed. "So you're saying there aren't any bones buried in your cellar?"

Her look was one of pure innocence. "Not that I know of, Sheriff. Of course, Buster may have buried a couple of prime rib bones down there, so I can't be one hundred percent certain. You know how dogs are."

Seth rubbed his jaw. "Then I guess you won't mind if I take a look."

Her voice filled with incredulity. "You want to search my basement right before Thanksgiving and the opening of my restaurant?"

"Afraid so. In matters like these time's of the essence, as I'm sure you know."

"That would be very inconvenient, to say the least."

"I can get a search warrant, if need be, but I'm hoping I won't have to."

She heaved a dramatic sigh. "That's not necessary. But I would think, Sheriff Murdock, that you would trust the word of someone you've known for many years over a stranger who is obviously distraught, not to mention vindictive."

"Dr. Donovan doesn't strike me as being irrational or prone to exaggeration."

"And I do? Well, thank you very much."

He twirled his hat between his fingers, looking extremely uncomfortable. "Well, no. You've always seemed very well grounded, Beth. But I can't say the same for your aunts, so I'm going to do a bit of digging and see what's what."

Crossing her arms over her chest and mustering up a look of defiance, she said, "Help yourself, Sheriff. You know where the basement is. Just be sure to lock the door behind you after you've finished. I don't allow my guests down there. I can't afford any lawsuits. I'm sure you understand." Reaching into her pocket, she withdrew a padlock key and handed it to him; the look of surprise on his face was almost laughable.

"I'll be expecting an apology when you've completed your search for buried treasure, Sheriff."

Seth nodded. "I'll just fetch my shovel out of the truck and notify Dr. Donovan that—"

"I won't allow Dr. Donovan down there, Sheriff. I'm afraid you're going to be on your own. You might want to wear your jacket. It's cold and musty down there. And the light's not working, so you'll need a lantern or flashlight, as well."

Not being a man who enjoyed manual labor, he looked visibly pained. "Very well, I'll let Donovan know he won't be accompanying me." He made to leave, but before he could make good his escape, Beth clasped his arm.

"Sheriff Murdock, you can do me a big favor by telling Bradley Donovan to go straight to hell." And with the lies she'd been forced to tell, she'd be joining him there shortly.

BRAD PACED BACK AND forth across the dew-laden back lawn, ignoring the fact that his loafers were getting soaked, while he waited anxiously for the sheriff to reappear and give him a full report on his findings.

Murdock had been down in the cellar for about an hour, but so far he hadn't heard a peep out of him, except for an occasional curse.

He'd spent a sleepless night, not quite able to believe that what had started out as one of the most enjoyable evenings of his life had turned into a nightmare of major proportions.

Beth had lied and he'd believed all of her falsehoods. He still couldn't believe, even now, in the light of day, with the town's sheriff digging holes in the basement floor, what had occurred the night before. And he wasn't talking about their lovemaking, which had been magical, but about what followed afterward—her startling confession.

On some level he understood her need to protect the old ladies; she was their guardian, for all practical purposes. But for chrissake! His father was still missing. And she should have been more forthcoming about the damn bones.

Her behavior had caused him to wonder if she'd made love to him only to throw him off track. But then he realized, she would have had to care about him a great deal to confide the truth and put her aunts in jeopardy.

But did she really love him, as she'd confessed?

And did it really matter now?

"Jesus, what a damn fool I've—"

"Hey, Dad, what are you doing out here? I thought you were going fishing this morning. Did you change your mind?" Stacy looked up at him, a questioning expression on her face.

"I am, but I'm helping Sheriff Murdock with something first."

"Cool. What is it?"

Brad didn't want to alarm his daughter, so he opted to stretch the truth a bit. "There's been a robbery in town. Sheriff Murdock thinks the kids that took the stereos may have hidden them somewhere close by, so he's doing a house-to-house search. He's down in the basement checking things out."

"And you're on the lookout for the bad guys?" His daughter seemed totally impressed.

"You could say that."

"Cool. But be careful that you don't get shot or something."

"I will, sweetie. What are you doing out here so early in the morning? Have you eaten breakfast yet?"

"Beth asked me to find Buster. She wants to give him a bath. He must have heard her say so, because he took off like a shot."

"You and Beth seem to be getting along much better." It was something he had hoped for, but now, he guessed, it didn't matter.

Stacy shrugged. "I guess she's okay. And I like her aunts and Buster a whole lot."

He forced a smile. "Well, don't get too attached. You know we'll be leaving here soon." Advice he needed to heed, as well.

"Maybe we can get a dog when we get home. I'd like to have a Lab just like Buster."

He tweaked her nose, which she hated. "Christmas is coming, so you never know."

Her eyes widened. "Really? That would be so cool, Dad. I'd promise to take care of him. You wouldn't have to do a thing. Beth says I'm really good with Buster."

"We'll see. Now go find the dog. I'm sure Beth is waiting for you."

"Yeah, she's in the laundry room."

"I'll see you later. Be good."

She ran off, yelling her goodbyes and waving as she skirted around the yard, which was fortunate, since Murdock appeared not a minute later.

The man was covered in dirt from head to toe. His usually immaculate shirt and pants were brown, his boots dusty as well. He looked tired and extremely agitated, which didn't bode well. "Any luck?" he asked.

"I didn't find a damn thing, Dr. Donovan. Are you sure Beth was telling you the truth? She might have just been teasing or something."

"You mean there weren't any bones down there?" Brad's forehead wrinkled in confusion. "But I don't understand." Why would Beth make something like that up? She wouldn't. He was sure of it.

"Well, that makes two of us, Doc. Beth said you were crazy for thinking there were bones buried in her basement, and now I've got to go and apologize to her for digging down there and making a mess. Hell, she might not let me and the wife have our Thanksgiving dinner here at the inn. And I can tell you right now Ethel will have my hide if that happens. She's been looking forward to it for weeks— says anyone who's anyone is going to be there."

"But Beth *told* me those bones were down there. She must have moved them late last night."

"The dirt down there's as hard as cement. I had a tough time digging in it and I'm a big man. I doubt a little thing like Beth could have even made a dent, let alone dig a big hole."

Brad cursed beneath his breath. "Then why would she tell me there were bones, if it wasn't true?"

"Hell if I know. Maybe you just dreamed it, or maybe she was pulling your leg. You know how women are. She said you two had a disagreement of sorts last evening. Maybe it was her way of getting back at you."

"We didn't have a disagreement. Well, not at first anyway." At the sheriff's renewed interest, Brad felt heat rise up his neck. "I mean, we argued after she told me about the bones. But that was only natural."

"Well, if you want to know what's going on in Beth's mind, you need to ask her. I gave up long ago trying to figure out the mind of a woman. My wife drives me nuts. Speaking of which…" He pulled a bag of beer nuts out of his jacket pocket and began to munch. "I didn't have time to eat breakfast this morning."

"I'm sorry to have put you to so much trouble, Sheriff. And I do appreciate your following up on the lead I gave you."

"That's my job, son." Murdock squeezed Brad's shoulder. "I know you're grieving for your dad, but you need to understand that he could be gone for good. That's the way life is sometimes. It doesn't always turn out for the best, even though we want it to."

Brad watched the sheriff walk away, then he stormed back to the house, intending to get his pound of flesh from Beth, who was either turning into the biggest liar in the world or a whole lot smarter and deceptive than he'd given her credit for.

BETH EXITED THE DINING room after making sure her guests were taken care of, then headed toward the laundry room at the back of the house, hoping to find Buster waiting for her so she could bathe him. For a dog who liked water, he sure did hate baths.

But what she found standing next to the washbasin wasn't Buster, but Brad, and he looked furious, which didn't surprise her in the least.

"What did you do with them?"

She shook her head. "I'm sorry. Do with what?"

"Don't jerk me around, Beth. You know I'm talking about the bones. What the hell did you do with them?"

"I have no idea what you're talking about, Brad. Are you sure you're feeling okay?"

He took a deep breath. "I realize you're quite an accomplished liar, and maybe even a very good actress, but you won't get away with hiding evidence. I'm going to find it, and when I do I'm calling the authorities."

"But I thought you already did that," she brazened out, having decided that complete denial was her only recourse at the moment. "I didn't appreciate Sheriff Murdock coming here so early in the morning and upsetting my routine, all because of some crazy story you told him."

"What are you trying to pull? I'm not crazy. I know what you told me."

"Well, I don't know what you're talking about, so

if you'll excuse me." She made to move past him, but he clasped her arm.

"Tell me the truth, dammit!"

"I am telling you the truth. You just refuse to believe me."

"You're driving me crazy!"

She'd been on an emotional roller coaster since last night, so she knew exactly how he felt. "I think it's better for both of us if we keep our relationship free of any romantic entanglements. It'll be better that way."

He rubbed the back of his neck and was about to say something, when the door opened and Stacy walked in, leading an anxious Buster by the collar. "I found Buster."

"That's great, Stacy."

The girl stared at the two adults with a questioning expression on her face. "Hi, Dad! What are you doing here? What's wrong? You look kinda funny. Did something happen with those robbers?"

Brad shook his head. "Everything's fine."

"Thanks a lot for finding Buster, Stacy," Beth said before scolding the dog. "You can help me bathe him if you like."

Stacy's face lit up. "I can? Cool. I might be getting a dog of my own."

"I'm sorry, Stacy, but we're going into town today, so you won't be able to help with the dog."

"But why can't I stay here with Beth? It's okay, isn't it, Beth?"

"I thought you wanted to go clothes shopping?" He looked at Beth for assistance.

"Of course it is, Stacy. But I think you should go with your dad. It's not every day you get an offer like that. And you can help me with Buster the next time I bathe him, if you're still here."

The fact that they would be leaving soon caused a physical ache inside Beth. She'd tried hard not to fall in love with Brad, to remain detached and sensible. But that was the thing about love—nothing ever worked out the way you thought it would. Emotions got tangled, hearts got broken and relationships fizzled.

"Okay. I'll run upstairs and get my purse, Dad. Be right back." She darted out of the room, slamming the door behind her.

"Thanks for helping with Stacy. I don't want her getting too attached to the dog, or anyone else around here, for that matter."

She swallowed the lump in her throat. "I understand."

He looked at her and sighed. "I wish I did." And then he turned on his heel and walked out the door.

And maybe out of her life.

CHAPTER FOURTEEN

"Ms. Randall, I was in the middle of taking a shower and the water's gone off. I'll have you know I'm quite upset about it."

Beth turned away from the brochures she was straightening to find Mrs. Frederick standing in the hallway looking as if she'd just sucked a lemon dry and clutching the edges of her red flannel bathrobe together. It was not a sight she welcomed seeing first thing in the morning.

She smiled apologetically. "I'm terribly sorry, Mrs. Frederick." She wasn't sure what else to say. She had no idea what might have happened to cause the woman's shower to malfunction. "I'll try and—"

"Beth, come quick!" Lori shouted from the kitchen. "There's no water coming out of the sink."

The older woman cast the innkeeper an I-told-you-so look and Beth promised she would have the problem fixed immediately.

"Is that all you intend to do?" Mrs. Frederick asked, arching an imperious eyebrow.

"All?"

"I expect a free night's stay for my inconvenience, young woman, or I won't be coming back to this inn. And I'll have you know that my husband, Archie, and I travel a great deal." With that, she turned and walked up the stairs, white fuzzy slippers flapping behind her.

Having bigger things to worry about at the moment, Beth bolted to the kitchen to find her chef standing at the sink, cursing loudly. "What's going on with the water?" She had just installed a new well last year and had no idea.

Lori threw her hands up in the air, looking more upset than she'd ever seen her. "Don't ask me! I turned on the faucet and nothing came out. And I'm in the middle of cooking pasta. I *need* water, Beth."

"I'll call the plumber right away."

"Don't bother. I just did. He said he couldn't get here until tomorrow."

"What?" Beth felt sick to her stomach. No water meant no showers, no toilets flushing, no cooking, no guests and no money! "But that's ridiculous. When I hired Mort he promised he'd make the inn his top priority and put us at the top of his client list."

"Mr. Toomis said he was booked solid and couldn't come till morning. But he said to tell you he was sorry."

"Son of a—"

Brad walked into the room just then, his face half-covered with shaving cream, a towel draped around his neck. If Beth hadn't been so upset, she would have laughed. It was not the doctor's style to appear in just his undershirt. Well, except when making love, but that topic was no longer pertinent.

"Is there a problem?" he asked.

"Apparently, we have no water, though I see you're already painfully aware of that."

Crossing to the sink, he turned the knobs on and off, then sticking his head under the sink he fiddled with the apparatus down there. "The shut-off valves seem to be on. I thought perhaps someone had turned them off."

"That's a relief," Lori said. "So why isn't there any water?"

"I'm not sure. Where's your well?" he asked Beth.

"Out in back. But the problem can't be with my well. I had a new one dug last year."

He thought for a moment. "It could be the pump. Sometimes they burn out, though that doesn't seem likely in this case. They would have installed a new pump when they dug the well."

"But what else could it be? I'm so upset. Why does everything have to happen all at once?"

"What else has happened?" Lori wanted to know, her gaze shifting from Beth to Brad.

Beth's cheeks heated. "It's nothing. I'm just being dramatic, I guess."

Brad cast Beth a searching look, then said, "I'll

check the breaker. Can you show me where the control panel is?"

Chiding herself for not thinking of such an obvious solution, she led him to the back porch where the panel box was hidden behind a small metal door in the wall. After a moment of messing with the switches, he said, "Looks like the one to the pump's been switched off."

"But who would have turned it off? That doesn't make any sense."

"Sometimes if there's a power surge, they flip on their own. It's a safety feature."

He flipped the switch to On and a moment later Lori called out, "It's working again! We have water."

Toilets began flushing, and she could hear the well pump start up again. Hopefully, Mrs. Frederick's shower was working as well. "Thank you, Brad. I don't know what I'd have done if I'd had to wait until morning. Most likely all my guests would have cleared out." Which would have been disastrous, as far as her finances were concerned.

When is Mr. Pickens going to get back to me about the loan? I need that money.

"I'm much better with a stethoscope than a wrench, so you should be happy I didn't have to use one. But you're welcome. I'm glad I could help."

When he made to leave, she clasped his forearm. "I'm sorry about the way things turned out, Brad. I hope you know that."

"Me, too," he replied, and she could see the pain in his eyes. "Well, I'd better get back upstairs and finish shaving."

"Okay. I—"

He paused and looked back, but she shook her head, deciding it was better not to say anything else.

Heaving a sigh, Beth watched him walk away. There was nothing she could have said to change things anyway.

THAT SAME NIGHT, BETH came rushing into the kitchen, newspaper in hand. "Guess what I've got, Lori?"

Looking up from the menus she was preparing for next week's meals, the chef shook her head. "You've got me. But after the water incident today I don't think I can take any more bad news."

"This is very good news—great, in fact. The *Philadelphia Inquirer* has picked up the story on the inn. We're going to be famous!"

Beth was grinning from ear to ear, but Lori's smile froze. Bill read the *Inquirer* daily. This was the absolute worse thing that could have happened. Of course, Beth didn't know that. "When did the article come out?" she asked. But what she really wanted to know was how much time did she have left before he found her?

"Let's see." Beth scanned the banner. "Five days ago. I just received this copy from Hilda Croft, who works for the historical society and is a big supporter of the Two Sisters. In fact, she's working on getting the inn listed in the Mediocrity Register for Historic Places. Isn't that exciting? I can't wait to tell my aunts."

Unwilling to put a damper on the young woman's joy, Lori mustered up some fake enthusiasm. "That's great, Beth! I'm happy for you. I know how hard you've worked to make this place a success."

"How hard we've both worked, you mean."

Beth squeezed Lori's shoulder affectionately, making her feel even more disloyal than she already did.

"Well, I've got to go. I think my aunts may have been the ones to cause the circuit breaker to flip. They're always plugging in stuff they shouldn't be, like that damn hot plate they use to brew their tea. I've tried to explain to them about the old wiring and all that, but they don't seem to get it."

Lori nodded sympathetically.

"And just this morning both my aunts complained that my mom's driving them nuts, which I can believe." She sighed. "I guess I need to find out what's going on. I've been so busy these past few days that I've practically abandoned them to my mother after she offered to keep an eye on them. I forgot that no one was around to keep an eye on *her.*"

"Well, good luck," Lori said, hoping she had some to spare. She was going to need all the luck she could get if Bill had discovered her whereabouts.

After she finished her menu preparation, Lori retired to her room and immediately checked her e-mail, her stomach knotting when she noticed another message from Bill had arrived. What she read made her blood run cold.

Lori, you haven't been an easy woman to track down, but I finally managed to locate you through the newspaper article printed in the local paper. I'll be coming soon to get my knives and recipe collection back. Bill.

Bill Thackery had found her. That was the first thing that sank into her brain. The second: she had to quit her job and leave immediately. She would give notice first thing in the morning. There was no way she wanted to have a confrontation with her former boss, especially in front of her new one.

But how could she leave Beth? The woman was depending on her. And she loved her job at the Two Sisters. The inn had become a real home to her, and she would miss everyone so much if she left, especially Beth.

"Dammit, Bill! Why couldn't you just leave me alone?"

If only she hadn't taken his stupid recipes and knives. But hindsight was always twenty-twenty, and at the time she'd run away, Lori hadn't had enough confidence in her abilities to go it alone. Now she didn't need Bill's recipes. Well, except for that yummy turkey stuffing. That one was too good to pass up, especially once she'd added her own touches to it. She'd developed her own unique style and had created her own set of recipes. Several of the guests had already begged her for copies, which had made her feel validated, not to mention thrilled.

Lori didn't need Bill anymore. And she certainly didn't need the trouble he could cause her and the inn if word got out that she was a thief.

ENTERING THE FRONT PARLOR later that evening, Beth found her mother with her shoes off, feet on the sofa, and reading a book that looked suspiciously like a romance novel. Margaret was engrossed in the story and Beth figured she'd just gotten to the juicy part.

"Mother, we need to talk."

Margaret looked up from the book and smiled, patting the space next to her, straightening herself as she did. "Of course we can talk, dear. I hope you don't mind that I borrowed one of your books from the inn's library. It's a romance novel. I've never read one before and I'm quite enjoying it."

"That's nice, though I must say I'm surprised. I can remember you criticizing me about my choice of reading material."

"I did? I wonder why. This is quite good."

Beth refrained from commenting, saying instead, "Aunt Ivy and Aunt Iris are very unhappy with your meddling, Mother. They said you've turned their rooms inside out, weeding through their personal belongings and bagging up old dresses, books and anything else you don't think they need any longer. They're extremely upset."

Her mother seemed astonished by the news. "But they never said a word to me. I just assumed—"

Beth sighed, wondering if the woman was dense or just a good actress. "The fourth floor is off-limits to guests for a very good reason. It's Iris and Ivy's home. They have the right to keep it the way they want it. And that goes for their collection of keepsakes as well. We may think it's junk, but they love all that stuff."

"But I'm family, not a guest. And I was only trying to make their suite more comfortable and roomy by getting rid of things they'll probably never use again."

"Those are *their* things, Mother, not yours or mine. And though you might mean well, you shouldn't have taken it upon yourself to clean and organize."

"You're right, dear. I'll make it a point to apologize to them. I was just trying to help and keep busy in the process."

"I realize that Mediocrity is not the most exciting place in the world, but it is what it is. You should know that better than anybody since you grew up here."

"You misunderstand me. I'm enjoying the slower

pace. In fact, I've given some thought to moving back here so I can be closer to you. There's nothing keeping me in California anymore."

The very idea of having her mother living in the same town sent spasms of nausea straight to Beth's GI tract. "Why would you want to move here? Isn't that a bit drastic?"

"Not at all, dear. I can find a small apartment or house, get a part-time job and be near my family. I'm not getting any younger, Beth, and the idea of dying alone doesn't hold much appeal."

"Quit talking nonsense, Mother! You're as healthy as a horse, and you know it." Margaret's gifts lay in aging others, not herself.

"Things can change very quickly, as you know. One minute everything's fine and dandy and the next you've been diagnosed with some dread disease or you drop dead of a heart attack."

Beth's heart had been attacked, and it hurt like hell. Her relationship with Brad had disintegrated before it had ever really gotten started. "Yes, I'm aware of that. You're not ill, are you?"

"No, dear, I'm fine."

Relief surged through Beth. She might not always get along with her mother, but she was the only one she had. "Good."

"Would you hate it very much if I lived closer to you? I'd like to be part of your life."

"Why? All you've done my entire life is criticize me. I could never do anything to please you. You even took Greg's side in the divorce. That hurt, Mother. I needed you to be on my side. I had no one except you and those two sweet old ladies. At least they stuck by me."

Her face a mask of guilt and pain, Margaret reached out, clasping her daughter's hand. "You'll never know how sorry I am for the way I've behaved. It's true. I haven't been a very good mother. I became very bitter after the divorce. And I guess part of me blamed you for my shortcomings and the hell my life had become.

"Your father loved you far more than he ever loved me. I think that was partly the reason I drove him away—to punish you both."

"But why would you do that? What did I ever do to you? I was only ten at the time—a small child who needed both her parents."

"I was a stupid, selfish woman. I still am, in many ways. But I'm trying to become a better person, to make up for my shortcomings. I want us to be a family again, Beth, to grow close, if you'll let me."

Beth heaved a deep sigh. "I—I don't know. So much has happened. I was hurt very deeply. I'm not—"

"Please give me a chance to make things up to you. Don't you think everyone deserves a second chance? I promise it'll be different this time."

"I can't give you an answer right now, Mother. It's

too much to take in all at once. I need time to think things through. And right now I've got a lot on my plate, with the opening of the restaurant and the number of guests in residence. Not to mention that the inn seems to be falling apart at the seams."

"If there's anything I can do to help, you need only ask. I meant what I said. I know I'm not much of a cook, but I used to wait tables when I was young, so if you need someone to help out or wash dishes or anything, just let me know."

"I appreciate the offer, and I may just take you up on it. I can't afford to allow things to unravel so close to the restaurant's opening."

"You're talking about today's water problem?"

"That's part of it."

"I don't have a lot of money in my savings account. I haven't been very thrifty over the years. But you're welcome to what I have, if it'll help get you over the hump."

Beth felt tears clog her throat. "Thank you, but I've already applied for a loan at the bank. I'm just waiting to hear if I've been approved or not."

"And what are you using as collateral?"

"The inn—it's all I have."

"I don't have to tell you that's risky. After working so many years in the banking business, I've seen a lot of people lose their homes and businesses."

"I know the risk, Mother, but I have no choice. If

I don't get the loan, I may lose the inn anyway." She couldn't believe she was confiding in her mother, but Beth had kept these things bottled up for so long that it felt good to share her burden.

"I understand, dear, and I'll keep my fingers crossed that your banker comes through for you."

"Better make that fingers and toes. Mr. Pickens is not the sentimental sort. And even though I've known him most of my life, I don't expect him to grant me any preferential treatment."

"Thank you for telling me this, Beth. It means a lot to me."

"I guess it's a first step in the right direction."

Margaret hugged her daughter close and Beth's eyes grew moist. "Yes, it is. And unlike before, I will be here for you."

"I'M AFRAID I'VE GOT some bad news, Beth."

Lori watched the innkeeper snatch an oatmeal-raisin cookie from the batch she'd just taken out of the oven. She prepared a different kind of cookie each day for the inn's afternoon tea.

Wiping crumbs from her pants, Beth talked around the cookie she'd just stuffed into her mouth. "I can't take any more bad news right now. Mort Toomis finally showed up and told me that the septic system is in danger of failing. Can you imagine what will happen if the toilets start backing up? It'll make the water problem seem like a piece of cake." She shook her head. "I can't bear to even think about it, or how much it'll cost to fix."

"What are you going to do?" Lori asked.

"What can I do? Toomis is arranging to have the waste pumped out and hopes that'll take care of the problem for the time being."

Lori wrinkled her nose in disgust. "I'm sorry."

Beth sighed. "It seems par for the course these days."

There was no way Lori could leave Beth in a lurch right now. The poor woman looked miserable. She had intended to give notice this morning, but decided she just couldn't do something like that to Beth, who'd been so good to her, taking a chance on an unknown commodity.

She'd just have to take the chance that Bill wouldn't come looking for her before the Thanksgiving holiday. Once she got Beth through the restaurant's opening, she would rethink what to do. But for now, Lori decided to stay put.

The news she had to give Beth was likely to send the poor woman over the edge, at any rate. "There's something I need to tell you."

"I'm sorry. I forgot. What's your bad news? Just blurt it out. I can take it."

"My supplier called early this morning. He can't deliver the fresh turkeys we ordered, due to some kind of shortage. We're going to have to settle for frozen."

"But we only have a few days left. Will they get here in time to thaw out?"

Lori handed the tearful woman another cookie. "Here, eat this. It'll make you feel better."

"I doubt it. I'm never going to feel better again. I wonder why I ever thought I could run an inn." She shoved the cookie into her mouth. "Nothing in my life ever runs smoothly. Why should this place be the exception?"

"I've got the turkey problem under control, so don't freak out about it, okay? They should be delivered late this afternoon. I wouldn't have even mentioned this, but I didn't want you to expect fresh when we were having frozen. And the frozen ones will work just as well. You'll see."

"I hope you're right. I've had about all the drama I can take for one week."

"Why do I get the feeling you're not just talking about the inn's problems?"

Heaving a sigh, Beth grabbed a whole handful of cookies, pulled out a chair at the kitchen table and seated herself. "Guess I'm not very good at keeping my feelings hidden. You're right—there's more to my misery than a bunch of frozen birds."

Lori set the cookie sheet aside, wiped her hands on her apron, and sat down, too. "I don't need a crystal ball to see there's something going on between you and the doc. Sometimes the tension is so thick between you two I could cut it with a knife. If you want to talk about it, I'm a good listener."

"I'm in love with Brad Donovan, Lori, and I think he feels the same way about me. But there are insurmountable problems that won't allow us to be together."

"Nothing can be that bad, Beth. Maybe you're just overreacting."

"I wish I were."

"Would you like to talk about it?"

Beth shook her head. "I'm sorry. I can't. Not right now anyway. But I appreciate your concern. At any rate, it doesn't really matter because whatever was between us is over. Brad will be leaving soon to go back to his life in Virginia and all I'll have left are some wonderful memories to cherish."

Clasping her hand, Lori said, "I haven't been entirely honest with you, Beth, and I feel terrible about it."

Beth's eyes widened. "In what way?"

"I ran away from my last position in Philadelphia. Bill Thackery was impossible to work with, and I needed to prove something to myself—to stand on my own two feet, I guess. Out of spite, I took his knives and recipes and left without explanation. I know it was childish, dishonest, and very unprofessional. If you want to fire me, I totally understand. I wouldn't hold it against you."

Beth took a moment to absorb everything Lori had told her, and then said, "Fire you? Are you insane? I would never do that. I understand the need to prove something to yourself. I lived in my ex-husband's shadow for years. How can I blame you for needing to escape so you could make a career of your own? If you had stayed in Philadelphia, you might never have realized how truly gifted you are."

"Thank you for understanding. I wasn't sure you would. It sounds so sordid when I tell it."

"Well, at least you didn't have sex in the hayloft with a man you'll never see again."

Lori's eyes widened and she gasped. "Ohmigod! I had no idea."

"That makes two of us. Apparently I had no brain at the time."

"I hope things eventually work out for you and Dr. Donovan. You're a great-looking couple."

"Even if things worked out between us, there's still Brad's daughter to consider. Stacy doesn't like me and she doesn't want her dad to remarry. And I'm not really sure I want to be married again, Lori. I don't think I have the stamina to do it a second time."

"We're a pair, and that's no lie. We've got man trouble, secrets up the wazoo and more drama than a Hollywood movie. But I sure do feel better for having confided in you."

Beth smiled. "Ditto. So what do you propose we do about our problems?"

"I don't see that there's a lot we can do, other than just sit back and see what happens. Bill may show up here, or he may not. There's no sense in worrying about it. We've got enough on our plates with this restaurant opening at the moment. For now, let's concentrate all of our efforts on that and forget about the rest."

Beth filled two glasses with milk and handed Lori one. "I'm going to toast to the successful opening of the Two Sisters Ordinary Restaurant. May the food be delicious, the toilets flush properly—"

"And may sleeping dogs lie."

"Amen!"

CHAPTER FIFTEEN

THERE WERE PROBABLY hundreds, maybe thousands, of restaurateurs who could claim that their Thanksgiving Day feasts had gone off without a hitch. Beth, unfortunately, was not one of them.

Murphy's Law had reared its ugly head many times over, before and during the restaurant's opening, beginning with the turkeys that hadn't arrived. Lori had called their supplier and given him hell. Fortunately, Brad had saved the day by driving to every grocery store and retail outlet within a hundred miles of the inn to purchase as many birds as he could find.

Margaret stepped up to the plate as well, waiting tables when two of the newly hired waitresses failed to show. Ivy and Iris had lent a hand in the kitchen, preparing pies, mashed potatoes and performing whatever chores Lori deemed necessary. And even Stacy had volunteered to help with this evening's cleanup and was, at the moment, washing dishes with Beth's mother.

Thinking how very lucky she was, Beth headed out the back door of the kitchen to fetch firewood from the woodshed so she wouldn't be caught short-handed in the morning. The temperature had fallen throughout the day and was well below freezing now. She had donned her parka to ward off the chill, though the glowing success of the restaurant's open-ing was enough to keep her warm.

The comments on the food had been more than generous. Everyone, including the mayor and his wife, loved the feast Lori had prepared and promised to come back again to dine very soon. Sheriff Mur-dock, who'd eaten three pieces of pumpkin pie, had declared the food to be the best he'd ever eaten. His wife had taken exception to that comment and had kicked him so hard beneath the table that she'd nearly broken her big toe.

For the first time in a very long time, Beth felt a real sense of accomplishment. She and Lori were planning to celebrate their achievement later on with a bottle of champagne.

The two women had grown close these past few days, confiding more of their hopes, dreams and dis-appointments, and Beth valued the friendship that was forming between them.

"You shouldn't be lifting that heavy wood, Beth. Here, let me do that."

Turning to find Brad standing right behind her, his

arms outstretched, Beth shook her head. "You're a guest, in case you've forgotten, Dr. Donovan, and I don't make my guests carry firewood. Besides, you've already done enough. Buying those turkeys was a life-saver for me. I never could have opened on time without your help. Thank you so much for everything!"

He smiled. "I was happy to help. You looked ready to cry when the delivery truck you were expecting never showed up, so I figured I'd better play the part of hero and rescue the damsel in distress. Besides, your aunts have been very generous with their time, helping Stacy with her studies and all. I really appreciate the time they've spent with her. She's blossomed under their attention and kindness."

"Well, I'm grateful anyway. And you don't need to carry firewood for me. Hank will be back on Monday, and then this chore will fall to him again."

"You'll have a sore back by Monday. Now let me have that wood and I'll carry it into the house for you."

Unwilling to argue over such a trivial matter, she dumped the wood into his arms, figuring the demand was another one of those "macho man" things. "Thank you."

"You and Lori should be very proud of yourselves. You really pulled it off tonight. Everyone was raving about the food, which was excellent, by the way. The turkey stuffing was delicious."

Beth grinned. "You don't know how relieved I

am to hear you say that. There were times when I thought about giving up and chucking the whole restaurant idea."

"I'm glad you stuck with it. There are always start-up problems in any business. That's just the nature of things. I'm sure it'll be smooth sailing from here on out."

"You're not only kind, you're very optimistic, Dr. Donovan. I wish I shared your hopefulness."

Brad reached out and caressed her cheek. "I've missed you, Beth. I know what happened between us was partly my fault. I'm sorry I let you assume all the blame for it. That was wrong of me."

Startled by the admission, Beth grabbed a few more pieces of wood and began walking toward the house. "There's nothing to be sorry for. I don't regret a single moment of what happened between us."

"That's good—because I wouldn't mind it happening again."

Beth pulled up short. "I don't think that would be very wise, do you?"

"Probably not, but I meant what I said when I told you I loved you. That's never going to change for me. I've done a lot of soul searching lately and I can honestly say that I believe everything you told me about your lack of involvement in my father's disappearance. And as far as your aunts go, well…they're strange, but I don't think either one of them is capable of murder."

Beth's heart leaped and she smiled widely. Brad's words filled her with hope and happiness. He dropped the load of wood he was carrying to the ground and she did the same.

They fell into each other's arms without saying another word, kissing deeply and passionately, trying to savor every precious moment as if it might be their last. When they finally pulled apart, both were breathing hard and Brad looked visibly pained.

"I love you, too, Brad. But as you know, that doesn't change much. You dad's still missing."

"I can see now that I was wrong to judge your aunts so harshly. After all, they were never convicted of any crime. Maybe I just let all the gossip and innuendo get to me."

Again, she was shocked by his admission. It was something she'd never thought to hear, especially since confiding in him about the bones. "I appreciate your saying that, Brad, and I'm very sorry about your dad. I wish there was more I could do to help." Brad's anguished expression tore at her heart. "Nothing concerning my father's disappearance makes sense to me. I've given it a lot of thought over these past few days and knowing how unhappy and depressed he was, I can't discount the possibility that he took his own life. And if that's the case, it means I failed him in some way."

She gasped. "Oh, Brad, please don't say such

things! You're not responsible for your father's problems, whatever they might be."

"I can't keep grasping at straws, Beth. There has to be a logical explanation for why he never came back. He's either had an accident, killed himself or someone has done it for him. We may never know what happened and I have to try and accept that."

"But you mustn't give up hope. He could still be alive, still come back. You have to believe that."

"I've always told Stacy that she needs to move on and accept her mother's death, and I need to follow my own advice. I can't put my life on hold any longer and give up a chance at real happiness. It's time I started thinking about the future."

Like a cascading waterfall, Beth's heart roared so loudly in her ears that she thought he could surely hear it. "What exactly are you saying?" But she already knew and it scared her.

"I want you in my life, now and forever."

She swallowed with some difficulty. "Oh, Brad, I'm not sure we would work. We're so very different, come from such diverse backgrounds. You're a doctor with a position to maintain in your community. I don't have the social skills for that kind of life. And even if I did, I'm…I'm just not sure that's what I want right now."

Would she ever be sure? Beth didn't know. After what had happened with Greg she wasn't certain she could give herself over to another man again and become just an extension of his life.

She wasn't sure she could give up the identity she'd struggled so hard to make for herself, to live in another man's shadow. And there was Stacy to consider. Beth wasn't cut out to be a mother, especially to a teenage girl with issues.

He looked confused. "But you just said you loved me. I don't understand."

"I do love you. But I'm not sure— I mean, this is rather sudden, you have to admit. And I—"

"And I've taken you by surprise?" He looked hopeful.

"You could say that. One minute you're accusing me of vile things and the next you're kissing me and confessing your love. I'm confused." And how could she be certain he wouldn't have a change of heart again?

And they say women are fickle. Ha!

"I understand. It's just now that I've finally figured out what I want, I needed to let you know."

She smiled softly. "I'm glad you did. It gives me a lot to think about."

"I won't pressure you."

"I appreciate that." She had enough pressure on her at the moment. Her relationship with Brad was only part of it. There was still her mother and their new bond to work out, the loan from the bank that hadn't materialized yet, the bones buried in her basement and her aunts' possible involvement with them. The list seemed unending.

"We'd better get back inside before we freeze to death and my mother sends out a search party."

"You and your mom seem to be getting along better."

"We are. We've been doing a lot of talking, a lot of sorting out of our differences. For the first time, I think I'm finally starting to understand who Margaret Shaw is, and I think the same is true of her. My mother never really allowed herself to get to know me as a woman. I think she always thought of me as a child."

His smile was downright erotic. "I can attest to the fact that you're all woman, woman."

"As I've told you before, Doc, you're good for my ego."

"And you're good for me. Don't ever forget that, Beth, because I don't intend to."

"No pressure, remember?"

"No pressure. But you've never had the opportunity to experience the potency of the old Donovan charm. It goes all the way back to County Clare, Ireland. Me ancestor Michael Donovan was quite the ladies' man, or so I'm told."

She laughed at his Irish lilt, completely charmed. "I'll consider myself warned."

"You do that, because I don't intend to give up easily."

Part of Beth hoped he wouldn't give up, but the other part, the frightened part, wanted to run away as far and fast as she could.

EARLY MONDAY MORNING, Aubrey, dressed in three-piece charcoal Armani, strolled up the front sidewalk of the Two Sisters Ordinary and rang the doorbell impatiently. He hadn't worn an overcoat—hated the damn things—and was freezing his balls off.

A few moments later, an attractive red-haired woman opened the door and invited him in. She was dressed casually in jeans and a sweater and looked too young to be the owner.

"May I help you?" she asked, smiling a practiced smile that couldn't possibly be genuine. No one was that happy in the morning, especially on a Monday.

"The name's John Connor."

"Oh, like in *The Terminator?*"

"I beg your pardon?"

She shook her head, her cheeks filling with color. "It's the name of one of the characters in an Arnold Schwarzenegger movie. I often connect things to movies I've seen."

Aubrey often used an alias when he didn't want to reveal his true identity. But he had no idea who this John Connor was. He rarely watched movies—a complete waste of time, in his opinion—and had never seen one featuring California's governor, at any rate.

"I'm here to see Elizabeth Randall. Do you know if she's available?"

The woman nodded. "I'm Beth Randall," she said, taking him by surprise. "Do we have an appointment this morning? If so, I've completely forgotten, and I apologize."

"We don't have an appointment, Ms. Randall. But I'm hoping you can spare a few minutes to speak to me. You see, I'm a real-estate investor, and I'm interested in acquiring property in this area. Yours is of particular interest to me. And I'm prepared to offer you a very handsome—"

Her eyes widened. "I'm not interested. I've no intention of selling this inn for any price, so you might as well save your breath. The Two Sisters Ordinary is not for sale."

"I don't think you should dismiss my offer so quickly, young woman. First, I'd like to explain how I intend to develop this property into a luxury condominium resort." She gasped, but he continued as if he hadn't heard her reaction. "I can assure you it would be a very upscale development." *Once he tore down this eyesore of an inn.* Of course, he had no intention of mentioning that.

"I don't care if you want to erect the Taj Mahal here, Mr. Connor. My answer is and always will be no. The Two Sisters is not for sale, at any price, for any reason."

"I rarely take no for an answer, Ms. Randall. A

man in my position is used to getting what he wants, and I want this property."

"I don't want to be rude, Mr. Connor, but you are obviously under the misguided impression that I'm willing to sell, which I'm not. I've spent years redoing this old place. The house has been in my family for generations. It's part of me and I won't give it up. Some things are more important than money. Now if you'll excuse me, I have guests to attend to."

Aubrey's lips slashed into a thin line. He hated doing business with women. They always let their emotions interfere with sound decisions. "You haven't heard my offer yet, Ms. Randall. I would think that four million dollars would be of use to a woman of your circumstance. I'm sure you aren't earning that kind of money as an innkeeper. You could live a life of ease, provide for your family, if you have one, and not have to worry about a thing for the rest of your life."

Eyes wide, her mouth gaped open before she said, "Four million dollars? Why on earth would you want to give me four million dollars for this inn? I doubt the structure or the land would appraise for that much. In fact, I'm positive they won't."

"Because I can, Ms. Randall, and because I see the development potential others don't. Rest assured I've done my homework. This area is ripe for development. I intend to put Mediocrity on the map as a major tourist destination."

"Although your offer is very generous, I'm still not interested. As I said, money isn't everything."

Was the woman insane? Money was the only thing that mattered! Money begat power, power influence, and with enough influence a man could do just about anything he wanted.

"An inn is only as good as its reputation. Rumor has it that you've been having money problems, which have led to water and sewage problems. Troubles such as this could greatly affect future bookings. Word of mouth can make or break a business such as yours. Can you really *afford* to let that happen?"

"Those matters have already been taken care of, so you needn't concern yourself. This inn is in fine shape and my financial affairs are no concern of yours."

Aubrey could tell the woman was lying, but he didn't call her on it. He'd always been fond of the element of surprise. "I'll leave for now, Ms. Randall, but I'll be back. When I want something I go after it. And I want this inn and the surrounding property, no matter what I have to do to get it."

Her eyes narrowed. "Is that a threat?"

"Not at all, but it is a promise of how I do business. I wouldn't be successful if I allowed a little opposition to stand in my way."

"As my aunts are fond of saying, Mr. Connor, you are barking up the wrong tree."

"And as I'm fond of saying, Ms. Randall, there is more than one way to skin a cat."

"I CAN'T BEGIN TO tell you how vile the man was. He stood in my front hallway and practically threatened me if I didn't sell him this inn. Can you imagine his audacity?"

Ivy and Iris exchanged a look of concern, then Ivy asked, "But why does he want this old house, Beth? That doesn't make any sense."

"What was his name?" her mother wanted to know. "He sounds like a crackpot."

Beth was still shaking from her encounter of moments before. After she had ushered the rude investor out of the inn, slamming the door behind him, she had rushed up the stairs to tell her aunts and mother about the strange encounter.

"He said his name's John Connor. He wants to build luxury condos here. Here, on my property! And when I told him no, he just smiled this smarmy smile, like I had no say in the matter whatsoever, and continued talking about putting Mediocrity on the map. It was awful. He made my skin crawl." She rubbed her arms against the chill.

"Do you think we should call the sheriff, dear?"

Aunt Iris asked. "Perhaps he can talk to the man, tell him to leave you alone."

Beth shook her head. "Sheriff Murdock would just say that the man hasn't done anything wrong, except to offer me four million dollars for—"

"Four million!" Margaret's eyes rounded. "Are you certain you don't want to reconsider? That's a lot of money."

Beth took a deep breath. "I'm quite sure, Mother. This inn means more to me than any amount of money he can offer. I told him flat out that it's not for sale at any price." And she'd meant it, even if he was too dense to understand the finality of her decision.

"But, Beth, perhaps your mother's right." Ivy glanced at her sister, who nodded her confirmation. "If you invest that money wisely, you'd never have to work another day in your life. And you work so hard, dear. You could travel, buy anything you wanted. This could be the answer to your dreams."

"I can't believe you're saying such a thing, Aunt Ivy. Mother I can understand, but this is your and Aunt Iris's house. You grew up here. It's part of you. And you know how much you both love it."

"It's just a house, Beth," Iris said. "Oh, we love it, don't get me wrong. And we're happy you love it, too. But if you can sell it and use the money to have a wonderful life, then you should reconsider."

From her position on the sofa, Beth bolted to her feet and began to pace. "I can't believe I'm hearing this!"

"Look at it sensibly, Beth," Aunt Ivy began. "Iris and I are old. We should probably be living in a nursing home and not underfoot, ruining your life."

"First of all, you two would probably be kicked out of any nursing home you tried to live in. And secondly, you are not ruining my life. I love living here with you. If it weren't for you two, I wouldn't have been able to cope after my divorce. I wouldn't have been able to make a fresh start and realize that I have talents for something other than being a man's companion and housekeeper."

"Being a wife and mother can be very rewarding, Beth. You shouldn't dismiss it out of hand," Margaret chimed in. "I realize you had a terrible time of it with Greg, but not all men are like him. Look at Dr. Donovan. He's a fine example of a man who would make an excellent husband and father."

Determined to keep their tentative truce and not say what was on her mind, Beth took a deep, calming breath. "Now, Mother, we've already agreed not to discuss marriage to Brad Donovan."

"I know, honey, but I've had the opportunity to spend time with Stacy and I think she really likes you. In fact, she told me as much the other day."

"Just because we're getting along better doesn't mean she wants me to marry her father. And I'm just not ready to get married again. Not now. I told Brad—" She snapped her mouth shut when all three women leaned forward.

"Did Dr. Donovan ask you to marry him, dear?" Aunt Iris wanted to know.

Beth shook her head. "Not in so many words. He just hinted that he'd like us to be together. And that's all I'm saying on the subject. I came up here to tell you about that awful Mr. Connor and now you've got me talking about Brad, marriage and things I'm not comfortable discussing."

"We only want what's best for you, Beth," Aunt Ivy stated. "I'm sure you know that. We've always known that someday you could meet someone and get married. And Iris and I would be delighted if that happened. We certainly wouldn't want you to give up a chance at happiness because you're worried about what would happen to us."

"Beth would have nothing to worry about in that regard, aunts, because I intend to move back here. And I am perfectly capable of taking care of you."

Iris and Ivy exchanged shocked glances at the idea of having their niece as a caregiver, but nodded in spite of their trepidation. "Well, there you go," Ivy said. "Your mother is here to lend a hand, if need be. My advice is to sell this old relic of a house for as much money as you can, marry Dr. Donovan, have lots of babies and live happily ever after."

Is no one listening to what I've been saying? Beth wondered, heaving a sigh. Everything wasn't as black-and-white as they seemed to think.

"Mine, too," Iris concluded with a delighted smile. "You would make an excellent wife and mother. You're a very kind and caring individual, Beth dear, and Ivy and I are very proud of the woman you've become."

Margaret knelt before her daughter's chair and took her hand. Expecting to hear a lecture, Beth was surprised by what her mother had to say.

"I'm not going to tell you what to do this time around, Beth. You're a grown woman with a mind of your own. Of course, I'd love for you to get married again and have children, make me a grandmother, but I promised to support you in whatever decisions you made from here on out, and that's what I intend to do. If you decide not to sell the inn, then I'm on your side."

Unable to believe what she was hearing, she swallowed hard, blinking back the tears threatening to spill. "Thank you. You don't know how much your support means to me."

Margaret smiled sadly. "Yes, I think I do. It took me a while to figure things out, but I'm learning from my previous mistakes."

"Well, amen! It's about time," Ivy said.

"Are you sure that keeping this inn is what you want to do?"

"I'm quite sure, Aunt Iris. I've worked hard to make a success of this place and I'll be damned if I'm going to allow some wealthy stranger to force me out of the only home I've ever loved."

"Then Ivy and I will back you up one hundred percent, too. We want you to be happy, and if keeping this old relic will make you happy, then so be it. We just don't want to become a burden to you, that's all."

"You'll never be a burden. I love you both and I'm happy that we're a family. And now that Mother's here, too…well, that's even better."

Margaret started crying. "I don't deserve to be this happy," she said, dabbing her eyes with a tissue.

"Hush, Margaret," Iris chastised, "this isn't about you."

"This is about all of us," Beth contradicted. "The Two Sisters is our home and no one will take it from us."

Well, except for maybe her creditors. But Beth would cross that bridge when she had to.

CHAPTER SIXTEEN

ALL OF THE GUESTS, with the exception of Brad and Stacy—Margaret was no longer calling herself a guest—had departed the inn that morning, providing Beth with some much needed time to relax. She was seated on the front porch reading a book. The sun was shining but didn't add much warmth to the brisk afternoon.

The front door banged shut and she glanced up to find Stacy approaching. The young girl sat down in the rocker next to Beth and smiled a rare smile. "Hi! Are you busy?"

Setting the book down in her lap, Beth replied, "Not really. I'm just catching up on my reading. I thought you and your dad were going into town to do some Christmas shopping. How come you're still here?"

"We are, but he had a couple of phone calls to make first."

"I see. So what are you going shopping for?"

"I want to get your aunts and mom something nice for Christmas."

Beth's eyes widened. "That's very sweet, Stacy, but not necessary. You should take your money and buy something nice for yourself."

"I really like your aunts. They've been very nice to me. Aunt Ivy lets me do eBay with her on the computer and Aunt Iris is always teaching me interesting historical stuff. I'm thinking about becoming a history teacher, like her. I used to want to be a singer like Jessica Simpson, but Aunt Ivy says she looks like a tart, and I think she's right."

Beth had no trouble believing the outspoken woman had said that. Ivy rarely minced words when it came to the youth of today. "That would be wonderful, Stacy. The world can always use more teachers. Music's nice, but you can really make a difference by teaching."

"That's what Margaret said. She's nice, too. I wasn't sure at first I was going to like her because she talks a lot and asks so many questions, but I do. She's a lot of fun."

"Are you talking about my mother Margaret?" Beth had never thought of the woman as fun, though the nosy part certainly fit her to a tee.

Stacy nodded. "She taught me how to do a French manicure and she lets me wear some of her eye makeup when my dad isn't around."

"She does?" Her mother had always been so strict about makeup and short skirts when Beth was growing up. Of course, that hadn't kept Beth from wearing them anyway. She just kept the items hidden in her locker at school and made sure she changed before going home.

Apparently, Margaret had mellowed big-time.

"I'm glad you two are getting along so well."

"Your mom told me you didn't used to get along, but that you've been working stuff out and things are better now. Margaret said she wasn't a very good mom. Is that true?"

"My mother had a lot to deal with when I was growing up, because of my parents' divorce and her own immaturity. I think she was just overwhelmed. Mom's not perfect, but then, none of us are. And we get along much better now. Talking about the past has helped us sort out a lot of issues."

"We've been talking a lot, too, about my mom dying and my dad getting married again. Margaret thinks he should. She said Dad's going to get lonely after I leave home to go to college. Do you think that's true?"

Ah. Margaret's motives for befriending the young girl were becoming crystal clear, especially in light of their recent conversation on marriage. "You mustn't let my mother influence you in any way, Stacy. She's very opinionated and likes to interfere in things that are none of her business." *Like my life.*

"Yeah, she told me that. But I think she's right

about some stuff. It was selfish of me to keep Dad all to myself. I know he likes you a lot, and I just want you to know that I don't hate you anymore. In fact, I think you're kinda cool."

"Tha…thank you!"

"Since I've been here I've watched you do all kinds of stuff, like making the holiday decorations and arranging the pretty flowers you put everywhere. I think you've done a nice job with this inn."

The unexpected compliment filled Beth with pleasure. "That's very sweet of you to say. But I thought you hated this place."

"I did at first, mostly because I missed my friends back home. But now that I've made new friends it's not so bad. Plus, I love Buster. I'm hoping my dad buys me a dog just like him for Christmas."

"You can visit Buster whenever you like," Beth found herself saying. "He likes you, too."

Stacy smiled widely. "Thanks! Aunt Iris said I could take the bus, if I ever wanted to visit. And Aunt Ivy promised she'd keep in touch through e-mail."

Beth nodded. "You can certainly take the bus, though you'll need your dad's permission first."

"My dad loves this place. He said if he didn't have a medical practice in Charlottesville, he'd move here in a heartbeat. Do you think you'd ever want to move to Virginia? You could bring your aunts with you. It'd be fun! I could show you around, introduce you to my friends. Maybe we could go to the mall together. We have a really nice one."

Surprised by her enthusiasm, Beth stammered, "I—I don't think that would be possible, Stacy. My aunts are old. Relocating them wouldn't be good. Plus, my business is here. It would be very hard for me to start over."

The young girl heaved a disappointed sigh. "That's what I figured, but I thought I'd ask anyway. Aunt Ivy says there's no harm in asking, just as long as I don't expect to get my way about everything."

Beth was saved from commenting when Brad appeared.

"What are you two ladies gossiping about?"

His daughter shook her head. "Nothing. Are you ready to go into town now?"

He turned to look at Beth, flashing a sexy smile that warmed her toes—and other areas you couldn't mention in front of children. "Would you like to come with us? I promised Stacy I'd take her Christmas shopping, *again.* She seems intent on looking at everything Mediocrity has to offer before making up her mind."

"Oh, Dad, I do not."

Beth smiled. "Thanks for the invitation, but I'll pass. You two go ahead and have fun. I'm going to savor the peace and quiet around here for a little while longer. It's been in short supply these past few days."

Just then a dilapidated car pulled up in front of the inn and two elderly people got out.

"I wonder who that can be? I'm not expecting guests today. At least, I hope not." Though addled as she'd been lately, it was entirely possible she'd forgotten.

Brad turned to look, and then so did Stacy, and their mouths dropped open in unison. Then Brad called out to the gentleman dressed in navy slacks and a red-and-white reindeer sweater, "Dad? Dad, is that you?"

Stacy squealed in delight and took off down the steps. "Gramps! Gramps, you've come back. But what are you wearing? It's, like, totally gross."

The older man smiled and waved, and Beth recognized Robert Donovan. The prodigal father had returned—and he wasn't alone.

When the older couple reached the porch, Brad said, in a not-too-pleasant voice, "Dad, where the hell have you been? I've been worried sick about you. I thought you were dead. Why didn't you call?"

"Watch your language, son. There are ladies present." Robert Donovan smiled at Beth and brought forward the lady standing next to him.

Brad finally noticed the older woman and smiled in apology. "Sorry. I didn't see you standing there. I was concentrating on my father."

"This is Opal Cosgrove," Robert said proudly.

"Opal Cosgrove *Donovan*," she corrected, smiling adoringly and winking at her husband's blunder. "I hope you haven't forgotten our marriage already, Robert."

"Never, my dear," he said, kissing her cheek.

At his father's besotted expression, Brad's mouth unhinged, and he shot a look of confusion at Beth that mirrored hers. "You're *married?* But when? How? I don't understand."

"I'll explain all of it, son. But first, Opal and I would like to come inside and get warm, if that's okay with Ms. Randall." He turned to face the innkeeper.

"I realize you weren't expecting us, but we were hoping you might have room to put us up for the weekend."

"It's Beth, and it's more than okay. And yes, I can accommodate you. Come inside and get warm. Everyone's been quite concerned about you, Mr. Donovan, especially Brad and Stacy. We'd almost given up hope of ever seeing you again."

She smiled at the new bride. "Welcome, Mrs. Donovan. You're quite a nice surprise, as well." She wondered if Brad thought so.

Stacy stared shyly at the gray-haired woman. "I'm Stacy. Are you my new grandma?"

Opal Donovan wrapped her arm about the girl's shoulders, her smile warm and kind. "Well, I suppose

I am. I'm so glad to finally meet you, Stacy. Your grandpa's told me so much about you and your father." She held out her hand to Brad. "It's nice to meet you, too, Brad. I hope we're going to be good friends."

Brad nodded dumbly, wondering what kind of explanation his father could possibly have for his recent behavior. Nothing short of amnesia was going to satisfy him for all the heartache and anguish the old man had put him and Stacy through.

Hell, not to mention that Brad had accused Beth of duplicity in his father's disappearance! And now here Robert Donovan was, living and breathing and making him look like the damnedest fool in the world.

AFTER COFFEE, doughnuts and chitchat, Beth escorted Opal Donovan to the bridal suite, while Brad and his father remained in the parlor to have a more serious discussion. Stacy had wisely opted out of the confrontation and had taken Buster for a walk.

"I can't believe you got married without telling me, Dad," Brad said, pacing the small, sunlit room in agitation. "We've been worried sick for weeks and you've been off honeymooning with Opal and enjoying the hell out of yourself."

An apologetic expression on his face, Robert took a deep breath, patting his knees nervously. "It wasn't quite like that, son. I know you've got reason to be upset, and I'm sorry. But let me explain why I left before you judge me too harshly."

"I'll say I have reason to be upset. Hell, I thought you were dead!"

"I've been doing my damnedest to avoid that eventuality, son." When Brad opened his mouth to question him further, Robert shook his head. "A short time before leaving Charlottesville I was diagnosed with prostate cancer."

Brad ground to a halt, unable to believe his own ears. "What? My God! And you didn't tell me?"

"I didn't want to upset you or Stacy by revealing my illness, not after what you'd gone through with Carol. I just couldn't bring myself to do it. You'd already suffered so much and just the word *cancer* scares the hell out of everyone, including me."

"So you just disappeared, without calling or leaving word. And you didn't think your actions would upset us?" Brad shook his head. "How could you be so inconsiderate, Dad? That's not like you at all."

"I sent you a postcard. Didn't you get it?"

Brushing impatient fingers through his hair, he replied, "Of course I got it. How do you think I found this place? But you never called, not once. I checked the answering machine at home a hundred times—checked in with my office, too. And I had my cell phone with me the entire time."

"I couldn't bring myself to call, so I sent you

word by e-mail, informing you of my whereabouts and letting you know I was okay. But apparently you left home without checking your mail."

"I did check my mail and there was nothing from you."

Robert heaved a sigh. "Hell, I hope I didn't screw up your address. I get things like that mixed up sometimes. But I was so sure… It was never my intention to worry you or Stacy. I thought I was making things easier on you, but I see now that I didn't, and I'm sorry for that, son."

"Where have you been all this time? It's like you disappeared off the face of the earth."

"I went to Pittsburgh, to the hospital there. I've been receiving treatment for my prostate cancer these past weeks. It's where I met Opal. She's a cancer survivor and volunteers her time at the hospital. We met and it was love at first sight. Never believed lightning could strike twice in one lifetime, but it has."

Heaving a deep sigh, and trying hard to keep his fears at bay, Brad sat down on the sofa next to his father. "What's your prognosis, Dad?"

"Good. Very good, in fact. Dr. Edwards, the physician who's been treating me, said the cancer was in the earliest stage. He's pleased with the outcome thus far. But, of course, I'll need to be tested every so often, to make certain the cancer cells haven't returned."

"Well, thank God you caught it in time and that

you were treated successfully." If only Carol had been as lucky.

"I was afraid I'd be impotent after the surgery, which is one of the reasons I didn't want to confide in you beforehand. I was embarrassed, even though you're a doctor. But it looks like I'm not." He smiled with equal amounts of pride and relief.

Brad finally smiled. "Opal seems like a nice lady. I think she suits you."

"She's the best. I never thought to fall in love again, after your mother. I've been lonely, Brad, even with you and Stacy around. I missed my independence and the companionship of a woman."

"I wish you'd confided in me. I feel badly that you didn't think you could trust me."

"Trust had nothing to do with it. But I couldn't stand the idea of your having to deal with another loved one who had cancer. And there was no way in hell I was going to put my granddaughter through that kind of pain again. Stacy needs to heal, not deal with more tragedy."

"I know, but—"

"I needed this time away, to sort things out and find myself again. The trip was good for me, on many levels. And meeting Opal was a bonus I never expected. Out of something terrible came something good. I hope you can forgive me, son. I never meant to hurt you or Stacy by my actions."

"Of course I forgive you. I just hope Beth can forgive me." He sighed deeply, thinking that was a long shot.

"Beth?" Robert's brow arched. "Oh, you mean Ms. Randall? So that's how it is, huh? I'm happy to hear it. She's a very attractive, hardworking young woman, from what I've seen. I like her aunts, too. They're good people."

"Speaking of Beth's aunts, did you happen to mention to them the reason you were going to Pittsburgh?"

Robert nodded sheepishly. "We were playing cards one evening and it just slipped out. They were upset for me and when I explained what I was going to do, they agreed to keep my confidence. I see they have and I'm grateful for it."

"I couldn't get a thing out of those two old ladies, and neither could the sheriff."

Robert's eyes widened. "You called the sheriff? I really did have you worried, didn't I?"

Brad explained about the disappearance of Lyle McMurtry and how he had believed the old ladies might have had something to do with Robert's vanishing act.

Chuckling, his father slapped his knee. "You thought Ivy and Iris had done away with me? Those two sweet old gals? Now that's a hoot. Wait till I tell Opal."

"I was distraught and everyone was acting very suspiciously! And you shouldn't be laughing, Dad. It's not funny."

"Guess I should have stayed missing, huh?"

"I'm relieved you're back. And I'm happy you've found love again. I hope you and Opal will be very happy together."

"Thanks, son, and I hope you'll be happy with Beth."

"My future with Beth isn't quite as secure as yours. We still have a lot of problems to work out." He just hoped they weren't as insurmountable as she seemed to think.

Patting Brad on the back, his dad said, "I've got faith in you, boy. It's time you got your life back together. Carol would want you to be happy."

"Carol will always have a special place in my heart. That will never change. But I love Beth Randall, and I hope I can convince her to marry me."

"Have you asked her yet?"

"Not in so many words, but I hinted at it."

"Well, go ahead and ask her, son. Nothing's going to happen until you do."

Brad intended to do just that, but first he needed to talk to his daughter.

THIRTY MINUTES LATER, Brad found Stacy down by the pond, tossing the ball for Buster. She was laughing gleefully and looked so grown-up that his heart ached at the thought of losing his little girl. Someday another man would have the right to call her his own.

He called out to her and she waved. "Have time for your old man?"

"Oh, Dad," she said when he approached, "you're not old! Though you do dress kind of old-fashioned, like when you wear those boring suits to work."

"Thanks. It's always nice to know your daughter thinks you have no fashion sense."

"How come you're out here and not inside with Gramps? You didn't have a fight, did you?" Her forehead creased with worry.

Clasping her hand, Brad led Stacy to the bench, remembering another time, another woman. "Everything's fine between me and Grandpa. You don't have to worry about a thing."

"Whew! That's good to hear. I like Opal. She seems nice. Do you think I should call her Grandma?"

Thinking about his own mother and how she'd always doted on his daughter, Brad's heart tightened at the thought, but then realizing he was being selfish, he said, "You should ask Opal what she'd like to be called."

"I think I'll call her Gram, if I call her anything, because I always called my real grandmother Grandma and I'd feel funny calling anyone else that."

Brad's heart lightened and he squeezed his daughter's knee. "Whatever you think's best, honey. I'll leave that up to you and Opal."

Picking up a handful of pebbles, Stacy tossed them into the pond, one by one. "So, are you and Beth going to get married?"

His eyes widened at her perceptiveness. "What makes you ask that?"

"I'm not stupid, Dad. I know you like Beth a whole lot, maybe even love her. And I don't want you to be lonely after I'm gone. Someday I'll be going off to college, you know."

"What makes you think I'll be lonely?"

"Margaret said you might be. And with Gramps married now, he might want to live by himself and not with us anymore."

Brad hadn't thought that far ahead. "You might be right about Grandpa and Opal. I guess they'll probably want a place of their own." And if he married Beth...

"I'll miss him if he moves out. It won't be the same without Gramps. And your cooking isn't as good as his."

"I'll miss him, too." And she was right about the cooking.

"So, are you going to marry Beth?"

"Would you be upset if I did?"

Stacy thought the question over for a moment and then shook her head. "Not anymore. I want you to be happy, and I like Beth. She's been very nice to me, even though I haven't always been nice to her. But you should know that she can't move to Virginia. She told me so."

"You asked Beth to move to Virginia?" Now he really was astounded by his daughter's foresight, not to mention her maturity.

"Well, not just because of her. I'd like Buster and Aunt Iris and Aunt Ivy to come live with us, too. I'm going to miss everyone. And now that Gramps is back, we'll probably be leaving here soon, right?"

Brad nodded. "You've got school beginning again on Monday. You'll have to make up the extra week you missed because of Grandpa's disappearance."

Stacy made a face. "Gross! I'll have tons of home-work. So when are you going to pop the question?" she asked again, unwilling to drop the subject.

"I wanted your blessing first. So I guess since you don't seem to have any objections I'll ask her very soon." He wanted to find the right time, a romantic setting, and most importantly, he needed to buy a ring.

"I hope she says yes. I think Beth would make a pretty cool stepmom."

He was relieved to hear her say that. If Stacy hadn't approved of his marrying Beth, he wasn't sure what he would have done. She'd been through a lot these past few years. "Let's not put the cart before the horse, okay? We don't know if she'll say yes."

"I know she likes you, Dad. Beth always gets all moony-eyed when you're around."

"She does?" He grinned stupidly. "I hadn't noticed."

"That's because you're a guy. Boys don't think like girls do. Aunt Iris told me that. She's been around for a long time, so I figure she knows what she's talking about."

"Do you think Beth's aunts and mother are in favor of us getting married?" Brad hadn't really thought about their objections. But he supposed Beth getting married would uproot everyone's life, not just her own.

Stacy shot him a look of disbelief. "Well, duh! They've wanted you two to get married since we got here. I heard Aunt Ivy tell Aunt Iris that she's going to buy a fancy lavender dress for the occasion. And she's going to wear that big red hat from the women's club she started."

Brad's eyes widened. "I had no idea."

Stacy patted his arm. "Don't look so surprised, Dad. When it comes to weddings, the groom's always the last to know."

CHAPTER SEVENTEEN

TOO SOON AFTER Thanksgiving came a day for good-byes. Beth had bid a tearful farewell to her mother earlier that morning. Margaret had flown home to California to settle her affairs before moving back to Mediocrity, but had promised to return in time for Christmas. Beth was really looking forward to spending the holiday with her, something she hadn't done in years.

Stacy had left an hour ago with her grandfather and Opal. They were driving back to Charlottesville, so she could start school the following day—a prospect the young girl wasn't looking forward to.

After giving strict instructions that they were not to be disturbed, Aunt Ivy and Aunt Iris had secluded themselves in their suite. Beth had no idea what the old ladies were up to, though she suspected that Stacy's departure had upset them more than they cared to acknowledge. Their goodbyes had brought tears to everyone's eyes, including the usually stoic Stacy's.

The only guest remaining at the Two Sisters was Brad, and he intended to leave first thing in the morning.

The inn seemed empty now that everyone had gone, and tomorrow would be even worse. Though she'd tried to prepare herself for Brad's departure, the reality of it was too painful to contemplate. She would miss him terribly. He'd become such an important part of her life in such a short time. And even though she'd still have the inn, her aunts, movies and books to keep her occupied, she wouldn't have the man she loved.

Some things just weren't meant to be.

"Beth, do you have a moment? I need to talk to you. It's important."

Turning away from the blazing fire, she looked up to find the object of her thoughts standing in the doorway of her private sitting room. Her heart ached at the goodbye she knew would be coming.

"Are you all done packing?" She forced a smile, motioning for him to join her on the floor in front of the hearth.

"I've just got the last-minute stuff to toss into my bag tomorrow morning," he replied, sitting down beside her on the braided rug. "Good night for a fire. It's freezing out. I hear we might get snow before morning."

"The weatherman's promising four inches and it's supposed to start late tonight." The first snowfall was something she looked forward to every year. Pristine and pretty, it painted the landscape into a winter wonderland and gave a festive air to the holiday season.

"Stacy's going to be upset that she missed it. She was hoping for snow the entire time she was here. I doubt she'll speak to me after I tell her."

"You'll have to bring her back for a visit, then. We get most of our snow in January and February, so there'll be lots more for Stacy to enjoy."

He nodded, then took a deep breath. "Beth?"

She gazed into his eyes, wondering why he appeared so nervous. "Yes?"

"I love you! I don't want to leave tomorrow, but I've got to get back to my practice."

Though her heart was pounding wildly, she tried to remain calm, knowing if she gave in to her tears, she would never stop crying. "I understand. There's no need to explain. We both knew this day was coming."

"I want you in my life. I want to marry you, so we'll never have to be apart again. I hope you want that, too." Rising to his knees, he reached into the front pocket of his jeans and pulled out a diamond solitaire ring, offering it to her. "Marry me, Beth. I love you. Life isn't worth living if you're not in it."

She gasped, tears filling her eyes at the unexpected gesture. "I don't know what to say. The ring is absolutely beautiful." The diamond dazzled in the firelight, beckoning her to take it from his hand. But she didn't. She couldn't.

"Say yes."

Heaving a deep sigh, she replied, "We've discussed this before, Brad. There are too many obstacles standing between us for our marriage to work."

"Look, I know I made a horrible mistake by accusing you and your aunts of wrongdoing, and I'm very sorry for that. I hope you'll forgive me. I intend to spend the rest of my life making it up to you, if you'll let me."

She stared intently at the ring. "It's not just that, though your lack of trust did hurt. But I've forgiven you."

His smile was filled with relief and gratitude.

"I love you very much, but I've made a life with my aunts. And now my mom's moving here, too. I can't just pack up and leave everything behind. I have responsibilities, to them, to this inn, to the people who work for me. I've made commitments. Surely you can understand that."

"But you made a commitment to me, as well," he reminded her. "You wouldn't have made love with me if you weren't serious about making a life together. I truly believe that."

Beth knew what he said was true. But everything had changed since their first romantic encounter. Reality had reared its ugly head, spoiling all of her dreams. "I've had time to think about things since then."

"What things?"

"Like children, for example. You know how I feel about having children. I've never wanted any. I'm not saying Stacy's not a great kid, because she is. But I don't know if I'm willing or able to take on the role of mother. And I know you want more kids, so don't try and deny it."

"I've never said that."

"You don't have to. You're a pediatrician. You love children. And you should have more. You're a terrific father, Brad. I've seen you with Stacy and I don't think you should be denied the joy of parenting."

"I love you more than I want children, Beth. Yes, it would be nice to have more, but I'm surrounded by children all day, so if you don't want any kids, I can live with that."

And what about the bones? She'd seen his reaction when she'd first told him about them. He'd been horrified, not that she could blame him; that had been her initial reaction upon finding them.

And what if they did turn out to be Lyle McMurtry's? What then? A scandal would ensue. His sterling reputation would be ruined. Their lives would become turmoil. She couldn't allow him to make that sacrifice, no matter how much it hurt.

"I can't marry you, Brad. I'm sorry. And my decision has nothing to do with love, because I love you more than any man I've ever known."

He looked confused by her answer. "Then why won't you marry me?"

"There are still unresolved issues."

"You're talking about those mysterious bones you found in your basement, aren't you?"

She heaved a sigh. "That's part of it. And they're *my* problem to deal with, not yours. And until I can resolve that issue—"

Where the hell was Ellen? Beth had expected to hear back from her by now. She'd left numerous messages on her voice mail, but so far there had been no answer.

"I don't care about any of that. I just want to marry you, make you my wife and grow old with you."

She caressed his cheek. "Oh, Brad, that's a lovely thought. And I do love you. But it would never work, not in a million years."

He put his finger to her lips. "Don't say any more. I'm leaving tomorrow and I don't want our last night together to end on a bad note. I want to make love to you, Beth."

She swallowed. "I want that, too." It would be a memory to cherish for the rest of her life. And memories were all she would have to keep her warm at night.

He reached for her hand and kissed it. "I want you to promise me something first."

"What's that?"

"Promise you'll think about my marriage proposal while I'm gone. Stacy and I will be back during the Christmas break and you can give me your answer then. Okay?"

Seeing the love and hope flaring brightly in his eyes, Beth couldn't deny his request, though she knew she wouldn't change her mind. "All right, I promise."

Brad pulled her into his chest, saying, "There'll never be any woman but you for me." Then he set out to prove it.

His kiss was exquisite, sweet and tender, shattering Beth's calm. Urgency swept through her, and the need to make him hers once more. She thrust her tongue into his mouth, tasting and teasing, and he responded in kind. Blood pounded in her brain and heated every one of her senses until all she could feel was pleasure—intense, mind-numbing pleasure.

"Beth, you drive me crazy!" He pulled up her sweater, unfastening her jeans and removing the remainder of her garments until she was completely naked. Gently he eased her down onto the rug, the firelight playing over her body. "You are the most beautiful woman in the world. Have I told you that lately?"

She smiled softly. "Not nearly enough."

His tongue caressed her sensitive, swollen nipples and they hardened instantly, desire flooding her thighs. Yanking at his shirt, she tried to help him out of it, needing to feel his warm flesh against her own.

"I love you so much it hurts," she whispered.

"I know, love. I know."

Suddenly he was naked and poised over her. The heat from the fire cast a burnished glow over his skin and yearning flared in his eyes. He kissed every inch of her—lips, cheeks, eyelids—and then he tasted from her most intimate place until she was writhing wildly beneath the onslaught of his mouth.

"Please! *Please!*"

Parting her legs, he eased into her burning flesh, entering slowly, exquisitely, filling her and making her flood with need. "Oh!"

He moved slowly at first, then increased his pace, riding her hard and fast and taking her higher and hotter than she'd ever been before. Suddenly, tremors began radiating from the core of her body.

"I love you." He rode the hot tide of his passion and with one last stroke, brought them both to climax.

Beth cried out, nearly passing out from the sheer joy of it before floating back down to earth.

"Wow!" he said, cradling her head in his hands. "That was incredible. You are incredible, not to mention delicious."

She could barely draw a breath. "If this is Nirvana, I'd like to visit more often." She smiled up at him and he kissed her nose.

"We're good together. You have to admit that," he said.

She sighed in complete contentment. "I do."

"Remember those words," he said, kissing her lips lightly. "You're going to be saying them again very soon. I promise you that."

THE SOUND OF SIRENS WOKE Beth from a deep sleep. Bolting out of bed, she hurried to her bedroom window to see sparks rising in the night sky. In the distance, flames shot up from the roof of the barn.

"Oh my god!" Grabbing her robe from the foot of the bed, she dashed into the hallway. Knowing it was useless to call out to her aunts, who were sound sleepers and wouldn't hear her anyway, she rushed upstairs to warn them.

When she reached their suite, she didn't bother knocking but barged into their living room, shouting, "Wake up! Wake up! The barn's on fire!"

Aunt Ivy called out from behind the closed bedroom door. "We're awake, dear. Go and see what's wrong. We'll be fine until you return."

Reaching the back of the house, Beth pounded on Lori's door, shouting for her chef to wake up, and then grabbed her boots and parka from the porch, hurrying out of the house toward the old building.

Five inches of snow had blanketed the ground earlier in the day, and it no longer looked quite as pretty as it had originally. It was slushy, which made walking difficult.

The fire truck was already at the barn when she arrived. Water pumped from the pond spewed forth from thick, long hoses as the volunteer firemen fought the blaze. The heat was intense, and she coughed several times, tears filling her eyes from the smoke, and from the heartache of losing the old barn she'd played in as a child.

Hank, her handyman, drove up. "What happened?" he asked, jumping down from his truck and wrapping his sheepskin jacket close around him. "Lori called me about the fire and I came as quick as I could."

Beth shrugged. "I don't know. I just got here."

Captain Clint Loomis from Mediocrity's volunteer fire department approached them, his expression grave. He was a tall, gangly man with a bushy red mustache that matched the hair under his helmet.

"Hello, Beth, Hank. Sorry about your barn. It's sustained quite a bit of damage, I'm afraid."

"Is the fire out?" she asked, relieved she didn't have horses or other livestock to worry about. The baled hay in the barn was sold to those who did, providing the inn with extra income.

"It's out. We think it started up in the loft. We found a broken kerosene lantern."

Hank shook his head, his brow wrinkling in confusion. "Don't know why that would have been up there. I haven't used kerosene in the barn for years. I bought a battery-operated lantern to use instead, so something like this wouldn't happen. These old buildings are like tinderboxes."

Captain Clint nodded. "Do you have any idea how the lantern got up in the loft, Beth?"

"No. Hank and I discussed using kerosene lanterns and opted against it. We've always been extremely careful. I rarely even use candles in the inn. But if we didn't leave the lantern, then who did?" she asked.

The fireman shook his head. "We didn't find any accelerant other than the kerosene. But that doesn't mean this couldn't be arson."

Beth gasped. "Arson? Why would anyone want to burn down my barn?"

"Don't know. At any rate, arsonists don't need much of a reason to start a fire. We'll need to do a bit more investigating before we figure out what's what. Is the barn insured?"

She nodded. "Yes, but I'm not sure the insurance money will be enough to rebuild it. I've never added to the original policy that my aunts took out years ago. I'm sure building prices have increased since then."

"Skyrocketed, I'm afraid," the captain said before walking back to his truck.

"I'm sorry about this, Beth. I hope you know I had nothing to do with it. I'm always very careful about fire," Hank said.

She patted the older man's arm. "I never thought you did, Hank. I just wonder who'd want to—" And then she remembered.

"What is it? Did you think of something?" he asked.

She shook her head. "No. It's nothing. I'm just thinking out loud. You'd better get home now. I don't want Willow worrying about you."

He grinned at the mention of his wife. "That woman worries about everything, not just me."

Hank departed and Beth made her way back to the house. As she walked, she thought about the man who wanted to get his hands on her property.

John Connor was the kind of man who would stop at nothing to get what he wanted. He'd said as much.

Did that include arson?

THE FOLLOWING DAY, Aubrey opened up the morning edition of *The Mediocrity Messenger* to read that a fire had consumed part of an old barn at the Two Sisters Ordinary. Arson was suspected, though not confirmed, as yet.

"*Tsk! Tsk!* Such a shame," he muttered, smiling

to himself. The fire couldn't have come at a more opportune time, as far as he was concerned.

Refilling his coffee cup from the silver pot that room service had just delivered, he pondered his next move while sipping the hot liquid, finally deciding that he would pay a visit to the inn this afternoon.

But this time he was not going to visit Elizabeth Randall, but instead, pay a call on his dear, duplicitous mother, Iris Swindel, to see if he could convince her to sell the property. And to satisfy his curiosity about whether or not he resembled the woman who gave him life.

"WHERE DO YOU WANT these ornaments, Beth?" Iris held out the box of delicate German glass tree ornaments that had been in her family for ages. She paused to admire the tree her niece was decorating. "What a lovely tree! I think it's our nicest one yet, don't you? Wherever did you find such a big one?"

A tall Douglas fir stood proudly in the center of the front hallway, waiting patiently for Beth to finish stringing tiny white lights on its branches. "Hank found it on the back of our property, so it didn't cost us a thing." Which made the tree even nicer, in her opinion.

"It smells divine. Fir trees are by far my favorite, I think, though I do like pines quite well, too. It's so difficult to decide."

Beth smiled. "Just set those ornaments on the table,

Aunt Iris. Is Aunt Ivy back from town yet? She said she'd help us string the popcorn and cranberry strands." It was a tradition the three women carried out every year without fail, and Beth always looked forward to it. Plus, keeping busy helped to keep her mind off her burned barn and Brad's marriage proposal.

"No, dear. Ivy called and she's not coming home until later this afternoon. She's having lunch with Louise and then they're going Christmas shopping. But we can get started on the strands without her."

"I thought Aunt Ivy was doing all of her shopping online this year." Parcels had already begun to arrive from retail outlets all over the country, thanks to the woman's penchant for shopping.

"She is. But you know how much sister loves to shop. I'm sure she'll find something to buy. Ivy always does."

"How's the new ladies' club coming along? Do you have many members yet?"

Iris grew animated. "Oh, yes! And it's been so much fun. Ivy said that at last count we had eighteen members. In January, we're taking a bus trip to Philadelphia to see the Chippendale dancers. Sister is over the moon about it. I haven't seen Ivy this excited since she discovered that *Peyton Place* had been turned into a movie."

Beth grinned, then rose to her feet, brushing fir needles from her hair. "I'm sure she is. Aunt Ivy's

· been dying to see those dancers for the longest time. And I'm glad you'll be going along with her—I think she needs a chaperone."

Iris nodded. "And don't I know it. I—" The older woman paused, making a face of disgust. "What an awful smell! Why, unless I'm mistaken, it smells like skunk."

Beth sniffed the air, noting the horrible odor. "I think you're right. It's totally gross."

"Now you sound like Stacy." Iris sighed. "I sure do miss that girl. I'm counting the days until—"

"Beth!" Lori called out frantically. "Come into the kitchen at once. There's a creature in here, and it's going to attack me."

Beth and Iris exchanged curious looks before hurrying into the kitchen to see what the inn's chef was so upset about. They found Lori standing on a chair with her hand over her mouth. She was pointing to the sink.

"In there." Her face was white with fright.

"What is it? What's wrong?" The stench was so bad Beth had to cover both her mouth and nose, to avoid inhaling.

"It's in the cabinet, below the sink. I heard scratching noises. I think it's a rodent."

Grabbing the broom, just in case their intruder wasn't a skunk, Beth threw open the doors and a black-and-white furry creature dashed out and ran toward the porch. "Oh, no!"

"Is it a skunk?" Aunt Iris wanted to know.

"Yes! And it stinks to high heaven!" Beth chased the creature toward the back door, shouting, "Quick, Aunt Iris, open the door and let it out. I'll block it from behind so it can't get back in."

Iris did as requested. "Merciful heavens! What a horrible stench! How on earth did a skunk get into the kitchen?"

Beth wondered the same thing and she didn't like where her thoughts were heading—straight for John Connor.

Once she was certain the skunk was gone, Lori hopped down from the chair, an apologetic smile on her face. "Sorry, but I'm deathly afraid of rats. I thought it might be one."

"City girl," Beth teased, and then wished she hadn't opened her mouth, because skunk fumes were going down her throat, making her eyes water.

She smelled a skunk all right, and it wasn't the four-legged variety.

CHAPTER EIGHTEEN

"I'M SORRY, Beth, but the committee has turned down your request for a loan."

Seated in Mr. Pickens's private office decorated with Civil War artifacts and old battlefield maps, Beth fought the urge to cry. Crying, as she'd learned during her marriage to Greg, never solved anything. It just made her eyes puffy.

"I don't understand. I own a business here in town. My family's lived here forever. Why won't you lend me the money? You know I'm good for it."

"I'm afraid it's not that easy, Beth. The loan committee feels that the bank has incurred enough risk, what with the monies you've previously borrowed and your fluctuating income. And the barn fire didn't help matters. It just made some of the members more nervous than they already were."

Phinneas Pickens looked uncomfortable as he delivered the crushing blow to her future and Beth was tempted to ask him to return her damson plum jam. The banker was so not jam worthy, at the moment.

And if it hadn't been for that stupid jam, and her attempt to butter him up, she never would have found those blasted bones in her basement and her life would not have become a soap opera: *As the World Turns on Beth.*

"I was counting on that money, Mr. Pickens, especially now that I've a barn to repair." As she'd feared, the insurance money would not be adequate. "Are you certain the bank won't reconsider? The inn is a valuable commodity to this town. You were at the restaurant's opening—you saw how successful it was."

"It's true we all love historical landmarks. I'm proud to be a member of the historical society. But as you know, the Two Sisters comes with a bit of *baggage,* for want of a better word."

At the veiled insult, she gritted her teeth. "If you're referring to that ridiculous fifty-year-old mystery, Mr. Pickens, it has nothing whatsoever to do with my inn." At least she hoped it didn't. "And it's unfair to hold it against me. I wasn't even alive then."

"If it was up to me, I'd have granted you the loan. I like you, Beth, and I think you've done a fantastic job with the inn. But I don't make the final decision. And these are conservative times. Though the bank would like to help everyone who walks through our doors…" He shrugged. "There's nothing more I can do. I'm sorry."

"Well, I'm not sure what I'll do now because I need that loan to finish off the repairs, landscaping and—"

"There is another option, though I hesitate to mention it because there is some risk involved. But if you're willing to entertain such a risk—"

A kernel of hope blossoming in her chest, Beth leaned forward in her chair. "I'm at the end of my rope, Mr. Pickens. If you have an alternative, I'm willing to listen."

"There is a private investment company the bank's had dealings with in the past. At my request, Trident Corporation has looked over your loan application, and they are willing to lend you the amount of money you require."

Beth's heart lightened. "But that's wonderful!"

"I must caution you that their terms are very stringent. Your property will be put up as collateral and a deed of trust will be issued in Trident's favor. If you should default for any reason, you could lose the inn."

"But if I don't get the loan, I could lose it anyway, so I don't see that I have a whole lot of choice." *Try none.*

"Well, of course, the final decision must be yours, though I want you to be aware of the risk involved. I'd hate to see you lose everything you've worked so hard to build."

"That's not going to happen," she stated firmly.

"Is Trident Corporation a legitimate company? I've never heard of it."

He nodded. "Oh, yes. Like I said, we've had dealings with them before. The bank considers Trident a last resort, as far as loans to our customers are concerned. As part of a larger corporation out of Philadelphia, they are willing to take a bigger investment risk than we are. Trident's been in business for years, and they have a very good reputation. We haven't received any customer complaints thus far."

"What kind of interest rates are we talking about?" When he told her, Beth paled. "That's high!" *Highway robbery, that is.*

"You're not a good risk, so the interest rate is higher. Your credit rating is low, and you haven't been operating an inn for that long, so your track record for success is still suspect. Plus, there were a few items on your credit report that threw up red flags."

"Those were Greg's debts, not mine! He's the one who defaulted on those loans. I paid all of my debts." And she'd worked damn hard to do it.

"But as his wife, you were still responsible." He went on to explain. "In banking everything is numbers. We try to factor in the human element, but sometimes we can't justify making the loan, as in your case. We have an obligation to our depositors, and we take it very seriously. As one of our depositors, you should appreciate that."

Beth understood, but that didn't mean she had to like it. She was between a rock and a hard place and had little choice but to agree to the loan with Trident. She'd just have to work extra hard to pay it off.

"When can I meet with the Trident loan officer? I'd like to get the ball rolling."

"Ms. Logan said she could meet with you today. She's in a meeting at the moment, but should be done—" he glanced at his wristwatch "—in about fifteen minutes, if you care to wait, which I would recommend. She's planning on returning to Philadelphia this afternoon."

"I'll wait. I need to get this over with as quickly as possible. Fifteen thousand dollars will go a long way to solving my problems." Well, some of them anyway. She still had the bones to deal with, and now there was that marriage proposal hanging over her head.

Mr. Pickens nodded. "I'm sorry my hands are tied in this matter, Beth. I would have liked to help you."

She sighed. "Your hands are tied and my feet are going to be held to the fire." Beth just prayed she wouldn't get burned.

KNOCKING ON THE DOOR of the inn, Aubrey felt nervous as he waited for his summons to be answered. He'd already made sure that Beth wasn't at home. In fact, he'd seen both her and Ivy Swindel in town not ten minutes before, so he knew now was a good time to visit.

The front door finally opened and a frail, white-haired woman appeared. She had eyes as blue as his own, and as he gazed into them, he felt a lump form in his throat at the realization that the woman standing before him was his mother. "Are you Iris Swindel?" he asked, tamping down the unwanted emotion that had taken him completely by surprise.

The woman's eyes widened and she replied haltingly, "Yes. Yes, I am. May I help you?"

"The name's John Connor. I came by a few days ago and spoke to your niece. I offered to buy your property. Perhaps she told you?"

Appearing nervous and somewhat flustered, the woman clutched her throat, but Aubrey chalked off her odd behavior to old age. "Yes, she did, Mr. Connor," she finally replied, taking a deep breath and regaining her composure. "But why do you wish to talk to me? Beth's the owner of this inn. My sister and I deeded it over to her several years ago. We merely reside here."

"I'm hoping you can convince Ms. Randall to accept my offer to purchase this property, Ms. Swindel. I want it very badly, for investment purposes."

She shook her head. "I'm afraid you're wasting your time, young man. My niece has made it clear to me that she is not interested in selling, and there's nothing I can say that will change her mind."

"So you've tried, I take it?"

"I encouraged Beth at first, yes. I felt your offer was a generous one and would give my niece a life that she wouldn't have otherwise. But she was adamant about not selling. I'm sorry, Mr. Connor, but there's nothing more I can do."

"I'm sure you have a great deal of influence with Ms. Randall. Perhaps if you spoke to her again, tried to make her see that she's making a mistake…?"

The fragile-appearing old lady suddenly grew steely eyed and determined. "This is our home, Mr. Connor. My sister, Ivy, and I grew up here. It's the only home we have ever known, and my niece is attached to it, as well. I'm sure you can understand our reluctance to part with it."

Sneering snidely, he shook his head. "No, can't say that I can. My home life was nothing to brag about. And I don't grow attached to things or people."

She looked visibly shaken by his answer. "I'm sorry to hear that. But as I said, my niece is not willing to sell. And I've said all I have to say on the matter. Goodbye, Mr. Connor. I hope you have a nice day." She shut the door in his face.

Aubrey couldn't believe that the sweet, soft-spoken old lady had actually slammed the door in his face. But why should he be so surprised? Iris Swindel had shut the door on him many years ago when she'd given him up for adoption. Mommy dearest, it seemed, didn't get too attached to people either.

Thank God she hadn't recognized him. For a few moments, he'd thought she had, but then realized he'd only been entertaining fanciful notions. If Iris Swindel had known his identity, she would have burst into tears and begged his forgiveness, become hysterical and made a nasty scene, like women were prone to do.

As he turned to walk back to his car, Aubrey thought how strange life was sometimes. One of his adversaries had turned out to be his own mother, and she didn't even know it.

FROM THE WINDOW, Iris watched John Connor walk away and the tears she'd been holding back began to fall. He was her son. She'd known it the first moment she'd laid eyes on him and it had been all she could do not to react.

He was the child she had conceived out of wedlock another lifetime ago and had been forced to give away at her parents' insistence. She had named him Aubrey, but she supposed his adoptive parents had decided to change his name.

"Oh, Aubrey, I'm so sorry, so very sorry. Can you ever forgive me?" she whispered, wishing she had the power to roll back time and be a mother to the baby she'd wanted so desperately but had been denied.

Young women of good breeding, especially living in a small town, as Mediocrity was then, didn't bear children out of wedlock, and they certainly didn't keep them. She would have been branded a loose woman, her child a bastard, and they'd have been outcast from society. And she would have brought shame upon her family.

Her father, a Methodist minister, and self-righteous to a fault, had railed at her daily for her sin, evoking God and the Devil, until she'd finally given in to his demands to leave town and have the baby in a discreet location before putting it up for adoption. She'd been young, and frightened, and it had been the second worst moment of her life.

Though Iris had never set eyes on her child before, she knew without a doubt that the man who'd stood before her today was her flesh and blood—her son. For Aubrey, or whatever he called himself, was the spitting image of his father, Lyle McMurtry.

BETH FOUND THE NOTE from her aunt as soon as she returned home. It was on the front hall table near the Christmas tree, and she thought it strange that her aunt had written instead of just calling down the stairs like she usually did when she wanted to see her.

Tossing off her hat, coat and gloves, she hung the garments in the hall closet, and then took the stairs two at a time to her aunts' quarters.

Knocking twice, she entered to find Aunt Iris pacing the floor, hands behind her back and looking more distraught than she'd ever seen her.

"Oh, there you are, Beth! Thank goodness you're home."

"Is something wrong? You look rather frazzled. Where's Aunt Ivy? Did something happen to her? Why isn't she here with you?"

Beth held her breath, until her aunt replied. "I've sent her downstairs to help Lori with dinner. I needed to speak with you alone."

She seated herself beside Iris on the sofa. "Now tell me what's happened to upset you so."

"John Connor came by to see me today."

"What?" Anger surged through Beth and she bolted to her feet. "I'm going over to the hotel this very instant and give that man hell for bothering you. How dare he come here and—"

"Please, dear, sit back down. There's more to the story, I'm afraid."

"He didn't threaten you, did he? I'm certain he's been behind all the problems we've been having lately."

Her aunt looked shocked. "You're referring to the fire?"

"And the skunk incident. But, of course, I have no proof. It's just a gut feeling." And she'd begun to wonder about her septic system failure, too, though maybe she was getting a little paranoid.

Iris sighed. "That doesn't seem to be his style, Beth. Mr. Connor goes after what he wants. He doesn't seem the type to just sneak around."

"You act like you know him."

Iris clasped her hand. "In a way, I do. You see, I knew his mother."

"His mother? But how?"

Taking a deep breath, Iris said, "I'm John Connor's mother, Beth. I knew he was my son as soon as I saw him today."

A moment of silence ensued, while Beth absorbed the startling revelation, then she shook her head, quite confused by the comment. "But I don't understand, Aunt Iris. How could John Connor be your son? We don't even know the man. And you've never been married." Had the woman been hitting the cream sherry?

"That's true. I'm ashamed to admit it, but I conceived a child out of wedlock when I was very young and gave it up for adoption. That child was John Connor, though I had named him Aubrey, after a favorite uncle of mine." She explained her parents' wrath and insistence in the matter. "My mother was of no help—she sided with my father completely. And for that, I never forgave her."

"But who was the father?" Although Beth thought she already knew.

Taking a deep breath, Iris said, "Lyle McMurtry and I were engaged to be married. It was announced in the newspaper and the wedding date had been set. Naturally being young and in love, I thought it would be all right to give in to my fiancé's demands that we consummate our wedding night ahead of schedule. I was so in love and foolishly believed that nothing could mar my happiness."

"I take it things didn't work out as you'd hoped."

Tears filled Iris's eyes and she shook her head. "No, it didn't. Two days before the wedding, Lyle got cold feet and left town. He jilted me."

Beth gasped. "The bastard!"

"In his defense, you should know that when he left he had no idea that I was pregnant."

"But why did he leave?"

"As the wedding date grew near, I'd sensed his misgivings about the wedding, but I'd hoped for the best, as all young ladies do, and dismissed his strange behavior as pre-wedding jitters. I knew Lyle loved me—that was never in question. But Lyle was a man who dreamed big and wanted to see the world. I think the idea of marrying and settling down in one place finally got to him."

"I'm so sorry, Aunt Iris. You must have been devastated."

"It was humiliating, to say the least. And after I discovered I was pregnant I was scared witless. But I was too proud to tell Lyle the truth, to use the baby to tie him to me. He wrote to me, you see, trying to explain his feelings and the reasons for his departure, but I didn't write him back to tell him about the baby. In fact, I never wrote him at all."

"But why? If he'd known, he might have come back and you two—"

Iris shook her head. "I didn't want to marry a man who didn't love me enough to stay." She got up and retrieved a leather box, handing it to her niece. "These are his letters. You can read them later if you like. And here is a photograph of Lyle. He really was a very handsome man. At least, I always thought so."

Beth stared at the black-and-white photo of Lyle McMurtry. She could have been looking at a picture of John Connor. The resemblance was unmistakable, though the real-estate investor was much heavier than his father. "I can see why you knew right away who Connor was. This is amazing." She should have made the connection after seeing the locket.

"Yes, it is. I'm sorry now that I kept Lyle from his son. But I was hurt, and—" She shrugged.

"Does John Connor know that you're his mother?"

"I don't think so, dear. How could he?"

Beth breathed a sigh of relief. Connor was a mean, greedy SOB and wasn't anything like her sweet, kind aunt, who would do anything for anyone. She had a difficult time believing they were mother and son.

"What happened to Lyle?" she asked. "Did you ever see him again?"

"No, never. Lyle ended up in Denver, and that's where he died. Someone—a stranger, I presume—found my address among his personal effects and sent me a copy of the obituary."

"So Lyle is buried in Denver?" Well, thank God for that! But if that was true, then who was buried in her basement?

"Since you're being so honest with me, Aunt Iris, I want to confide something in you."

"Of course, dear. You know you can tell me anything."

"Remember the day I went into the basement to fetch the jam for Mr. Pickens?" Her aunt nodded. "Well, that same day Buster uncovered some bones buried there, and a small gold locket with your and Lyle's picture in it."

Iris's eyes widened. "Oh, you found my locket! I've been looking for it for years. I must have dropped it down there ages ago. The clasp was never very good."

"It's in my room, if you'd like me to get it."

"Maybe later, dear. I've waited this long for it, a few more minutes won't matter."

"I didn't know what to think when I saw the bones and the locket," Beth admitted, and her aunt started to laugh.

"You thought the bones might belong to Lyle? Oh, that's rich! Wait until I tell Sister. She'll be in stitches. That damn rumor has haunted us forever."

"But if you had the obituary, why didn't you show it to the sheriff? It would have cleared up a fifty-year-old mystery." *And it might have helped me get the loan with the bank.* But she had no intention of saying anything to her aunt about that now. The poor woman had enough on her plate at the moment.

"Why should I have done that? I didn't do anything wrong. Just because there are some folks in this town who are small-minded and want to believe the worst about a person, doesn't mean it's true."

Beth's cheeks heated. "But if those bones aren't Lyle's, then whose are they?"

"We had a handyman named Sirus Heslop. He used the cellar to dress out his deer during hunting season. I guess the lazy cuss must have buried the bones down there, instead of disposing of them properly. Sirus was always into shortcuts. He died jaywalking, as a matter of fact." Iris *tsked* her disapproval.

Relief flooded Beth, followed by an equal measure of guilt that she'd suspected her aunts of wrongdoing. "I didn't know what to think when I found the bones and locket, so I guess I'm as guilty as all the other small-minded people in this town."

"Don't worry about it, dear. Ivy and I have always

taken great delight in our notoriety. Being murder suspects is not an everyday occurrence. It's added a little spice to our lives. And I've no doubt that deep down you knew we weren't capable of such a heinous crime."

Beth wrapped her arms around her aunt. "I did, I swear! I defended you to everyone, even Brad."

Iris's eyes widened. "Oh, dear! You mean Dr. Donovan thought—"

"He was worried about his father."

She grinned. "Our behavior must have certainly appeared very peculiar to him, poor man. How is Dr. Donovan? Have you heard from him?"

"He calls me every night before bedtime." *And tells me how much he loves and misses me.* Beth sighed, thinking about the episode of phone sex they had shared last night. It certainly wasn't as good as the real thing, but they'd had fun being naughty.

"Do you love Dr. Donovan, Beth?"

She nodded "Yes. But I can't marry him, even though he's asked me a hundred times."

"Why ever not?"

"I'm not sure I want to be married. I wasn't very good at it, if you remember."

"Trust me, my dear. From someone who has never been, I can tell you that I would have much rather lived my life with the man I loved than all alone."

"But you had Aunt Ivy."

"Yes, and she's a dear. But if I had to choose between Ivy and Lyle, the choice would have been easy. Ivy's my blood, but Lyle was my heart. You should think about that before you go putting everyone else in front of the man you love. Growing old alone isn't much fun."

"But you always seem to enjoy yourself, keep so busy."

"I've made the best of my life that I could. It would have been foolish not to. I have my hobbies and such. But they're a poor substitute for a warm body lying next to you at night. You read romance novels—you should know that."

Noting the twinkle in her aunt's eyes, Beth smiled. "I'm never sure who is more incorrigible— you or Aunt Ivy."

"It's definitely Ivy. I'm tame by comparison."

"I'm not so sure about that," Beth said, kissing her aunt on the cheek. "There are times when you definitely give her some serious competition."

CHAPTER NINETEEN

Two WEEKS PRIOR to Christmas, Beth was in the middle of hanging greenery and lights on the front porch when she spotted the mailman coming up the front walk. He was laden with packages and a stack of holiday cards an inch thick.

"Morning, Beth," Mr. Jessup said with a cheery smile, despite the fact that his cheeks were ruddy from the cold. Beth, who was also chilled to the bone, was grateful she had an occupation that kept her indoors for most of the winter months. "I've got a certified letter for you. You'll have to sign for it," he said.

Climbing down from the ladder, she scribbled her name on the required form and was surprised to find another letter from Trident Corporation. She'd already received her loan documents, along with a check for fifteen-thousand dollars, which she'd promptly given to a contractor for repairs on the barn.

She'd had that money earmarked for many other

things, but the barn was now the most pressing matter, especially with inclement weather and cold temperatures upon them.

"Those garlands and bows look mighty pretty. Christmas will be here before you know it and I'm not the least bit ready. Good to see you're getting a jump on things. You have a good day now."

"Stay warm, Mr. Jessup," she said, waving goodbye, and then moving into the house to deposit her mail.

Reading the certified letter from Trident, her mouth dropped open and she stifled the scream threatening to erupt. "This can't be! There has to be some mistake." She read it again, just to make sure she hadn't misunderstood.

Dumping her outerwear on the floor, she marched into her office and dialed the number on the letterhead, asking to speak to Ms. Logan, the loan officer she'd dealt with. A moment later, the woman came on the line.

"This is Nora Logan. How may I help you, Ms. Randall?"

"I've just received a letter stating that I've defaulted on my loan. There must be some mistake, Ms. Logan. As you know, my first payment isn't due until the end of the month."

"Hold on." There was a pause, some shuffling of papers, and then the woman came back on the line and said, "Have you read your loan documents carefully, Ms. Randall? I have them right here in front of me and you've agreed to make bimonthly payments. That's every two weeks, not once a month."

Beth gasped. "I've never heard of such a thing. Surely that can't be legal."

"I assure you it's very legal. We are a private investment company, not a bank or mortgage company. And if you recall, I went over the details of your loan, including interest rate and repayment schedule, when you signed the final documents. The repayment schedule clearly stipulates bimonthly payments. We made full disclosure to you."

"But I don't remember you mentioning it. Perhaps you're mistaken." Beth would have remembered such an odd requirement.

"I don't usually make mistakes, Ms. Randall. I have your signature right here, agreeing to our terms. I'm sorry you didn't understand the nature of this high-risk loan, but the stipulations are very clear."

"But—"

"Because you have defaulted on your loan payment, you will have thirty days to pay off the loan plus interest in full, or risk losing your property, which you have put up as collateral against the monies loaned to you."

"Thirty days! But that's impossible." There was no way she could repay that much money in such a short time. Hell, if she'd had that much to begin with, she wouldn't have needed the stupid loan.

"I'm sorry, Ms. Randall, but since you were not considered a good credit risk we were forced to make the repayment terms stricter than we usually do, to protect ourselves. Didn't Mr. Pickens explain any of this to you? He knows our policies very well."

Beth nodded mutely, recalling the banker's warning. "But I've already spent the money. I need more time to repay the debt." Like the rest of her life.

"I'm sorry," Ms. Logan restated, though she didn't sound the least bit contrite, "but you have thirty days to repay or we will be forced to foreclose. This is company policy, and there's nothing further I can do."

A strange ringing began in Beth's ears and then everything went black; she landed on the floor in an unconscious heap.

WHEN SHE OPENED HER eyes a few minutes later, she found herself in the parlor. Both of her aunts were hovering over her, staring down at her with concern. The two women had dragged her lifeless body to the parlor and had deposited her on the sofa.

"What happened?" she asked, and then remembered, tears filling her eyes.

"You fainted, dear," Aunt Ivy said, patting her wrist. "We were on our way to the kitchen when we saw you lying on the floor. You gave us the most dreadful fright, I promise you that. Shall we call the doctor?"

Beth shook her head. "Not unless he has fifteen thousand dollars to loan me." She explained about the letter from Trident and her subsequent telephone conversation with the loan officer. "I'm totally screwed."

"I realize things look rather bleak right now, Beth dear," Aunt Iris said, caressing her cheek and ignoring the kind of language she didn't normally approve of, "but rest assured we will find a solution to this problem."

She sat up. "I appreciate your trying to make me feel better, but there is no way I can repay the loan in thirty days. Perhaps you didn't understand, but I used this inn as collateral and they're going to take it away from me...from us."

Beth's eyes filled with tears, Ivy's with determination. "That is not going to happen. You must have faith, Beth. We are not without contacts and resources in this town. And we'll use them."

"Do you have fifteen thousand dollars, by any chance, or know someone who does?"

"Well, no," Iris admitted, "I'm afraid we don't. But we do know that the people in this town, for all their peculiarities, love this historical house as much as we do. I have no doubt that once Hilda Croft and the historical society hear of our plight—"

"And don't forget the mayor," Ivy interjected.

"And Mayor Lindsay," Iris added. "They will all come to our aid, you'll see."

Beth hoped her aunts knew what they were talking about, because right about now she needed a knight on a white charger, hopefully one with fifteen thousand dollars to spare.

LATER THAT EVENING, Beth was in her sitting room, brooding in front of the fire, trying to figure out what to do about the impending foreclosure when the phone rang. She answered on the first ring. It was Brad. The sound of his voice made her heart ache.

"How are things?" he asked.

"Not good. In fact, they're terrible." She went on to explain about the letter she'd received from the investment company.

"Those bastards! I wish I'd been there when you'd received that letter. I'd have told them where to stick it." She heard his sigh. "I feel helpless being so far away."

"Just hearing your voice makes me feel better," Beth admitted. "But enough about me. How are Stacy and the newlyweds doing?"

"Everyone's fine. Stacy's counting the days until Christmas break, and so am I." His voice grew husky with desire. "But for entirely different reasons, of course. It won't be long now."

She laughed, and he added, "Dad and Opal

won't be coming with us. They're still looking for a house to buy."

"But I thought they were happy living with you."

Sounding a bit evasive, he replied, "I guess they want their privacy."

"That's understandable, especially since they've just gotten married."

Suddenly Brad's tone grew serious. "Listen, Beth, I can loan you the money to repay your debt. You can pay me back whenever you can. I'm not in any rush for it."

"That's very kind of you, Brad, but I won't let you do that. I know you've been saving for Stacy's college education and I won't touch her money. Don't worry. I'll figure something out."

"I'll be there very soon and then we can figure it out together—two heads and all that. I want to help."

"I appreciate your support, really I do, but I've gotten myself into this mess and I'm going to get myself out." She wouldn't take Brad's money, no matter how desperate she was. And she was pretty damn desperate!

"Well, if you change your mind, the offer is always open."

"Thank you. That means a lot to me."

"I love you, Beth. I want to be there for you, now and forever."

"I know." Why couldn't she commit, tell him what

he wanted to hear? He was such a kind, decent man. And she loved him so much. But she was still afraid. And now that her life had become even more of a disaster she couldn't burden him with that. It wouldn't be fair.

"Not to change the subject," he said, "but have you heard back from your friend about the bones?"

Beth's mood lightened instantly. Finally, she had something positive to report. "There's no need for Ellen to get back to me. Aunt Iris explained everything." She told him the story that her aunt had relayed and he chuckled.

"Don't I feel like a damn fool?"

"You and me both. I did my share of eating crow."

"Those poor old ladies. To think they've been unjustly persecuted all these years for a crime that never even existed."

"From what I gather, they've enjoyed being infamous. After all, they had the proof to exonerate themselves and chose not to use it."

"I can't wait to get a look at this John Connor. Hard to believe he's Iris's son."

"He's a disgusting pig. I hate him!"

"Don't be too hard on him, Beth. He's probably always sensed that he was different from his adoptive family, but never knew why, until now. Kids are intuitive about stuff like that. His childhood might not have been a loving one, and that could be the reason he's like he is. It's not easy for any kid to understand why his real parents didn't want him, no matter the explanation."

Beth grew alarmed. "Do you think he knows Aunt Iris is his mother?"

"It's entirely possible. I don't believe in coincidence. My guess is that he learned the truth and came to Mediocrity to sort it all out. He'd be curious to find out about his birth parents."

"I hope my aunt won't be hurt by this situation more than she already has been. Her guilt is tremendous."

"Iris is a tough old gal. She can take whatever life throws at her, even a vindictive son."

"I certainly hope you're right, because I won't let Connor hurt my aunt, no matter what I have to do to prevent that from happening."

THE FOLLOWING MORNING, Lori was bent over in front of the oven, taking out a batch of Christmas cookie cutouts when she heard the back door open and close. Thinking it was Beth, who'd come to discuss the menu for the restaurant's Christmas dinner, she called out over her shoulder,

"Be right with you, Beth." She placed the cookie sheet on the counter and turned. But it wasn't the innkeeper who'd come to visit and her mouth dropped open, her eyes widening at the visage of Bill Thackery—the man she'd hoped never to see again.

His smile was borderline nasty. "Hello, Lori. Judging by your shocked expression, I'm guessing you didn't expect to see me here."

Panic filled her. Damn! She didn't need this right now. "What are you doing here?" Bill never took time off from the restaurant during the holiday season. He was a control freak and ran his kitchen like an army drill instructor, which, of course, was one of the reasons she'd left.

"I think you know the answer to that question." He came farther into the room, taking off his jacket and seating himself at the table, as if he belonged there. "Mind if I have a cup of coffee?" He didn't wait for her response but poured himself one.

"Help yourself," she said, unable to mask her sarcasm. "I suppose you've come for your recipes and knives?"

He stared at her intently. "They're mine, after all, but not the reason I'm here. I came for you, Lori. We were a great team. I want you back."

His answer surprised her—Bill never needed anyone. She tried to keep her calm. "I can't work for you anymore, Bill. I need to be on my own. I'm sure you can understand that."

"I can. But what I don't understand is why you left the way you did, with no word of explanation and stealing my belongings. I thought we were friends."

What was she supposed to say, that she couldn't

stand working with him day after day, that he stifled her creativity, made her feel stupid and inept? He'd probably laugh in her face. Bill wasn't a man who accepted excuses.

"I admit my behavior was childish. But I did help you develop some of the recipes. They were partly mine, though you never gave me credit for them."

His right brow arched. "And the knives?"

"The knives were a whim." Because she knew he loved them so much. "I took them to spite you, I guess."

"Spite me? Was it really so awful working for me?"

"The truth? Yes. You stifled my creativity! You of all people should understand that."

"Do you like your new position?" he asked, and she nodded enthusiastically.

"I love it! I have total control over the kitchen and menu preparation, though I do consult with the owner, to make sure we remain on the same wavelength."

"That's probably wise."

"How did you find me?" Though she already knew he'd read the article about the inn in the newspaper.

"The *Inquirer*. That was quite a nice article. You and the inn are already gaining a good reputation. It's become *the* topic of conversation in Philadelphia food circles."

His words pleased her. "Beth will be happy to hear that."

"Will she also be happy to hear that her chef is a thief? When word gets out, it might not be too good for business."

Her eyes flashed fire. "You bastard! Even you can't be that vindictive." But she knew he could. "I won't let you ruin everything Beth's worked so hard to establish."

"Then come back to Philadelphia with me and we'll call it even. Nothing has to be said about the stuff you stole."

She shook her head. "You don't get it, do you? We have artistic differences, Bill. We're just too headstrong and opinionated to be working together. We argue about everything. I can't do it anymore."

Rising to his feet, he crossed the room to where she stood by the stove, reaching out his hand to caress her cheek, which surprised her. He'd never touched her in that, or any other, way before.

"And here I thought arguing with you was fun, a way to left off steam. Creative people always have differences, Lori. And I care about you. I don't want to lose you."

Her eyes widened. "Because I'm a good chef?"

"Of course you're a good chef. I trained you, didn't I? But there are…other reasons. I—" He looked vastly uncomfortable and turned away to reclaim his seat.

"What other reasons?" Could Bill have feelings

for her that had nothing to do with friendship or work? Lori felt as if she'd been poleaxed. In all the time they'd worked together, he'd never even hinted at forming a personal relationship.

And how would she have felt if he had? She wasn't sure.

Bill shrugged. "There's no reason for us to break up a successful working relationship, Lori. You're just being stubborn. Now say you'll come back to Philadelphia with me."

"I can't. I just told you that."

"I'm not leaving here until you change your mind."

"Are you crazy? Who's going to run the Philadelphia restaurant if you're not there? This is the Christmas season. Have you lost your mind?"

"No more than you've lost yours."

Lori heaved a deep sigh. "I won't be bullied any longer, Bill. I'm an independent woman and I'm making a life for myself here. I won't leave. I have responsibilities and people who are counting on me."

"A life based on lies and half-truths?"

"Everything I told Beth was true. And my talent speaks for itself."

There was a spark of admiration in his eyes. "So you finally grew a spine, huh?"

"What the hell is that supposed to mean?"

He jumped up from the table, crossed the room in three long strides and grasped her shoulders, looking intently into her eyes. "It means—" He took a deep breath. "It means I miss you, goddammit! And that's all I'm going to say." He released his hold and spun on his heel.

Lori's mouth dropped open as she watched him storm out of the room. And for the first time since meeting Bill Thackery, she could think of nothing to say.

CHAPTER TWENTY

TRUE TO THEIR WORD, the Swindel sisters enlisted the help of Hilda Croft and Mayor Lindsay. Two days later, the mayor called a town meeting to discuss how to save the Two Sisters Ordinary.

Beth was seated in the front row of the packed council chamber, her aunts seated on either side of her lending their love and support. "I can't believe you pulled this off," she whispered to them. "I'm so grateful to both of you."

"Not everyone in this town thinks we're a couple of loonies," Iris stated, making her sister chuckle.

"A good friend is worth far more than riches, Beth dear," Ivy said, "but right now I wouldn't mind having the riches." She winked at her niece.

The gavel banged, gaining everyone's attention, then recording secretary Lilly Reynolds announced, "The meeting of the Mediocrity Town Council for Historic Preservation will now come to order, the honorable Mayor Frank Lindsay presiding."

Mayor Lindsay approached the podium and

tapped on the microphone, which screeched with feedback. "It's been brought to my attention," he began, "that one of, if not, *the* most important homes in our town is in jeopardy of falling into the hands of developers. I regret that we did not act soon enough to declare this home a historical landmark."

Gasps and loud murmurs ensued, and then someone called out, "Damn carpetbaggers!"

Beth turned to see who had made the comment, and her gaze fell upon none other than John Connor, who smiled spitefully, making her blood boil. Damn parasite! she thought, turning away quickly and saying nothing to her aunts about the man's attendance, hoping to avoid upsetting Iris.

"In order to save the inn we must raise in excess of fifteen thousand dollars," the mayor explained, "and we only have thirty days in which to do it. Does anyone have any comments or suggestions as to how we can accomplish this?"

A man at the back of the room stood to be recognized, and the mayor pointed at him. "Go ahead, sir."

"My name is Aubrey Fontaine, though some of you know me as John Connor."

Iris gasped aloud, and Beth reached over and clasped her hand, giving it a gentle squeeze.

"I am the CEO and owner of Trident Corporation."

"Oh my God!" Beth exclaimed, suddenly feeling sick to her stomach.

"I hold the lien on the inn and would like to develop the land into an exclusive upscale resort."

"Over my dead body!"

"Ivy, sit down." Iris tugged her sister's sweater hem. "You are making a spectacle of yourself."

"As I was saying," Aubrey continued, "I will not allow Ms. Randall any additional time to pay back the loan. Either she pays the note in full or the inn and property revert to me. It's what she agreed to."

"You crook," someone shouted, and many of the town's residents nodded in agreement.

"Let me assure you that this is all perfectly legal." Trident's CEO looked smug as hell. "And what I intend to do with the property will be very good for this community. I'm going to put Mediocrity on the map. You'll all be making a lot more money, and—"

Loud booing and derogatory comments followed his announcement and Aubrey sat down.

The mayor took control of the meeting, purposely ignoring the man's comments. "I propose that we hold a series of fund-raisers to help raise the money Beth needs to retain control of the inn. Does anyone *else* have any ideas?"

Ivy jumped up again. "As you know, I am the president of the Red Hat and Roses Club. Our members intend to hold a bake sale next week. Fern Reynolds is making pecan pies, and you all know how good they are. And Iris and I will prepare our award-winning coconut cakes. I hope everyone will buy generously."

Max Greeley, accompanied by his wife, stood. "Margie and I are donating the proceeds of twenty haircuts to this good cause, so come on over to the barbershop and get your hair cut. Everyone's welcome to participate, not just the men."

"What about us bald guys?" Roger Owens, the town's pharmacist, asked, making everyone laugh.

"You'll get a deluxe scalp massage," Margie informed him. "Or a manicure, if you're tender headed."

Ideas to raise money began pouring in from various individuals in the audience and the secretary began taking notes as fast as she could write.

The lump forming in Beth's throat had grown so large at the generous offers she could barely swallow. Tears filled her eyes, but she didn't start crying in earnest until the side door opened and she turned to find Brad coming toward her with a disarming grin on his face.

Smiling widely, Ivy scooted over to make room for him, and Beth could hardly believe her eyes. "What are you doing here?" she asked. "I just spoke to you a few hours ago."

"I'll explain everything later. I told you I wanted to help." He squeezed her hand. "Trust me."

"But—"

Suddenly, Brad stood. "I'm Dr. Bradley Donovan from Charlottesville, Virginia. I've been fortunate enough to stay at the Two Sisters Ordinary recently and have gotten to know Beth Randall and her two lovely aunts."

Ivy and Iris tittered at the compliment.

"It's heartwarming to see that so many of you are willing to give your time and efforts to saving this historic building, which Beth has worked so hard to turn into a first-class establishment. And so I would like to start the fund-raiser off by donating one thousand dollars."

Beth gasped and clutched her throat. "Brad!"

"I hope others will join me in this worthwhile cause. I'm going to be visiting each of you in the next few days to collect your donations in person."

A huge cheer erupted and Beth's mouth fell open, then she covered her face and began sobbing, unable to believe how kind and generous everyone was being, especially Brad.

Wrapping his arm about her shoulders, Brad lowered his voice and said, "We're going to kick that bastard's ass, you wait and see." Noting Iris's shocked expression, he added, "I'm sorry, Iris. I was speaking metaphorically."

"Don't worry about me, Dr. Donovan. You take

good care of Beth and see that she gets home safely this evening. I have someone I need to talk to."

"Aunt Iris, don't! He might be cruel. I don't want you going alone."

"Posh!" She waved away Beth's objection with a flick of her wrist. "I've handled bullies all my life, dear. I'm not afraid of Aubrey Fontaine. I'll be home as soon as I can, but don't wait up for me."

"Do you want me to come with you, sister?" Ivy asked, equal measures of worry and respect shining in her eyes. "I don't think you should—"

Iris shook her head. "No. This is something I have to do alone."

IRIS WAS EXTREMELY NERVOUS when she entered the Excelsior Hotel a short time later. She had no idea if Aubrey Fontaine was in residence, or whether he would agree to talk to her, but she'd decided to wait all night if necessary, because she intended to talk to him. She might not be successful in making him understand why she had given him up for adoption all those years ago, but she was going to have her say, one way or another.

It was painfully obvious that Aubrey was trying to get back at her. And she couldn't allow her niece, who had worked so hard to turn that dilapidated old house into something worthwhile, to take the brunt of his wrath, which rightfully belonged to her.

At the front desk, she spoke to one of her former

students, George Worman, asking if Aubrey Fontaine was presently in his room.

"He is, Ms. Swindel, but I can't give out his room number without Mr. Fontaine's permission. It's hotel policy—"

"Listen to me, George, I knew you when you stuck gum in your classmate's hair and started a fire in the boy's bathroom. And I won't take some mealy-mouthed excuse about why you can't give me some-one's room number. I intend to surprise Mr. Fontaine, not murder him."

The graying man's eyes widened. "Yes, ma'am." He gave her the information she needed and Iris nodded.

"Thank you, George. It's nice to see that you've acquired a bit of common sense over the years. I was beginning to wonder."

"Yes, ma'am, thank you, ma'am."

Iris smiled as she made her way to the elevator. It wasn't often that she got to play the role of self-righteous schoolmarm, and it was certainly fun, es-pecially with George, who'd been the terror of her sixth-grade history class and the cause for many of her white hairs.

As she approached the suite her former student had indicated, she paused outside the door and took a deep breath. No doubt Aubrey would not be happy to see her, and she could hardly blame him.

"Only one way to find out, Iris," she muttered to herself, tapping lightly on the door several times.

A moment later an irritated voice rang out. "Who is it? I'm busy. I don't recall ordering room service, so go away."

"This isn't room service, Aubrey. It's Iris Swindel. I'd like to speak to you."

The door opened and Aubrey Fontaine stood in the threshold, wearing a white terry-cloth robe and looking quite surprised. "I was getting ready for my bath. Sorry I'm not dressed appropriately for visitors."

"May I come in? I promise not to stay too long."

He ushered her into the living room, indicating the brocade sofa. "Would you care for some coffee or tea?"

Well, at least the man had some manners. "No, thank you."

"So what can I do for you, Ms. Swindel? Have you changed your mind about selling the inn? It's too late, you know. I don't need to buy it from you now."

Iris shook her head. "I'm well aware of that, Aubrey, and I think we both know why I'm here. I recognized you the moment I laid eyes on you. You are the spitting image of your father."

His cheeks filling with color, he looked very uncomfortable. "My father is dead."

"That's correct."

"I was speaking of my adoptive father."

"I'm sorry to hear that. Please accept my condolences. Your real father is also dead. Lyle McMurtry died many years ago."

"Why should that concern me now?"

"Because, as I'm sure you know, I'm your birth mother and I've come to explain why you were given up for adoption. I'm certain you've wondered over the years."

"Actually, I found out only a short time ago that I was adopted. It was after my mother died that I discovered my original birth certificate and some old newspaper clippings in her desk. Neither she nor my father ever told me."

Iris's heart ached at the pain registering on his face. "I'm very sorry about your mother and the fact that you were never told about the adoption. You must have been upset by the discovery."

"I was more shocked than upset. But it made me understand a bit better why my mother was always so aloof, so cold toward me. I'm not sure she ever loved me. Most likely it was my father's idea that they adopt a child."

Iris heaved a sigh, trying not to let guilt overwhelm her. "I'm sure your mother loved you. People just have different ways of showing affection. And she did leave you the means to finding out about your birth parents."

"Why didn't you want me?" he asked, unable to mask the hurt in his eyes.

"Oh, Aubrey, I did want you, very much. But I got pregnant out of wedlock and then Lyle ran off and jilted me shortly before we were to be married. My parents were adamant that I could not raise you by myself, though I begged them to let me. I even offered to move away, to spare them my disgrace, but they wouldn't hear of it."

His brow lifted. "That seemed rather harsh, under the circumstances."

"My father was a minister and a hard man. He saw things in black and white, never gray. I imagine he thought he was doing the best thing for me. But it broke my heart. At the hospital, you were taken away before I could get a glimpse of you. I never expected to find you." It would have been easier if she hadn't, because now she had to deal with a son who obviously hated her, and she didn't know how to fix that.

"So you've come here to clear your conscience, is that it? Well, you needn't have bothered. None of this matters to me anymore. I'm a practical man. What's done is done. I don't believe in crying over spilled milk."

"I'm sure you don't think very well of me, and that's understandable. But you shouldn't take your bitterness and anger out on my niece. Beth has never done anything to harm you. She didn't even know I had a son until after your visit to the inn. I decided then that I needed to tell her the truth."

He smiled, but it never reached his eyes. "So that's what this visit is all about—your precious niece. I should have known. Well, let me assure you that when it comes to business I don't let emotion rule my head. I'm not pursuing your property for revenge, but because it's a good investment. I see the potential for making lots of money down the road. People get hurt in life and in business. That's just the way it is."

"But don't you see it doesn't have to be that way? You could change the terms of the loan agreement and allow Beth more time to pay off the monies owed to you."

"I don't care about the money. I want the property. You're sitting on a gold mine and you don't even realize it."

Iris heaved a sigh. "You look so much like your father, Aubrey. And I can see that you've inherited many of Lyle McMurtry's selfish traits. I loved him more than anything in the world, and he ruined my life, you see. He stole my love, my child, my chance at happiness, and he never thought another thing about it.

"Lyle thought only of his own happiness, his desires and needs." Why had it taken her so long to admit that? She'd been grieving for a man who was really just a selfish bastard. "I can't allow you to do the same, Aubrey. No matter what I have to do I will protect my family."

"Are you threatening me, *Mama?*" he asked, his eyebrows lifting.

"Why yes, *son,* I do believe I am."

"I THINK YOU'RE MAKING a huge mistake. The duck will be too expensive. You'll be much better off going with chicken or game hens."

Lori stared daggers at Bill, who'd insisted on helping her, despite her vehement protests, with the two-hundred-dollar-a-plate benefit dinner they were giving on Saturday evening. "I'm the chef here, in case you've forgotten, and I've decided on duck."

He shook his head. "I'm telling you, Lori—"

"This is what I'm talking about. You are too damn opinionated, and we don't see eye-to-eye on anything. It's a recipe for disaster as far as a working relationship goes. Surely you must realize that."

He held up his hands in surrender. "Okay, okay, I'll keep my mouth shut. We'll have the duck."

She smiled to herself, surprised he'd given in so easily. Bill prided himself on being right one hundred percent of the time. "Good. And we'll do a bing cherry sauce and maybe some wild rice."

"Or we could do risotto."

"Or risotto." She sighed, wondering why she had to work with such an exasperating man.

Beth entered the kitchen just then and grinned at the sight of the two chefs, who'd obviously been arguing, again. That's all they'd been doing since Bill Thackery's arrival a week ago.

"Everything all set for Saturday night?" she asked, and Lori looked up, her cheeks rosy in embarrassment.

"We're sold out. Bill and I were just going over the last-minute details of the dinner. We want to make sure everything goes off without a hitch."

"I appreciate your helping us out, Mr. Thackery. Lori's told me a bit about your expertise in the kitchen. I'm honored to have such a celebrated chef cooking for us."

He looked pleased by her compliment. "It's Bill, and I'm happy to do it. Helping Lori gives me an excuse to stay here a while longer. I like to think she needs me, though I know she doesn't. She's an excellent chef in her own right."

Lori's cheeks flushed again. Bill wasn't one to lavish compliments on anyone, but he'd been heaping them on her this past week. Now that she was on her own turf, and in charge, things between them seemed different—better. In those rare moments when they weren't disagreeing, she actually enjoyed his company. He had a great sense of humor, and she'd seen a side of him he hadn't shown before—a softer, less combative side. Perhaps not having to deal with the day-to-day stress of running the Philadelphia restaurant had improved his disposition.

"How's Brad doing with the door-to-door collections?" Lori asked finally.

"The man is amazing. I'm not sure what Brad's been telling folks, but he's already raised over two thousand dollars. When you add in his donation of a thousand that makes three thousand he's collected so far."

"Wow! That is impressive," Lori agreed. "How much have you taken in altogether?"

Beth tapped her chin while she calculated the donations. "Let's see, the bake sale my aunts held collected close to a thousand dollars." She had a feeling Ivy and Iris browbeat their friends into purchasing more than they wanted to.

"Max and Margie donated five hundred and the historical society has given us five thousand dollars." Ellen had finally arrived home from her extended working vacation and had sent Beth a check for one thousand dollars, with a lovely note of encouragement, and even better, a copy of the medical examiner's report—the bones in Beth's cellar were *not* human.

"The money we'll collect from Saturday evening's dinner should put us almost at goal." At least, that's what she hoped, because if it didn't, she wasn't sure what else she could do to raise the money. The well was running dry.

"That's terrific," Bill said. "You're a lucky woman

to have such great supportive friends. I don't think we realize how important our friends are until we lose them." His eyes turned toward Lori, who blushed.

Beth nodded. "I do feel fortunate and I'm so very thankful to everyone. In fact, I'm starting to feel a little bit like George Bailey in *It's A Wonderful Life*. 'No one is a failure who has friends.' Remember that line?"

Bill nodded. "I sure do. That's one of my favorite holiday movies."

"Mine, too," Lori admitted, smiling at Bill, who winked at her.

"Hey, you two have actually agreed on something," Beth remarked with a grin. "I think we're finally making some progress."

LATE SATURDAY NIGHT, after the benefit dinner was over and everyone had left, Beth and Brad were sequestered in her private sitting room counting the receipts.

After all of the expenses were paid, including food, wine and help, Beth figured they'd clear about three thousand dollars, which would still leave them short.

"It won't be enough," she said with a deep sigh, gazing over at Brad. "I'll still be short by about two thousand dollars."

"I can make up the difference," he said. "I don't want you to worry about it."

It was a tempting offer, but one Beth couldn't accept. "I won't take any more of your money. You shouldn't have donated the thousand, though I'm grateful for it. Don't worry. I'll find another way."

He lifted her chin with his forefinger. "Did I happen to mention what a stubborn woman you are, Ms. Randall?"

She smiled. "Once or twice, Dr. Donovan."

"Did I also mention how much I love you?"

"*Hmm.* Once or twice."

He kissed her then, a deep soul-searching kiss that sent her pulses racing and her toes curling upward. "Just in case you've forgotten."

Beth sighed. "You're a wonderful man, Bradley Donovan. I feel lucky to have you in my life, and I love you very much. I hope you know that."

"Then why won't you marry me?"

Say yes, she told herself, but Beth knew she couldn't. She still had debts to pay and family matters to attend to. "Please don't pressure me, Brad. I have so much on my plate right now. And to top it all off my mother called to say her affairs in California are settled and she'll be arriving next week. I haven't told her about the loan problem. I didn't want to hear her lecture on how irresponsible I am."

"You should give Margaret the benefit of the doubt. She might be willing to help you."

"Maybe, but I don't want to borrow money from

her. She's already incurred a lot of expense with the move she's making, and now that she's retired…"

"I understand."

She caressed his cheek. "I thought you would."

"I have an idea," he said. "Why don't we grab a bottle of wine and go up to my room? I'm sure I could think of ways to take your mind off your troubles."

She kissed him softly. "You're the doctor, and that sounds like the perfect prescription."

CHAPTER TWENTY-ONE

BETH HAD ONE WEEK LEFT to come up with the rest of the money to pay off the loan or her inn would be forfeit.

As she walked alone down by the edge of the pond, she felt the guilt of her stupidity weighing heavily on her shoulders. The cold air slapped her cheeks, making her nose run, and she wiped it with the back of her sleeve.

She should never have taken out such a risky loan, never put the inn up as collateral. Her foolish actions had put everything she loved in jeopardy—the Two Sisters Ordinary, her aunts' welfare, even her relationship with Brad.

But hindsight was always twenty-twenty, as Aunt Ivy was fond of saying. And there wasn't much she could do at this point but eat humble pie and borrow the money from her mother or Brad, something she was loath to do.

"Beth! Beth! I've come to get you. Dad says you're needed in the parlor right away."

She waved at Stacy, who'd arrived with her grandparents the previous evening. Beth had been surprised by how happy she'd been to see the young girl again. She had missed her infectious smile and nonstop questions. Her aunts, too, had been over the moon. They'd all missed Stacy a great deal.

"I'll be right there," she called out, wondering what catastrophe awaited her. At this point, she wasn't sure she could take any more bad news. Her aunts counseled that God tested a person only as much as he or she could take. Well, Beth was definitely flunking her present test, and she didn't know what God thought of that.

"Okay. I'll go and let everyone know," Stacy told her, running back toward the house.

Beth's brows drew together. *Everyone?* What did she mean by that? With Bill Thackery, Brad and Stacy, the elder Donovans, who had arrived late last evening, and her mother, nearly all of the rooms at the inn were occupied.

It was fortunate that the three couples she had previously made reservations for had canceled. Normally that would have freaked her out, especially this time of year, but not now. This year she was grateful to be surrounded by people she knew, just in case she experienced a nervous breakdown, which, at this point, seemed rather likely.

Wiping her feet on the back porch mat, Beth hung up her jacket. Then she grabbed a handful of cookies off the platter on the kitchen table and made her way into the parlor, where she found all of the Donovans, Lori and Bill, Aunt Iris and her mother in attendance. It looked as if they were having some type of meeting.

"What's going on?" she asked, handing Stacy a gingerbread cookie and then one to Bill, who was holding out his hand and looking hopeful.

"My son's told me about your difficulty, Beth. Opal and I would like to help. We've put some money aside and—"

She shook her head. "Oh, no, Mr. Donovan! I couldn't accept your money. That wouldn't be right."

"Of course you can," Opal insisted. "Why, we're practically family. And family always helps each other. I'm sure your aunt will back me up on this."

Smiling in conspiratorial fashion, Aunt Iris nodded. "That's true, dear."

Beth's eyes widened at the woman's assumption and glanced over at Brad, who was grinning like a hyena.

Robert handed her a check for five hundred dollars. "It's not much, but we hope it helps."

"It will help very much. Thank you so much. I can't begin to tell you how grateful I am."

Stacy stepped forward. "My dad told me you were

in trouble and needed help to save the inn, so I took all of my pennies down to the bank and cashed them in. It's only twenty dollars, but you can have it, Beth."

Beth's heart squeezed. "Oh, Stacy, thank you!" She hugged the child to her, tears filling her eyes. "I don't know what to say. That was such a nice thing for you to do."

"I know," Stacy admitted, making Beth smile.

Then Aunt Iris handed her niece an envelope. "Mr. Pickens said to give you this, dear, and tell you that he feels just awful about what happened. It's a hundred dollars. I'm sure he would have given more, but Finnola is a tightwad and always has been. I really can't abide that woman."

Beth's mouth dropped open. *Mr. Pickens* had given her money? That was too astonishing for words.

"Before you go into overload, honey," her mother said, rising from the sofa and coming forward. "I want you to know that I paid a visit to your miserable ex-husband and his wife. Their house is the most appalling thing I've ever seen, by the way." Margaret shook her head. "Anyway, Greg has donated four hundred dollars for the cause."

"Greg Randall gave me money?" Now that was the most shocking thing of all! Her ex-husband was the cheapest man on earth and probably beyond; unless, of course, he was spending the money on himself or something he deemed an absolute necessity, like sports equipment.

"Yes, apparently the rat took your skis, bowling ball and some other items when he left and never paid you for them."

All gifts from him she had never wanted in the first place and had never used. No doubt Greg had appropriated them for wife number two. "And he's suddenly developed a conscience? I find that hard to believe."

"Well, let's just say he was made to see the error of his ways." Margaret grinned, and Beth hugged her tightly.

"I love you, Mom. I love all of you," she said, arms thrown wide. "Thank you for everything you've done. For once in my life, I am speechless."

Ivy rushed in. Her eyes were sparkling and she was breathing deeply. "Don't go giving away all your thanks just yet, dear. Wait until I tell you what I did."

The older woman looked so pleased with herself, Beth was almost afraid to ask what that was.

IN THE LOBBY OF THE Excelsior Hotel Aubrey stared at the check he'd just been handed and his look was inscrutable. "Well, you are certainly full of surprises, Ms. Randall. I never expected you to pay off the loan so quickly."

Brad had come with Beth to lend moral support

and was standing next to her as she faced Aubrey Fontaine. He squeezed her hand in encouragement. "To be honest, Mr. Fontaine," she replied, "I didn't think I'd be able to, either. But the residents of this town were overly generous with their donations and quite determined to keep the inn intact." *And away from you,* she thought. "And quite surprisingly, my aunt Ivy sold her antique jewelry on eBay.

"So needless to say I am feeling truly blessed, not to mention relieved, at this moment and quite happy that my aunts' property will remain as it always has, in the family."

He masked his hurt as best he could, but Beth had seen the sadness and felt badly that her thoughtless comment had caused it. She still had a difficult time remembering that the cold, bitter man before her was a relative.

"I assume now that our unpleasant business dealings are concluded, Mr. Fontaine, you'll be leaving Mediocrity and going back to Philadelphia."

"I haven't decided as yet. I like the tenacity of this town. And I haven't given up on the idea of developing property here. There may be other pieces of land to buy that would suit my purposes."

Beth hoped not. She wanted Aubrey Fontaine to get as far away from her aunt as possible, though she knew Aunt Iris wanted just the opposite. Her aunt felt the need to make up for lost time with her son.

"I wish you luck in your endeavors, Mr. Fontaine. My aunt has extended an open invitation for you to visit her whenever you're in town, if you so desire."

"I take it you're not quite as eager for me to be around my birth mother, Ms. Randall?"

Brad squeezed her hand again, to caution her, she assumed, and Beth swallowed what she was tempted to say. "As long as you don't intend to hurt my aunt, Mr. Fontaine, I have no objection to your visiting her. I know it's what she wants."

He nodded. "I appreciate your honesty. And you may as well call me Aubrey, since we're related, however strange that may be."

"Well, as they say, you can pick your friends but not your relatives." She smiled, and then so did Aubrey, who actually chuckled.

"I think you and that inn are going to do just fine, Beth. You've got grit. It must run on the Swindel side of the family. There aren't many men, let alone women, who can claim they beat Aubrey Fontaine in a business deal. Congratulations!"

Surprised at how gracious he was being in defeat, Beth shuffled her feet for a moment, took stock of the older man's sincerity, and then found herself saying, "I'm having a party on New Year's Eve, to thank everyone for their help in saving the inn. I know Aunt Iris would love it if you could come, Aubrey. I think it might be nice for you to get to know your family. We're not all that bad, despite what you might have been led to believe."

His eyes widened at the invitation. "Thank you. I may just do that, if I'm still in town."

Beth turned to leave, and then paused and looked back. "I hope you know that my aunt's decision to give you up for adoption was because of her unfortunate circumstances and not because she didn't care for you. Aunt Iris was a product of her times and had little choice in the matter."

"I understand that and hold no animosity toward her. I admit I did at first, but she explained everything to my satisfaction. I admire her for having the courage to say what needed to be said. Your aunt—my *mother*—is loyal, and I put a lot of stock in that."

"Thank you. Aunt Iris is the kindest woman you'll ever meet."

"Then it's nice to see, Beth, you're following in her footsteps."

CHAPTER TWENTY-TWO

NEW YEAR'S EVE WAS a time for new beginnings, for making resolutions and then breaking them the following day.

This New Year's Eve had surpassed all others, as far as Beth was concerned. Her "Thank You, Mediocrity!" party had been a huge success. It seemed everyone in town had come, including Aubrey, who'd fit in surprisingly well, considering all that had happened.

Everyone drank champagne, ate delicious food and danced until midnight, and then they rang in the New Year together, with kisses, the singing of "Auld Lang Syne" and nonstop laughter. It had been a joyous, unforgettable evening.

It was much later now, and Brad and Beth had retired to her room, hoping, as Brad had teased, "To start the New Year off with a bang."

"Penny for your thoughts," he said, kissing her naked shoulder as they spooned in her small bed.

"They're going to cost you a lot more than just a

penny, but if you really want to know, I was just thinking that you're the first man I've ever allowed to make love to me in this bed. This is the bed I slept in as a child, so to me it's sacrosanct."

He ran his hand up her thigh to her buttocks and she sucked in her breath at the exquisite torture. "I'm honored, truly. Does this mean I'm special?"

Turning in his arms, she smiled and kissed his chin. "You're very special, Dr. Donovan. My aunts and mother have given you the Good Housekeeping Seal of Approval, or you wouldn't be in here right now."

"They know we're in here doing this?" His cheeks reddened at the idea, and she found his reaction quite endearing.

"You don't know much about women, do you? My aunts and mother know everything that goes on in my life. Why, Aunt Ivy is probably listening outside the door at this very moment," she teased.

Brad's head swerved to stare at the door, and then noting her impish grin, he smiled. "I hope she gets an earful."

"Tonight was perfect, wasn't it? Aunt Iris was so happy that Aubrey came to the party. They seemed to get along quite well. He even danced with her a time or two. And she told me he kissed her on the cheek at midnight. She was absolutely thrilled."

"I'm happy to hear that. I hope they'll be able to

make up for lost time. It'll be an adjustment for both of them while they're getting to know each other better."

"I can't tell you how relieved I was to hear from Sheriff Murdock that Aubrey had nothing to do with the barn fire or the other incidents we had. Apparently, the Mullin twins were responsible for the mischief. Their parents are going to pay for some of the damage their sons caused."

"Good. Maybe it'll teach the kids a lesson."

"And it looks like things are going well for Lori and her chef, too," Beth continued, "though she's not about to make any commitment right now. She says she wants to see if Bill's really going to change his domineering ways."

"Bill told me tonight that he's planning to open up a restaurant here in town, so I guess you're going to have a bit of competition."

She nodded. "Lori told me, and neither of us is upset about it. In fact, we welcome the competition. It'll be good for the town, and she intends to kick his butt in the cooking department anyway."

Brad laughed, then his tone grew serious when he said, "Beth, now that things seem to be working out for everyone I'm wondering if you've given any more thought to the two of us getting married."

She sighed. "I think about little else. But I don't see how we're going to make this work, Brad. I live here, while you live in Virginia. And as I explained, I can't move there."

He kissed her lightly on the lips and took her hand. "I want to marry you, Beth, and I've given our dilemma a lot of thought over the past few weeks. I've come up with a plan that I think is going to work."

Her heart started racing. "You have?"

"I intend to apply for a medical license here in Pennsylvania and open up another practice. I've decided to divide my time between the two practices, taking in a partner to run the one in Charlottesville."

Her eyes widened. "Does that mean—?"

"Stacy and I will be living here with you at the inn after we're married, if you'll have me. My dad and Opal will take over the house in Virginia. It's the perfect solution."

"I…I don't know what to say. You'd be making such a huge sacrifice." Tears filled her eyes and she was so happy she thought she might burst with the love she felt for this man.

"All you have to say is yes. Leave the rest up to me."

She threw her arms about his neck and kissed him soundly on the lips. "Yes, yes, yes, I will marry you, Brad Donovan. And I will love you and Stacy for the rest of my life."

Brad reached over to the nightstand and pulled out the ring he had hidden in the drawer. "Then I guess

you should wear this, as a token of my love, love."
He slipped it on her ring finger.

Beth sighed as she gazed at the exquisite diamond. "I love it, and you. But are you sure about the baby thing? I don't think I'm going to change my mind." In fact, she knew she wasn't. Her life was perfect; she didn't need a child to make it more so.

"I'm quite sure. All I need in my life is you and my daughter. And I'll be getting quite an extended family, as it is, so that's not going to be an issue."

"I love you, Brad. And I'm going to try and be the best doctor's wife I can. Just don't expect too much at first, okay?"

"You're perfect just the way you are. I don't want you to change a thing—except the size of this bed. It's too damn small. I like a lot of room when I'm making love and this isn't going to cut it."

She giggled. "Kiss me, and then make mad, passionate love to me."

"Well, that's a relief. I thought for a moment that you were going to talk me to death."

She reached between his legs and caressed him until he gasped with pleasure. "You're asking for trouble. I hope you know that, Doc."

He grinned. "I do."

And they did.

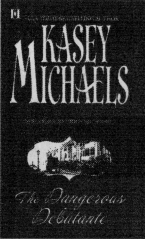

If you enjoyed what you just read,
then we've got an offer you can't resist!

Take 2 bestselling
love stories FREE!

Plus get a FREE surprise gift!

Clip this page and mail it to Harlequin Reader Service®

IN U.S.A.	**IN CANADA**
3010 Walden Ave.	P.O. Box 609
P.O. Box 1867	Fort Erie, Ontario
Buffalo, N.Y. 14240-1867	L2A 5X3

YES! Please send me 2 free Harlequin Romance® novels and my free surprise gift. After receiving them, if I don't wish to receive anymore, I can return the shipping statement marked cancel. If I don't cancel, I will receive 6 brand-new novels every month, before they're available in stores! In the U.S.A., bill me at the bargain price of $3.57 plus 25¢ shipping & handling per book and applicable sales tax, if any*. In Canada, bill me at the bargain price of $4.05 plus 25¢ shipping & handling per book and applicable taxes**. That's the complete price and a savings of 10% off the cover prices—what a great deal! I understand that accepting the 2 free books and gift places me under no obligation ever to buy any books. I can always return a shipment and cancel at any time. Even if I never buy another book from Harlequin, the 2 free books and gift are mine to keep forever.

186 HDN DZ72
386 HDN DZ73

Name	(PLEASE PRINT)	
Address	Apt.#	
City	State/Prov.	Zip/Postal Code

Not valid to current Harlequin Romance® subscribers.
Want to try another series? Call 1-800-873-8635
or visit www.morefreebooks.com.

* Terms and prices subject to change without notice. Sales tax applicable in N.Y.
** Canadian residents will be charged applicable provincial taxes and GST.
   All orders subject to approval. Offer limited to one per household.
   ® are registered trademarks owned and used by the trademark owner and or its licensee.

HROM04R   ©2004 Harlequin Enterprises Limited

Millie Criswell

77011	BODY LANGUAGE	___	$6.50 U.S. ___	$7.99 CAN.
77064	NO STRINGS ATTACHED	___	$5.99 U.S. ___	$6.99 CAN.

(limited quantities available)

TOTAL AMOUNT	$_____
POSTAGE & HANDLING	$_____
($1.00 FOR 1 BOOK, 50¢ for each additional)	
APPLICABLE TAXES*	$_____
TOTAL PAYABLE	$_____

(check or money order—please do not send cash)

To order, complete this form and send it, along with a check or money order for the total above, payable to HQN Books, to: **In the U.S.:** 3010 Walden Avenue, P.O. Box 9077, Buffalo, NY 14269-9077; **In Canada:** P.O. Box 636, Fort Erie, Ontario, L2A 5X3.

Name: _____

Address: _____ City: _____

State/Prov.: _____ Zip/Postal Code: _____

Account Number (if applicable): _____

075 CSAS

*New York residents remit applicable sales taxes.
*Canadian residents remit applicable GST and provincial taxes.

HQN™

We *are* romance™

www.HQNBooks.com

PHMC0406BL